Twin Legends

Twin Legends
Prelude to War

JASON PAULL

Twin Legends

Published by Tate Publishing & Enterprises, LLC
127 E. Trade Center Terrace | Mustang, Oklahoma 73064 USA
1.888.361.9473 | www.tatepublishing.com

Tate Publishing is committed to excellence in the publishing industry. The company reflects the philosophy established by the founders, based on Psalm 68:11,
"The Lord gave the word and great was the company of those who published it."

Cover design by Junriel Boquecosa
Interior design by Jomel Pepito

Published in the United States of America

ISBN: 978-1-63268-751-7
Fiction / Fantasy / Epic
14.07.11

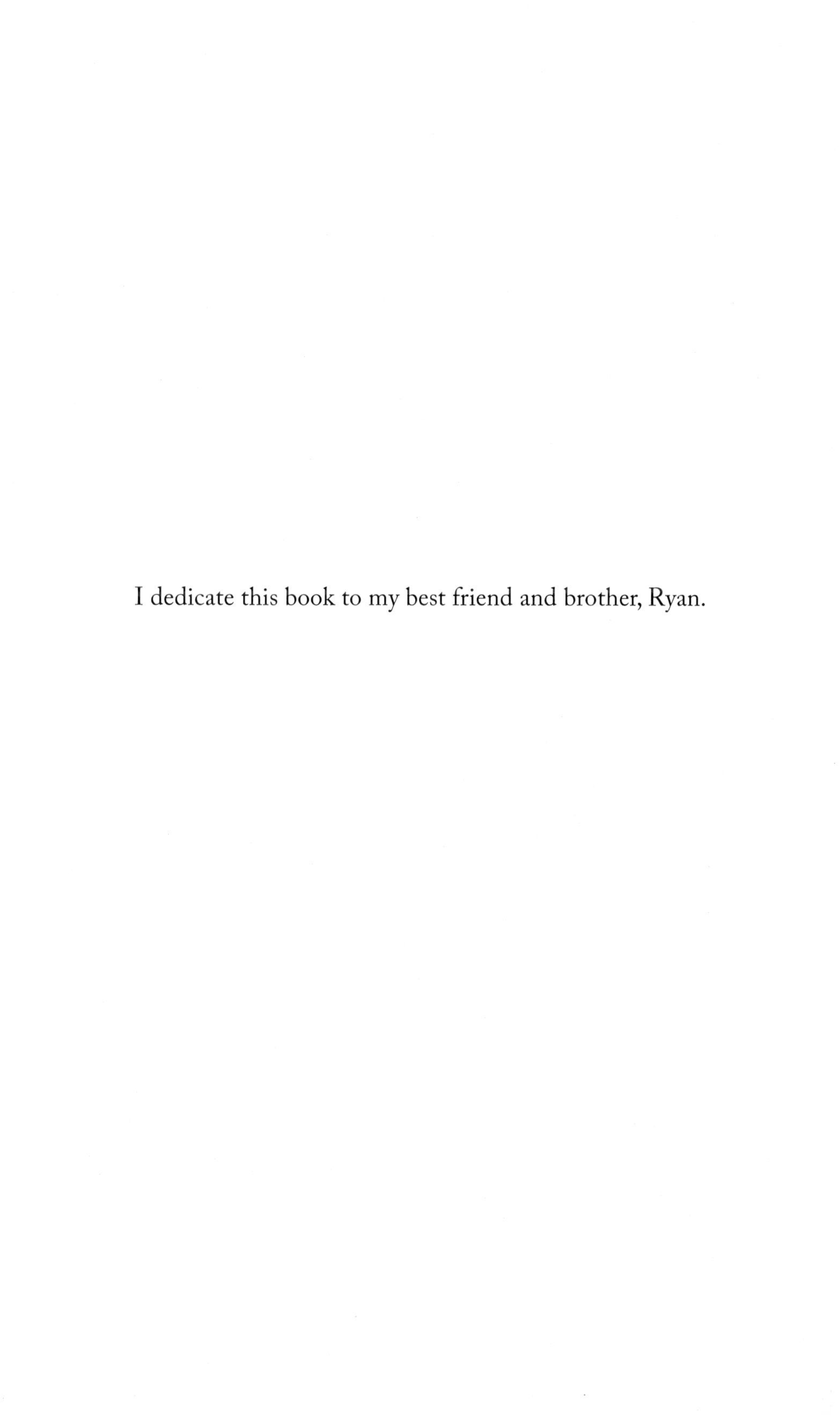

I dedicate this book to my best friend and brother, Ryan.

200 m

100 m= 5 days / caravan
2 days / riding
1 week / walking

Sanferin
Daley
Calm Sea
Calm Port
Viltress
Ganders Forest
Taris
Orgath
Gildell's Vale
Glimmershrine
Fog Bluffs
Long-leaf Forest
Mt. Saithane
Toranten

- Taris
- Daley
- Ice Dome
- Sanferin
- Orgath
- Calm Sea
- Viltress
- Mt. Saithane
- Long-leaf Forest
- Glimmershrine
- Toranten
- Fog Bluffs
- Gildell's Vale

Prologue

"Dryx, Weylor, it's time to go!" Alruin Stormcaller called to his two sons, eight-year-old twins, as they were running around the yard behind their small, two-bedroom home. He smiled as they came running around the side of his little home; they were his most prized possessions and his greatest achievements.

Alruin was thirty years old but his young face hid his years. He had coal black hair and a clean shaven face. His green eyes matched those of his young, blond son, Weylor. Being raised as a blacksmith, he was strong and lean.

"Load up, team," he said to his sons; their eyes shot open with enthusiasm.

They loved when he spoke like that; they always felt as though they were leaving on some grand adventure that would be full of surprises and new stories. Like every other child in the kingdom, they had heard most of the old stories floating around their small farming village of goblins and wars and dragons and all sorts of weird and exciting creatures. They had heard the stories of the ugly goblin beasts that were supposed to live in the mountains just to the east and how they shouldn't enter Gander's Forest, the only thing between them and the mountains. They heard of giants, man-like monsters as tall as trees that could destroy a house in a single blow.

"Ok, off we go!" Alruin said, spurring on the horse pulling the wagon.

Alruin thoroughly enjoyed his children's fascination with adventure and "the wild." When he saw their eyes light up, it made him remember how he felt when he crossed the Calm Sea himself; an only child in the care of a blacksmith, a family friend. He remembered how free he felt when they were on the open sea and how he longed to feel that freedom again, but he had responsibility now; a wife and children.

Alruin and his family lived in Halsgrove, a small farming village on the eastern edge of the kingdom. Only recently had they come to live so far away from Taris, the main city in the area.

Alruin had only recently acquired the land to farm, which lay even further east than Halsgrove, and so his and the twins' daily work consisted of clearing and preparing the land for planting. Dryx and Weylor, always full of energy and ever curious, found a way to enjoy their part of the clearing away. Alruin had given them the "command, from their captain to his men, to find all the rocks they could and clear them from the field."

"This is a vital part of our labor today, my sons. These rocks stand in the way of our victory, and food," he said, adding in the last part with a wry smile. "So, I shall advance whichever of you takes care of the most enemies!" he said, his tone encouraging and command-like.

They looked at each other perplexed; not understanding what 'enemies' he spoke of.

He walked over to the east side of the field and placed an empty barrel where he wanted the rock pile. He picked up a white rock and drew on the barrel the face of an ugly beast. "*Good enough,*" he mumbled to himself.

"Okay, for every rock you throw that hits this foul beast, one enemy is vanquished. Keep track, and be honest!" he said as he walked past them. He wore as serious a face as he could muster and almost gave in to laughter when he saw the surprised looks on their faces.

He walked back to the wagon and began unloading his tools; the finest in the entire town. He had been a blacksmith in Taris until he was asked (and bribed) to come to the outer unfarmed east and 'tame the land.' He made all of his tools and, for some extra work, made and repaired the other farmer's tools. It had only been a week since they left the walls of Taris and came out to Halsgrove but their work continued at a steady pace with no interruptions.

The morning passed as it did every other day; Alruin chopping down trees and clearing away sections for his farm house and barn while listening to the laughter and conversations of his sons. Every so often he would take a break and watch his sons at work, or play as it seemed to them. Instead of heavy competition which usually arose among brothers, they laughed and applauded at each other's 'kills'. Sometimes they would work together by throwing rocks at the same time and from different angles to make it harder to dodge. It put a smile on his face when he saw this because he knew that this unity between them would help them overcome any obstacle put in their path.

"Lunch time, come regain your strength my young warriors!" he called, with a satisfied look on his face.

Dried meat and bread with water was their 'meal befitting a king.'

"So, how goes the battle?" he asked in a calm tone.

"There are too many! We keep finding stones and throwing them, but the monster is still there every time!" Dryx said in an exasperated tone.

"I don't think stones can hurt it," Weylor whispered to his father in such a serious voice that Alruin could not contain himself and burst into laughter, causing the twins to do the same.

They finished eating and Alruin told them of his journey across the Calm Sea and of his 'adventures' on the water. Every time he told them stories of his adventures in a mysterious place that they weren't familiar with he could see their eyes glaze over and knew that their imaginations were flying, putting together in their minds all the details as best young children of their age could.

Alruin himself, whenever he told stories of his childhood, couldn't help but to fall into his youthful memories. He had been born in a village, on the other side of The Calm Sea, which was part of the city of Daley. His parents were fisherman and Alruin had gone out with them on their boat often. He was told, when they did not return after a fishing trip, that they were lost in a storm.

They finished out the rest of the day until just before night fall; it was dangerous to travel at night so far from the village. Dryx and Weylor fell asleep almost as soon as the wagon left their farm. It wasn't too far of a ride but it was long enough that it fell dark about half way back to town which always put Alruin on edge. It wasn't only the lack of vision that came with the darkness that brought Alruin the fear he felt, at times he felt as though eyes were on him while he worked.

Alruin, being a master blacksmith, had made his own sword, which he never left more than an arm's reach away. It was longer than a short sword but he had curved the blade slightly and kept the blade narrow, keeping it light. The blade was made of a rare metal that was difficult to smelt and manipulate, but once it hardened it was harder than most metals and kept its edge longer.

They arrived safely at home and Alruin carried his sons into the house and to their beds.

"How long until we can move out to the farm house?" his wife asked when he came out of the twins room and sat down to eat. She would rather live out at the farm, away from Halsgrove, and be with Alruin all day than be away from everything she loved all day, every day.

"We're making good progress. The twins are clearing out more rocks than you'd imagine and I've about cleared away the section for the farm house. I'll be able to use most of the trees I cut down for it but..." Alruin dropped his gaze, not wanting to share his fears with his wife.

"But what?" his wife asked, a little on edge; she had never known her husband to fear anything.

"There's something out there, it just feels wrong. I haven't seen anything, and nothing has gone missing; it's just too close to them cursed mountains. They're still out there, somewhere," he said. He had been a young boy when Taris was attacked and sieged by the goblin army that had lived somewhere in the Giant's Steppes, the mountains on the other side of Gander's Forest.

His wife understood. She would rather starve and beg on the street than have all the family she has run the risk of being attacked and never coming back.

"Have you let the guard know?" she asked. She knew how much they needed the land and the farm. The bribe money from Taris for 'taming the land' would only last them so long.

"No, there's nothing to report. They wouldn't give a goblin's black heart about reports without any evidence to show. They have grown comfortable with so many years of peace. They won't do anything. Once the boys clear the field of the rocks they'll be staying here," he replied.

She could see how serious the situation was to him. She knew when that day came, once her boys were staying home while Alruin went to the farm, that she would fear more than ever for him.

Alruin and the twins got up the next day, and every day that week, and worked the same schedule; getting to the farm just after dawn and working until the sun started to fall in the sky. By the end of the week, the twins couldn't find a single rock in the entire field and Alruin began leaving them at home while he worked; he wished the twins were big enough to help him but they had nothing else to do out there and Deli, his wife, needed the company.

Alruin, for his own fears and to lessen the stress on his wife, began to leave and came back earlier every day. His same fear was almost tangible in their little village of just over a hundred people. No one spoke of it, but they all felt it; all of them besides the guards. No one had any evidence, but they all felt that something was wrong.

"Hey, Alruin!" Jack, his neighbor, called to him just before he reached his door on Saturday after returning from the farm.

"Hey Jack, what's going on?" He could see from Jack's expression that something was bothering him as he walked back out to the road.

"It's nothing…I just wanted to see how your farm is coming along?" The words came out as though the question had been thought up on the spot; small talk.

"Everything's on schedule, Jack. My sons have cleared out all the rocks and I'm getting ready to plant the seed and I've just about got all the trees cleared to start building the farm house." He decided not to mention anything about his suspicions; he didn't want to cause panic or make a scene out of something he had no proof of.

Jack started scratching the back of his head awkwardly and kicking at the mud clumps on the ground.

"Is there something you want to tell me, Jack?" He suspected Jack had the same worries as he did. His and Jack's farms were the only two that butted up against the tree line that began Gander's Forest. They were about a mile apart; Jack's farm south of Alruin's.

"Alruin, have you noticed anything out of place? I haven't seen anything and maybe I'm just crazy, but there's something out there. I work alone at my farm, as you do, but I can feel eyes on my back. When I look, there ain't nothing there; nothing that I can see at least. I'm not for complaining and bringing the guard out there to complain about nothing, but we ought to do something," he said to Alruin.

Alruin held his gaze, staring right into Jacks eyes for a long moment. He knew how Jack felt and, though he shared the same fears, he didn't want to talk about it until there was something to talk about.

"We are the furthest farms from Taris, Jack. We are butted up right against that damned forest and it's playing tricks on our minds. We've been here almost a month now and not a single thing has happened. Let's not make a panic out of something we can't prove," Alruin said.

Jack just stood there, surprised. He thought that Alruin felt the same way since he wasn't bringing his kids out to the farm anymore and he had started coming back earlier. He still thought Alruin felt the same, but agreed with his judgment. He knew that any rumors of something in the forest would bring nothing but panic to the people of the village. He nodded his agreement and left disappointed.

Alruin watched as Jack turned and headed toward The Farmer's Refuge, the local pub. He agreed completely with Jack and shared his worries, but he wouldn't make a decision until something happened, he just wished that waiting until something happened wouldn't be too late.

Chapter I

Signs

"Shh, quiet!" Dryx shot at Weylor.

"It's like I told you before, Jack, there is no reason to panic," Jarol told him, yet again. "There hasn't been a sighting up here for over twenty years now and I don't reckon there'll be another for twenty more! I was there when we drove'em off, Jack. You should've been there!" he let out a booming, drunken laugh as he recalled the last war with the goblins. "A surprise that they came it was, but we beat them back all the same! Had those beasts running like there was no tomorrow!" Jarol let another booming laugh as slammed down his mug in The Farmer's Refuge.

Dryx and Weylor looked at each other from under the floorboards, both faces dirty from crawling halfway under the tavern.

"Goblins attacked us before?" Weylor asked Dryx, who shrugged his shoulders at the question.

They heard the men above them, of whom they only knew Jack, get up and walk over somewhere in the tavern; probably to refill their drinks. The boys waited until there were no feet by the door then crawled back from under the tavern and ran home.

"So, what'll it be Jarol?" Jack asked uncertainly. He knew the guards disbelief that there was something out there other than animals and that anyone who thought there was would be called crazy. "Look, I'm not for saying that there are goblins in the woods, but something just feels off. Lots of the townsfolk have the same feeling, Jarol. I just think that it would be a good idea to prove that there's nothing out there, you know, calm everyone's nerves."

Jarol sobered up a bit at the thought of easing the tension in the town, and also of being the one to 'take matters into his own hands'. He was a drinker and a brawler, which was no surprise to anyone that knew him or had seen him in a bar or tavern, but outside the tavern he enjoyed the peace and cared for the people of Halsgrove.

"Give me a few days," was all he responded. Jarol left Jack at the bar and headed back to the guard station.

That's enough for one day, Alruin thought to himself.

After a month of cutting trees down, stripping the bark and drying the timber, he finally had enough wood and rocks to lay the foundation for his farm house. He had all the logs he thought that he would need and all the rope and metal he could gather to help set the wood in place.

The sun had just started its descent in the sky when Alruin started home. A few minutes after leaving, however, he felt that same, familiar feeling of being watched and all the hair on the back of his neck stood on end. He saw nothing but knew he shouldn't urge his horse on faster; he knew that if something was watching him he would be just as vulnerable as if he let on that he thought something was there. So he decided to not act at all, but continue on the same course at the same speed.

Casually he glanced to the right and, seeing nothing, looked ahead again. He took off his wide brimmed farm hat and scratched his head, acting like he was stretching out his neck to be able to look to the left. Alruin was no tracker, no ranger that could see a footprint three days old but he knew there was something out there; one tree stood out. A branch was swaying faster than the others, as if something landed onto or jumped from it. Judging by the bushes and the rest of the nearby trees he knew that it was not the wind, and there were no animals, to his knowledge, that would be so jumpy from a person so far away. Whatever it was, it didn't want to be seen. He wouldn't let his suspicions get too big, though, knowing that he would only scare himself into doing something stupid.

Alruin arrived to Halsgrove before the sun set as usual. He tied up his horse at the local inn and entered to buy some bread and cheese before going home. He didn't want to tip his wife off that something had bothered him and getting food the family seemed like a normal enough thing.

He knew how much Deli loved him and needed him, and he knew she would worry too much if she knew how he felt. As hard as this decision was for him, he knew it was necessary to keep quiet and continue working to provide for his family.

"Alruin, you're home early," his wife said with a relieved smile on her face. She knew he was a hardworking man so she didn't doubt that the work was coming along as planned, although she was scared every day that he left, worrying all the day long about his safety and thinking about how life would change if he was taken from her. And every day when he returned home her fears were quelled and she could go to sleep in peace in his arms.

"I'm just about ready to start building the farmhouse," Alruin replied, hoping his voice stayed even to belie his calm. "I've got all the timber and rope I need, and I've got the foundation cleared for building. Nothing left but to dig the holes and start with the walls." He tried keeping his tone light, but he couldn't hide completely what he had seen that day.

"What is it?" she asked.

It lingered still in the back of his mind, but he knew that logic was against him. Deli wasn't the smartest woman in the kingdom, but Alruin knew that she knew just about everything there was to know about him. They had been together for more than ten years and she was the only person he had ever opened up to and confided in. He knew she knew there was something.

He gave a barely audible laugh and looked into her eyes, knowing that he could hide nothing from his perceptive wife. His smile was one of defeat and he put his hands on her shoulders, and then let them fall down to take her hands in his. His face tightened a little, the smile almost completely fading.

"I will do whatever it takes to keep my family safe. I know it's pointless to tell you not to worry," he chuckled a little at how true that actually was, "but there isn't anything to worry about that I've seen. It is strange out there, I'll admit, and the forest plays tricks on my mind, but more people will be coming over to farm soon enough. It's just being so far away; we'll get used to it."

She knew he hadn't admitted his true fear, but she held her silence knowing that he would tell her if it were important enough. He pulled her in for a hug and then led them both inside.

His demeanor changed almost completely when he saw his sons across the room, play-fighting with sticks and acting out the adventures their father had so often amused them with. Back and forth they ran, acting out both sides of the fight.

He went to bed that night leaving all his worries outside, happy to have one more day with his family.

"Well you are awful silent this morning, Jack." Alruin noted his grim mood as soon as they started off before sunrise to their farms. They had started riding together in the mornings towards their farms until the road split, Jack going right and Alruin left. Both farms were about half a mile from where the road split that led to Halsgrove.

Jack didn't want to respond, but he knew that if he didn't he would only put Alruin on edge.

"I got Jarol to come out and scout out the area for us…uh… for me," he said, instantly noticing the change in Alruin's mood; he could see the obvious frustration on his face building. "Now before you get angry with me, I know what you told me about leaving the guard out of this, but Alruin,"he said, trying to sound confident, "it'll put my nerves to rest and those of the townsfolk, too. When he gets done and hasn't found anything the word will spread like fire that the guard came and checked it out and all is safe."

Alruin, without realizing it, had stopped his horse. He sat there on his horse, contemplating what he had just heard. He hadn't considered that side of getting the guard involved. He knew that, if it worked out like Jack said, it would put everyone's minds at ease; except for his.

"He knows that it's just to scout out around our farms, right?" He had to be sure of the guard's motives for coming out.

"Yea he knows, I explained it to him just as I told you, Alruin. He probably won't come alone, so we'll have the word of a few guards and not just his. Those guards don't think anything is out there." Jack relaxed a bit seeing that the logic was working out some of Alruin's stress and anger.

Without responding Alruin kicked his horse along at a trot at the same, normal pace as always. This new information did nothing to ease his tensions, though. But he was comforted in knowing that the guard's report of finding not a single trail or footprint would put his wife at ease. He knew her as well as she knew him and he knew she worried everyday he left.

It wasn't long before they came to the end of the road and, like usual, they parted ways with a wave and nothing more.

All day Alruin was thinking about those two things; the tree branch from the day before and the guards that would be coming out to scout out the area. He had never been in a war before, although in his youth he went through the basic military training to learn how to use a sword. Despite his inexperience with battle and danger, he knew that trusting in his gut instinct was right. He knew what was on that branch was no animal; no bird had just flown from that tree, no bear had been climbing. It was something else, something intelligent. He worked with his sword girded and sheathed on his belt and instead of letting his horse graze about, wandering where it would, he tied it to a near tree. He started taking shorter and more frequent breaks to check his surroundings and his horse.

"Alright, here is the plan," Jarol headed down to Jack's farm the next morning with two other scouts, Tannon and Will.

Tannon was a tall and slender, less coordinated guard. Some thought he was too easy-going and not serious enough. His thin chain-mesh shirt hung loose around his skinny features and his leather jerkin didn't quite cover his midriff. He was twenty years old with short, blond hair.

Will was shorter and thicker; he had taken the Fighter School's training a bit more seriously than Tannon, who graduated with him the previous year. Will didn't talk much, he preferred to keep himself reserved unless it was necessary to speak. His dark hair matched his thick, trimmed beard. He had moved to Halsgrove with his wife and young daughter after graduating; it was his first paid job.

"There is nothing out here but the townsfolk seem to think there is. They say they feel eyes on them and just don't feel right out there. So," he continued, "we are going to camp out on his farm for a night. One night, that's it. During the day we'll look for tracks and such and at night we'll set up a trap and see if anything bites," he chuckled at the end, playing out the absurdity of anything actually being out there.

The two guards nodded their agreement, not that they had any say in it anyway. They were less experienced guards, only a year out of Taris' military school, but looked at each other when Jarol turned back to the road and smiled. They were both just excited to be leaving Halsgrove for a bit and be doing something and the thought of lying traps and camping out was exactly what they needed to release all their boredom from sitting in the town day after day with nothing to do.

They reached the forth in the road at mid-day, where Jack and Alruin had parted some hours before.

"To the right; Jack's is to the right." Jarol led them down the same kind of straight and narrow path that they had just come down, evidence that the trail saw only limited use. This trail was a little harder to navigate, though; the underbrush was thicker and, though, for a man he could pass through without touching a single bush, it was not so easy in a wagon. They followed the same wheel marks as Jack's but still found it to be a slower ride than the main road.

"Next time we come down here we leave the wagon and ride horses! Curse this trail!" one of the guards complained from all the bumping up and down of the wagon on the trail, rubbing his sore backside.

"Not a bad idea," Jarol muttered to himself.

After a few more turns and bends around thickets and tree groves too thick to cut a decent path through they could see a clearing just ahead of them. There was no farm house to be seen but they knew he couldn't have built it yet; one man building a farm alone takes time.

"Mama?" Weylor called from outside.

"What is it?" she answered, stepping outside but paying only little attention; she still had chores she wanted to get done before Alruin got back.

"Why did that wagon of guards go down the road to daddy's farm?" he asked with a confused look on his face; he and Dryx had overheard Jarol and Jack's conversation but thought Jarol didn't want to go out there.

"Are they going for daddy?" Dryx cut in, just as curious as Weylor.

Deli just stood there, looking down the road. She forgot about her chores; she forgot about dusting, she forgot about getting firewood, she forgot about all the dirty clothes she had to still wash. All she could think about was Alruin.

She stared down the road leading to Alruin, for how long she couldn't remember, before absentmindedly telling Dryx and Weylor to go play inside. They stood staring at her; not moving, staring down the road with a worried look.

"Is daddy okay, mama?" Dryx asked.

She forced her gaze and thoughts to come back to Halsgrove and her children and chores. "Yes, daddy's fine. Now, why don't you play inside, I have a lot of chores to do."

Brozek sat there, high up in a tree, watching the unfamiliar wagon make its way down the winding road that led to the southern farm. He knew the farmer from the northern farm was wary now, always carrying his sword around and keeping his horse close, but he didn't know why the southern farmer had a wagon of guards coming to him.

Brozek was sure he hadn't been spotted, although he thought the farmer from the north farm had caught a glimpse of the branch he was on the day before. He had very strict orders; be invisible or be killed, either by the humans or by Grol, his vicious and merciless captain.

Brozek remembered well his place and his mission; to scout out the farms and village to the north along the forest and see what kind of defenses the small farming village had. For more than a month he had been inspecting the farms and the farmers, trying to find out anything that would be worthy of reporting. Twice he had gone up to Halsgrove at night, memorizing the layout of the town and the biggest building that the people would gather into. He noted the lack of patrols and the few armed guards that he occasionally spotted leaving a building at night. He knew the population was very small and that there were many women and children, more so than men.

Now, though, he watched from fairly far away, and under heavy foliage, as the three guards greeted the farmer and began unpacking their wagon. He saw that they didn't unpack much gear; they weren't there to stay long.

Brozek wasn't bright even by goblin's standards but he understood the purpose of the guards; they were here to scout out the area. He feared that he had been seen but didn't understand why there weren't more guards if they knew goblins were in the area.

As carefully and slowly as he could, he climbed down from the tree and left to the south to find his camp. He had no desire to run into those guards; if they didn't kill him Grol would for having been spotted. Deeper into the woods he walked, being careful not to leave any signs of his passing.

The night soon stole the light from the land. Jarol and his two scouts had found nothing that day, not a single foot print or broken branch out of place.

Jarol had Tannon and Will set up the tents around the fire. He made the campsite look comfortable; with a small pile of wood and some food lying out.

They sat around the fire, eating and talking, until the fire burnt down to coals. At about midnight they all slipped into their tents, supposedly to go to sleep; but this was just part of their scouting plan. They had previously cut a line in the bottom of the back of their tents just big enough to slip out of. They all put on cloaks to cover their chain mesh to quiet its clinking. They had placed their tents so that the shadows cast by the fire would give them a direct line of darkness to a nearby tree or bush where they could crawl to and leave the campsite without being spotted.

They circled around in the underbrush and met on the north side of the farm and started a sweep of the woods, working in a simple weaving pattern to scare out anything in between them.

Every now and then they would stop to listen but they never heard anything. They found a few places where something, or someone, would be able to hide, especially during the day, but found no evidence of anything ever having been there.

By the time they came back to camp they had done three full sweeps around the farm, each sweep further out than the last. They found no fire pits, no marks on any of the trees and didn't find a single footprint of anything near the many muddy areas they came across; they found nothing.

The two scouts were more than happy to go in their tents and fall asleep but Jarol couldn't; he felt uneasy for some reason he hadn't yet discovered.

Later on that morning, as the sun was just coming over the mountains, Jack rode in to the farm. He was shaking slightly, nervous to find out what had happened during the night and to hear their findings.

He spotted the guards tents and rode over, stopping just before he reached them and dismounted from his horse.

"Morning, Jack," came Jarol's voice from a tree branch hanging just over Jack's head as he passed under it. Jack jumped back as he looked up into the tree where he heard the voice come from, breathing a sigh of relief when he saw Jarol.

"Well? What did you find? What happened?" Jack was anxious to know all the details and didn't appreciate being surprised.

"Now settle down, Jack," Jarol told him, climbing down limberly from the tree. "I've been up all night and nothing has happened. We did three sweeps around your whole farm and not a single sign of life out there. Jack, there is nothing out there." Jack stood there for a long moment, thinking through everything that he heard. They had done 3 sweeps around his farm and had nothing to show for it.

Am I going crazy? he thought to himself. He felt awkward and uneasy that nothing was found. He might have felt better if his suspicions were proven, because at least he would know that he wasn't going crazy and they would know that there is something out there. But to find nothing just put him on edge more than ever. He knew there would be enough talk about him for bringing them out there to find nothing so he dismissed himself from them and began his work around his farm.

"So, what now Captain?" Will asked Jarol, who was watching Jack walk away with more than passing interest.

"Pack up, we're going," was all he replied and left to get the wagon.

They set off down the winding trail that led back to the road to Halsgrove. As they approached the turn Jarol stopped the wagon. He didn't tell Jack his true feelings, not wanting to let on that he was feeling the same and put the whole village even more on edge.

"Tell me, what did you notice about last night? What was out of place?" Jarol asked as he turned back to face the two younger guards.

"I didn't notice anything, Captain, not a single trace of anything! These farmers are going crazy way out here all alone," he said through his laughter, thinking the captain was trying to press the point further that Jack was crazy and that nothing was out there.

Will looked at Jarol with a little more interest in the question, seeing his captain's serious tone and visage. "Did you see something Captain?"

"No, not a thing; and that's just it," he said.

Tannon's laughter ended abruptly when he heard the captain's tone.

"I've been out here in the eastern lands for nearly twenty years now and I've always known these parts to be full of animals. Two months ago you couldn't go an arrow's flight without spotting a deer or a bear, let alone rabbits and birds. We didn't see a single one yesterday, day or night. These farmers aren't hunting anything, I checked. There was no blood, no skins, not even a fire pit in

Jack's whole farm. Something has spooked away all the animals, and whatever it is, it doesn't want to be seen."

Tannon and Will couldn't believe what they were hearing. They never thought of the absence of animals or activity as a sign that something was there, but the more that they sat there thinking about it the more sense it made.

Only the Captain had ever seen combat against goblins and knew what it would mean if they had started coming out of the mountains again. Jarol sat there, letting this new information sink into his younger guards.

"So, what are we to do?" Will asked.

This was the very question that Jarol had been turning over in his mind since noticing the absence of the animals. He knew they had no evidence, except for the lack thereof which, to him, was evidence enough. He regretted not having taken the matter more seriously when he first heard about it. Now it was up to him to prevent both panic and a raid, because that is how it started last time; goblins raiding small farming villages.

"It's been so long," he began, his eyes losing focus as his memories took him back to the last war with the goblins.

He remembered seeing the vast hosts of goblins from the top of Taris' walls; the goblins had seemed countless. They had raided the outer farming villages for years as their numbers swelled, although their attacks were uncoordinated and sporadic. That is why Taris was able to beat them and drive them back into the caves beneath their city, Orgath, in the southern mountains of the Giant's Steppes; they were uncoordinated and easily separated, giving Taris' military and vital advantage in splitting the goblin's force.

"Twenty years ago," Jarol said, his thoughts still in decades past, "there were regular scouting parties patrolling the outer areas of the kingdom. Taris' army was active in its military training and the king was always sending out patrols to know what was happening." When he came to he saw fear in the scouts' expressions.

"Are they back, then?" Tannon asked with a shaky voice.

"I don't know, but this is more serious than I thought. We need to get back to Halsgrove," he said. He spurred the horses on and headed down the main road back to Halsgrove.

The next few months passed by uneventful. The cold winter chill deepened with each passing week and the work on the farm was slowed by the snow, though in comparison to former years it seemed to be a mild winter.

Alruin was able to clear enough snow away from his laid foundation, though, to start constructing the walls to his farm house. It took him only a few weeks, trading days with Jack when he needed another hand to lift the logs, to get his small farmhouse finally built. It wasn't much to look at but he was proud of his work.

Two more months passed by and the snow had almost all but melted with the coming spring. He hadn't been able to work on his farm much due to the snow, and decided not to move his family out to the farm until the spring.

On the last day of winter, a Saturday, just before leaving for Halsgrove, he did an inspection around his property, like he did every day before leaving.

His land was now very distinguishable as a farm and not as just piece of ravaged forest. He could see the visible lines going down his field, free of rocks and weeds; although he knew that the weeds would spring up as soon as what snow was left had melted. He had dug a foot-wide, six inch deep trench around his field, filling it with the rocks Dryx and Weylor had pulled out of the field. It wasn't a traditional farming technique to line a field with rocks but he thought it would, at the least, put a barrier between his field and the wild grass. He filled in the space around the rocks with salt, which kept the weeds from growing in between and through the rocks to his field.

He was turning onto the southern side of his farm when he saw it. It had rained the day before and so the ground was moist and soft and a lot of the snow had melted away near the tree line.

There, at the base of a tree only twenty feet from his field, was a footprint. His hand flew to the hilt of his sword and he looked up the tree. There was nothing there, but he knew there wouldn't be; it was daylight. He knew the print before he walked closer to exam it. The print was like that of a human, except there were only three toes and it was smaller.

Alruin noted that the print hadn't sunk too far into the mud, telling him it wasn't a heavy creature. He looked around, his nerves causing him to shake with fear; not out of being attacked by a single goblin, but of the implications of goblins in the area.

He ran over to his horse and untied it. There was still an hour or two of sunlight, Alruin guessed, but when he saw the rain clouds gathering in the distance he knew he couldn't bring the guard back in time to see the track. It would be gone and he would have nothing to show.

He didn't care if no one believed him; he wouldn't risk his family's safety. He saw the print and he knew what it was from; a goblin.

He didn't know what he was going to say to the guard but he knew he had to try; Alruin knew the safety of the entire kingdom was now at risk.

Chapter 2

Halsgrove

Alruin made Halsgrove with the light quickly fading due to the approaching storm. He rode his horse right up to the guard station and tied it quickly to the post outside. He walked up to the door and pounded on it impatiently.

Ryker was on duty in the guard station and answered the door. He had lived in Halsgrove for almost four years and knew the name of everyone in the town. He had been a scout for a few years but decided to take the job of being a guard to stay in one place. He almost a foot shorter than Alruin but his tight clothes hinted at his muscular features underneath.

"Howdy, Alruin," Ryker greeted him with a smile, always in high spirits.

"I need to speak to Jarol immediately, Ryker. It can't wait," Alruin said in as serious a tone as he had ever used.

"Of course," Ryker replied and opened the door quickly, motioning for Alruin to enter. "Follow me."

Alruin followed Ryker back through the entrance room and down a hall to the right. The hall ended in a doorway that led into a room filled with tables and maps.

Ryker knocked on the open door to get the captain's attention. "Captain, Alruin is here. He needs to speak with you, he says it's urgent," he said.

"Come in," Jarol said.

Alruin walked straight up to Jarol's desk and Jarol motioned for him to take a seat. Alruin remained standing.

"I saw a footprint today," Alruin said.

Jarol's eyes widened at the blunt statement. "What kind of footprint?" he asked, already knowing what Alruin would say by the expression on his face.

"A goblin footprint; it had three toes and was smaller than a man's. I saw it clear as day not twenty feet from my field.

"Damn," Jarol muttered. His suspicions were finally confirmed.

He had traveled to Taris the day after visiting Jack's farm months before, but Captain Strongshield, the captain of the guard, had told him to return when there was actual evidence; he wouldn't risk scaring the entire kingdom into fleeing to Taris on suspicions. Captain Strongshield had ordered him to not say anything to anyone to keep the suspicions from spreading to other villages.

"You saw this footprint tonight?" Jarol asked, wanting to make sure he had the facts exactly right.

"I rode here as soon as I saw it," Alruin answered.

"Ryker, get the rest of the guards," Jarol said, his voice sounded determined. "Alruin," he said, now turning back to Alruin. "I need you to grab some men and bring everyone here, have them wait just outside the guard station."

Alruin nodded and left.

Jarol pulled out a map of the area that encompassed Alruin and Jack's farms and stared at it until Ryker returned with the rest of the guards.

A dozen guards, Jarol thought. It won't be enough.

"Ok," he said, standing up. He walked around his desk to stand in front of his men. "Alruin found a track, a footprint, of a goblin at his farm today. It's confirmed; there are goblins in Gander's Forest. I am going to leave tonight for Taris; all of you are to remain on duty. Six of you will stay here in Halsgrove; I want a pair at both the east and south entrance and the other two I want to stay here in the guard station, ready to ring the bell and help everyone get in should there be an attack." He looked around at his men, all of them stood wide-eyed, surprised at the sudden claim.

"Goblins, Captain? I thought they were all beaten back into the caves?" One of the guards asked, his voice anxious.

"It looks like they've come back out of the caves," Captain Jarol replied. "Now, the other six of you I want in pairs. Will and Tannon, since you two are more familiar with Jack's farm and that area, I want you two to scout out to the east. You get out of there if anything happens; anything. I want another pair to the south and the other to the south-east," he said. "If an attack is coming, you are the only ones able to give Halsgrove enough time to gather to the guard station."

Jarol looked around, waiting for any questions. He made his orders clear and simple; he would only be gone a few days.

"I'll ride as fast as I can but I need you all here. Any questions?" he asked the dozen guards.

None of them answered. They looked around at each other, sobered by the news.

"Ryker," Jarol said, turning to look at him directly. "I need you to talk to the townspeople and explain what is going on and what to do if the town is attacked."

"We will keep Halsgrove safe, sir," Ryker said, nodding at Jarol.

Jarol nodded his head at Ryker and with that, left for the stables to saddle his horse.

Ryker, now the guard in command of Halsgrove, turned to the rest of the guards. "Those of you leaving to scout, I want you on the road by dawn."

The guards nodded their agreement and left.

Ryker waited at the entrance. It wasn't long before the townspeople arrived at the guard station. Alruin didn't have time to explain anything to them so they waited with puzzled and confused expressions on their faces.

"What's going on?" one of the townspeople asked from somewhere in the crowd.

"Yea, what's all this about?" another said.

"Everyone," Ryker said in a loud voice, wanting them to quiet down and pay attention. "I need you to pay very close attention to what I'm going to say." He waited a minute until the crowd was quiet before he continued. "We found evidence that there are goblins in the area," he said, the crowd burst into commotion and noise, everyone mumbling in disbelief at the claim.

"Please!" he yelled, trying to get their attention back.

It took a minute but the crowd again quieted.

"Jarol left for Taris. He won't be back for almost a week. Guards will be sent out in the morning to the outer farms to scout out the area in case there are any goblins coming this way. If that happens, everyone needs to get to the guard station as quickly as possible. Bring all the supplies you can but get here as quickly as possible. If you hear the bell ring," he said, pausing a moment to let everything he said sink in, "you need to get here fast. No one is to leave town until Jarol returns. Any questions?"

There was silence for a moment and then every villager at once seemed to have a question. Jarol answered questions for nearly an hour before the villagers returned to their homes.

The village was quiet, eerily quiet. The pub and inns were closed and not a single person was outside, except for the guards who posted up in pairs around the village to keep watch through the night.

Jarol rode through the night. By sunrise he could smell the salt of the Calm Sea, letting him know he had reached the inner kingdom. It was a three day journey to Taris on horseback, five for a wagon.

Reluctantly, Jarol had to stop twice to give his horse time to rest. The anticipation kept him on edge and too anxious to sleep.

"Bring me Brozek," Grol growled at the two goblins standing guard at his tent door.

Grol was an orc and the leader of the goblin scouting party. He stood almost six feet tall, a full head and a half taller than any goblin he commanded. His skin was a lighter shade of green and he weighed more than twice what a goblin weighed. His muscular features, easily visible to anyone who saw him, set his race apart from that of the goblins.

Anger burned in Grol's eyes. Grol was staring at the goblin scout before him, who was shaking more than a little, being careful to not look higher than Grol's toes for fear of death.

He had just brought word to Grol that the farmers to the south of Halsgrove hadn't returned to their farms for two days.

"You better be sure about what you saw," Grol's words rolled out like venom, causing the scout to fall to the ground. A few minutes later Brozek, followed by the two guards, entered the tent.

"Brozek, what are the farmers up to? I told you not to be seen," Grol's tone threatening the small goblin with his life. "Why are they staying away from the farms now?" Grol yelled in Brozek's face.

Brozek didn't understand, he knew he hadn't been seen; but that wouldn't save him from Grol's anger if he thought that Brozek had been seen.

"I scouted. I left when group came. No one saw'd me. I swear!" Brozek fell to his knees and was shaking violently at Grol's feet.

"What group?" Grol asked, his curious tone hinted that he was even angrier that Brozek had kept something from him.

Brozek knew he was dead. "Before the snow, scouts went to the farm. They stayed the night and left and never came back. The farmers, they kept coming back. They didn't see Brozek!" Brozek's voice was a high-pitched squeal by the time he finished the sentence, he knew death was only moments away but that same fear paralyzed him to where he couldn't move even if he wanted to try and run away.

Grol knew he hadn't been seen. There would be scouts all over the forest. An echo of thunder off the mountains reached Grol's camp and he thought of something. "When was the last time you spied on them?" Grol asked, in a deceptively calm tone.

"I, I…I came back three days ago…so…so…the night before that…," he replied, his words sounding more like whining than talking. He couldn't see Grol's face from his prone position on the ground or he might have tried to run.

"It rained that night…" was all that Grol said; Brozek had left a track in the mud.

"I was not…" was all he managed to say before he felt Grol's heavy foot blast the consciousness from him. His eyes would never open again.

Grol grabbed his axe and decapitated the little goblin in front of the other goblins. He kicked Brozek's severed head out of the tent for all the rest of the goblins to see, who promptly backed up far away from the tents entrance, not wanting to confront Grol if he came out in a rage.

He walked out a moment later, his bloodied axe in hand. One goblin's life was worth re-affirming his dominant position. He figured the village wasn't too on edge or there would be scouting parties all about the woods. *Just like last time,* he thought.

It would be a day's travel with the whole raid party through the woods to get to the village, a slower route to stay unseen; but if they gained the advantage of surprise…a wide smile spread over Grol's face.

Now just as a show of force, Grol kicked the severed head again and it flew a hundred feet through the air, splattering against a tree.

"We leave tomorrow for the village," Grol said in a loud voice and returned to his tent to get ready.

Jarol started off early the third and last day of his flight to Taris. He could tell his horse was tired but he had to keep going, there was no time to rest.

At midday, riding over a hill, Jarol caught view of the tall mage tower that marked Taris for anyone traveling from the east.

To anyone outside its walls, Taris appeared as a brilliant city of white stone. Walls twenty-five feet high surrounded the city to the east and south. The city had been strategically placed on a cliff that made up Taris' western and northern sides.

It wasn't long before Jarol made the gates and entered Taris. He noticed that there were only a few dozen guards walking lazily around the top of the wall; this only spurred him on faster down the road heading north towards the keep.

The keep stood in the middle of the city, made of immense white stones. The Wizards Tower shot up like a spear, forming part of the eastern wall of the city.

Familiar with the layout of the keep, Jarol entered, passing the guards who recognized him and allowed him entry, and ran up the stairs that led up on the right side of the entrance chamber.

A guard stopped him at the top of the stairs.

"Hold," the guard said, raising a hand to stop Jarol. Jarol had never seen this guard, which meant that the guard didn't know him.

"I am Captain Jarol of Halsgrove, I must speak with Captain Strongshield immediately," Jarol said to the guard impatiently.

"Sorry, Captain. Of course, right this way," the guard said sheepishly when he realized Jarol was his superior.

"Captain Strongshield, Jarol from Halsgrove is here to see you, he says it's urgent, sir," the guard said after he opened Captain Strongshield's door halfway.

The Captain looked up at the guard that brought him the news then motioned with his hand to let Jarol in.

"Jarol, it's been a while since I've seen you up here in the city. I hope you haven't brought more of your suspicions?" He liked Jarol despite his suspicions and unfounded fears; he was still a good man.

"It's confirmed, Captain," Jarol said, ignoring the slight insult.

"What's confirmed?" Captain Strongshield replied, now serious

"Goblins, sir. One of our farmers, Alruin Stormcaller, found its footprint in the mud near his farm," Jarol said quickly, fear obvious in his voice.

"Has a goblin been spotted yet? I'm not for sending a war party out to the edge of the kingdom on suspicions, Jarol. You better be sure of what you are saying, this is matter I'll have to take up with the King. If we send out a war party it'll start rumors and panic across the rest of the kingdom and everyone'll be scared to go out and work the farms," Captain Strongshield replied. He asked because he had to be sure before he brought news to the king that the goblins had returned, but he believed Jarol's claim as soon as he heard that it was Alruin who made the claim.

Captain Strongshield knew Alruin; he was the blacksmith that had made his own personal sword. He knew Alruin was a sober man and trustworthy.

"No, at least no one has come forth yet that has seen one, but I'm not one for waiting to act until dangers at the door. I'm not asking for a war party, Captain, but send out a team of scouts. It won't be of any surprise and no one will be talking about it," he was desperate now. He understood the Captain's hesitancy; for those same reasons he was slow to listen to the rumors spreading around Halsgrove before visiting Jack's farm.

Captain Strongshield could see the desperation in Jarol's eyes. He knew Jarol was sincere and the possibility of goblins being seen again was enough for the captain to agree to send out the scouting party.

"Ok. Go get some rest, Jarol. You look like you've been on that horse of yours for a tenday. You leave tomorrow morning at dawn. I'll have a scouting party ready tonight. If there is anything out there, they'll find it," Captain Strongshield said and dismissed Jarol, who, much relieved to hear the news, left for The Traveler for the night.

Jarol awoke in the morning to the roosters call and, looking out the window from his bed, saw the first rays of the sun creeping over the mountains towards Taris. He didn't want to get up; the inn's bed was surprisingly more comfortable than his own and his body ached from the long ride from Halsgrove. But he got up, pushed on by the thought of his village being in danger. He took personal responsibility for Halsgrove's safety.

He got ready and ate a quick, but filling, breakfast of fresh milk and cheese with bread. The inn keeper brought around a new horse; courtesy of Captain Strongshield, Jarol presumed.

He mounted the horse and road down to the city gate where the scouting party was already ready and waiting. Captain Strongshield was there, giving his last instructions to the men.

"We do not know if there are goblins out there, men, but we need to know if there are. Your mission is very simple; if they are out there, find them. Only engage the enemies you know you can overtake, otherwise, scout out the whole region before returning. You are our eyes out there, do not let your kingdom down! Follow Captain Jarol here to Halsgrove, learn what you can from the village, then do what you have been trained to do." Captain Strongshield said. "It is possible that we are about to face our old enemy again; do not fail your city."

He knew many of them personally and the others had left their chosen school with outstanding marks. He trusted completely in their loyalty and sent them off with naught more than a nod of his head.

Jarol, shaking hands with Captain Strongshield before he rode out, was ready. He kept a pace that would allow the party to reach Halsgrove before the end of the week. So he rode, confident that he would be able to bring peace to his town. He hoped.

Chapter 3

First Encounter

"Do you think they're out there?" Tannon asked Will. They had gone to Jack's farm and started south, leaving their horses in the farmhouse so that they could scout out the area.

"Captain sure seems to think so," Will replied, not caring for the conversation; he didn't want any distractions.

"Stop!" Will said to Tannon. "Look!" he pointed, motioning for Tannon to look where he was pointing.

Tannon hesitantly walked over, not sure what he was looking for until he saw it. There, in the mud, was a foot print; a three-toed foot print. Fear crept over them and they began turning about and looking in every direction, thinking that it was a trap. A minute went by and nothing happened so they continued on, trying to follow the same direction as the foot prints, which were becoming easier to spot and follow the deeper into the woods they got.

It wasn't long before Tannon and Will sat atop a hill a few hundred yards from the goblin camp. The goblins had already begun getting ready to move; tents were being taken down and weapons and armor was being readied. They could not tell how many there were from all of the trees in the way but they guessed that there were well over a hundred by the size of the camp.

They came upon the camp a few hours before sundown and decided to stay to see what the goblins would do. From the goblins on the outer edges of the camp, closer to where Tannon and Will were hiding, they noticed that all the goblins wore a red mark on their chest piece; a red print of a large lizard claw.

"We need to leave and get word back to Halsgrove," Will said as calmly as he could to mask his fear.

"What do you think they're up to?" Tannon replied, stills staring at the goblin camp without paying attention to what Will said.

Will, not responding, started down the hill on his hands and knees and dropped suddenly to his chest; his eyes flying wide with fear.

Tannon turned when he heard Will drop to the ground to see what was going on. There, coming out of a copse of trees only a hundred yards away, were two goblin scouts.

Both Tannon and Will, as quickly and quietly as possible, tried to conceal themselves. Through the underbrush Will could see them walking casually; they hadn't been spotted. He quickly retrieved his bow and knotted an arrow.

Tannon copied his movements.

Will motioned to Tannon, then to the goblin on the right then to himself and the goblin on the left.

Tannon nodded and slowly raised himself just high enough to bring up his bow and take aim. He closed his eyes and inhaled deeply, settling his nerves and his shaking hands to aim. He had never felt so afraid. He never dreamed that he would actually have to fight, let alone against an enemy he had never before encountered. He opened his eyes and steadied his hands, knowing that Will and his life depended on it. He waited for Will's arrow to fly, and then released his own.

As still as a statue, Alruin sat on his back porch and watched his sons at play. It didn't bother him that they were acting out wars and battles; he actually enjoyed watching his sons play fighting, picking up sticks and running through an imaginative war that seemed to come alive in their eyes.

The scene took him back to his childhood days once again, running around the deck of his father's ship when he was no older than his sons, yelling out to the crewman how to defend against the imaginative pirates that were closing in. He remembered how they would laugh, not mockingly but thoroughly enjoying his young spirit. Often times they would give him scenarios and hint at the right way to defend.

He missed the sea; the smell of salt and fish on the breeze, the feel of the water spray kicked up by the prow bursting through a high wave on its descent. He longed to sit atop the nest and see nothing but open blue water, a hint of land in the distance and the feel of a chase when 'pirates' were spotted.

As his mind came back to the present, he saw that same spirit of his youth in Dryx and Weylor. A smile broke across his face, just like a strong wind blows across a sail and fills it, as he saw their spirited battle coming to a crescendo with Dryx and Weylor chasing off the last of their enemies; their faces lit up as they did the day he gave them a real enemy to fight, the bucket out on his farm.

He wanted nothing more than for them to keep that same spirit, to grow up and be able to do what he never was able to. As that dream of his took on shape in his mind, he realized to his dismay, that that day may never come; or if it did, it would not come in the way he would have it come. He knew that something was coming. Everyone could feel it.

He resigned himself to the fate that he might never see his farm again, the only proof of his hard work for that past six months. The thought didn't bother him nearly as much as the thought that what was coming would steal his son's innocence to the world, that their adventurous spirits would be formed around real enemies.

The most painful thought of all, he realized as Dryx and Weylor started a new "quest," was that someday those stick would become much more real, that those enemies they fought against would no longer be imaginative, and that those grins on their faces would turn from the pure joy of their imaginations to frowns of fear and despair in the eyes of real enemies. As bitter as that thought was to him, he knew that the world would steal their innocence away no matter how hard he tried to preserve it. As much as he would like that they never take up weapons of war, he knew that the knowledge of how to do so could save their lives; for he knew that that day would come. Their life was far more valuable than their innocence to truth, and he would rather have them prepared for what was coming than to try and shield them from the inevitable.

"Dryx, Weylor," he called over to the twins.

Their imaginative quest disturbed, they dropped their sticks and ran over to their father. They stopped in front of him, side by side, as he sat on the steps leading into their home. Their smiles and laughter vanished as they viewed their father's visage. By the serious look on his face they thought that he was angry with them, though they had seldom seen him angry.

"Sorry, father. We..." Weylor began but Alruin cut him off by raising his hand.

He was fighting an internal battle; he was torn between teaching them of the reality of their imaginations or letting them enjoy their innocent bliss as long they could. It did not take long, though, for him to decide. The slightest thought of them having to wield weapons in real combat settled his internal debate. He would not have his sons cut down because of their fear and inability to use a weapon.

"I called you over here, my sons," he began, ideas rolling through his mind as though he had been thinking hours upon the subject, "but you have forgotten your weapons! What if I had set an ambush here for you, you would be caught without a way to defend yourselves. Go," he said to them, now playing the role of commander, "get your sticks, let's see how well you wield them!" he said, his voice ending in a challenge to his young twins.

They looked at each other wide eyed, smiles creasing their cheeks from ear to ear and they hurried back to fetch their sticks.

Alruin picked a bough that was nearly as tall as him and slightly curved, somewhat resembling his own sword.

Dryx retrieved his two, equal length sticks and Weylor, never one to leave his brother alone in a fight, picked up the nearest stick and was at his brother's side in an instant.

Alruin went through the motions of a fight, though much slower to let his sons practice how to counter his moves. He almost felt like a young boy again, letting his imagination come alive, narrating the battle commencing before them. He never thought he would enjoy teaching his sons how to fight, though it was only play to them; for they were too young to be taught real combat. But he would guide them, telling them how to better take advantage of fighting against a single foe. He blocked all of his son's attempts to get a stick through his guard, letting them try to learn how to readjust to an opponent and try to find his weak spots.

As the sun sank lower in the sky Alruin realized they had been playing for quite some time. The twins were sweating from head to toe, though the breeze grew cooler as the sun sank lower; it was a welcomed feeling against their hot bodies.

He brought the battle to an end, kneeling down and clasping his son's shoulders as they stood together before him. "Well done, my sons! Surely no foe would stand against both of you and walk away!" he said in a most proud tone. All of his stress and worry flew from him as they took his compliment, once again lighting up their tired faces.

As he stood to lead the twins into the house for the night he saw Deli in the doorway, leaning against the frame with a content smile on her face. He paused, motioning for the twins to go into the house and met Deli's eyes.

A long moment passed, and to Alruin it seemed as though they had an entire conversation before she came out and stood beside him.

"I haven't seen you so happy in years," she told him, looking up into his eyes with the most genuine of smiles. She knew her life would be nothing without him, like a tree that was burnt and stripped of all its leaves yet still alive to live out its barren shame the rest of its days. "It's nice letting all the worry leave our house for a few hours. And besides, by the look of the twins, they'll be asleep before dinner," she added with a chuckle.

Alruin let out a short laugh; he truly did enjoy playing around with his sons. Alruin knew that Deli could see further into his time with the twins than just play-fighting.

Deli could see as much as he thought she could. She had been watching them almost from the beginning. She could see how he played on their imaginations, to keep it as light as possible, but also that he was more serious in their combat. She thought she knew the reason; that if something were to happen it would be better for them to know what to do than to grow up without knowing. The thought scared her as much as it did him, but she agreed with his intentions for the same reasons he did. Alruin kissed her forehead and led them inside, his arm around her shoulder.

"We must stop and make camp, sir. Our horses will need the rest for the final ride tomorrow and the night grows dark," Veredus told Jarol, unwilling to over-exert his men and horses when there was no apparent need to.

Jarol didn't respond, but nodded his agreement while looking east towards Halsgrove. He did not fear that Halsgrove would be attacked in the few days he had been gone, but he was anxious to get a real scouting party out to the eastern reaches of the kingdom. He needed proof, as much for himself as for his village, that they were safe and that all of their worries and fears were no more than wild imaginations that had risen up from the shadows of the Giant's Steppes and their proximity to Gander's Forest.

He dismounted his horse, a beautiful gray horse with a mane as white as driven snow. He truly appreciated the gift, though he already decided to return it with the scouting party.

The smell of the ocean, the salty breeze blown in from the north, cleared his mind of some of the stress he had. Jarol missed the ocean; but the thought was pushed far out of his mind almost as quickly as it entered as he began unbridling his horse. The campfires and smell of cooking venison brought him back to reality.

He looked over the group; the majority were young and, though well trained, he feared were too inexperienced if they should happen upon anything on their scouting route. The scout leader, Veredus, and a handful of other scouts were old enough to remember the war and had been in the guard for a long time.

After stowing his saddle and gear with the rest of the patrol's gear and eating a quick dinner, he found some low hanging branches in a nearby copse of trees and hung his hammock; sleep falling over him long before the hammock stopped swinging.

"Don't let it get back to camp!" Will hissed at Tannon, as loudly as he dared.

They had watched their arrows fly; Will's arrow pierced the chest of the goblin on the left, knocking it back a step. It looked down with a most perplexed look and raised its hand to touch the arrow before falling to the ground.

Tannon's arrow hit the bigger goblin a second later in the shoulder. It screamed in agony. It saw its comrade dead on the ground next to it and started turning to run back to camp.

Will saw that the goblin was going to run back quickly notched another arrow and shot, the arrow pierced the goblins left leg right above the knee and it fell down.

The pain in its shoulder and knee almost completely immobilized it, but it tried to crawl. Its breathing became hard and quick, not allowing the goblin to take a deep enough breathe to scream again.

Will was up in a flash, though running as low as he could to the ground to keep from being spotted. He dropped his bow and unsheathed his sword, heading straight for the goblin. He ran as fast as he could, knowing it would be only seconds before the goblin was able to scream again.

Tannon watched the goblin try to scurry away in pain, his own arrow sticking out of the back of the goblin's shoulder. He couldn't believe what was happening; he was paralyzed, crouched there on the ground, watching Will run forward and ready his sword.

In a matter of seconds Will was upon the goblin. It was in too much pain to hear the coming scout. All of his training flew from his mind, his fear and adrenaline blocked it. He moved on pure instinct, putting the sword straight through the goblins back. He realized his mistake, though, only a second after plunging the sword through the beast, as it let out a blood curdling scream; the pain forcing all the air out of its body. Will, as quickly as he could, stepped on the back of its head, forcing its open mouth into the ground to cut off its scream. He knew he had to think fast, fearing its scream had been heard in the camp not too far away.

He looked back and saw Tannon still kneeling in the same spot, bow hanging from his hand at his side, staring at him in shock. He started back but stopped when a sudden idea came to him as he passed the goblin he killed with his bow. Goblins weren't big creatures by any means, standing a full head-and-a-half lower than a human, but Will knew he would not be able to carry the dead goblin back to Halsgrove if the other goblins heard its scream. So, he bent down and severed its head clean off. He grabbed the repulsive head by its long, thin greasy hair and ran back to Tannon.

"What are you doing?! Let's go now!" he shot at Tannon as he passed him.

Tannon still couldn't move, though. So, after sheathing his sword and replacing his bow over his shoulder, Will grabbed the back of Tannon's backpack and pulled him along.

"We could have died," Tannon breathed, finally coming out of shock enough to run on his own.

"We still might if you don't hurry up!" Will hissed. He understood Tannon's fear, though, and agreed with his reasoning, but could not allow them to be caught up at the moment; he didn't know if they were being followed.

"We did what we had to do," Will said, trying to give Tannon some confidence. "They would have warned the camp and attacked us. Now, forget about that and focus on getting back to Halsgrove alive!" As much as Will wanted to sympathize with Tannon, he knew that it would slow them down and they could afford no delay. After what seemed like hours to them, they found Jack's farm, bringing a considerable amount of relief to both of them.

They quickly saddled up their horses, mounted up, and rode as fast as their horses could carry them back to Halsgrove.

"Where are they?" a goblin complained to his partner, waiting to relieve the missing scouts.

The other goblin, feeling slightly on edge, decided to leave and look for them. They all followed the same trail around the camp so they couldn't be far.

Only a few minutes later the two goblins came screaming back into camp.

Grol came out of his tent in a hurry. He was already on edge about the scouts report of the missing farmers so he wasn't too surprised to learn of the dead goblins they had just found.

Grol had to make a decision; attack or retreat. *If it had been a scouting party they would have attacked the camp,* he thought. It must have been a small group who fled when they saw how big the camp was.

"To the village!" Grol screamed. The goblin that had been scouting to the south of the village led the way through the thinner, less dense forest; Grol was not worried about trying to surprise the town, they already knew the goblins were there. He would attack them before they could get help from anywhere.

Chapter 4

Grol

The guard station bell sounded clearly against the calm spring evening, a sound the farmers and guards had never heard before. Regardless, they knew what it meant as soon as they heard it.

Alruin knew this day would come but he had hoped that it wouldn't. He had already gone over what they would do with his wife and the twins. He prepared a new box of fresh food every night that week and set it just inside the door in case they had to leave in a hurry. His wife grabbed the twins and followed Alruin, carrying the box of food, to the guard station.

Dryx and Weylor didn't know what was going on but understood that it was bad. Their father had told them how everything would happen in the guard station and what they were to do; be strong and stay with their mother. So, they ran next to their mother, their father following behind them. They didn't cry, Alruin told them not to.

"Deli, when we get in, take the twins to the back of the guard station," Alruin said to Deli as they neared the guard station. Although he trusted her completely, he wished he could stay with her and his sons; however, he knew a fight was coming and he would protect them, even with his life.

They reached the door and, as he had instructed, Deli took the twins into the guard station and down the hall to the back room.

Alruin smiled, though barely, at the sight of his scared sons; not crying as the other children, but following his order as he had told them to.

"Follow your mother," he called after his sons as they moved out of his sight into the building. Alruin quickly found the room that the guards had set apart for food and water and placed his boxes in the corner then went to find Ryker.

The two guards at the front door waited for the last villager before closing the large, wooden door. They pulled down a heavy wooden beam and set it across the metal door frame, further fortifying the door against being rammed.

Almost a hundred people were in the guard station, the entire population of Halsgrove. The women and children were crammed into the rooms at the back.

An hour went by in silence in the guard station before they could see, through the small arrow slits, the smoke that began rising into the air; Halsgrove was burning. At the same time as the rising smoke, the villagers began hearing the screams and yelling of the goblins, sending shivers down every single one of their spines. Not a person in the entire building was unafraid.

From inside they could see the approaching mass; a horde of goblins carrying torches and screaming from knowing they would all soon sink their weapons deep into the hated humans hiding in the big building in front of them.

They came on like a tidal wave, searching for any footholds to climb up to the top or holes to stick their weapons into. The yelps and screams came from all around the guard station, but the guards stayed in the entrance chamber and the hallway leading to it from both sides; that was the only way in.

The guard station had been built shortly after the last war, when Taris' villagers were able to return to their farms and villages. It was made of solid stone, virtually unable to be breached except through the front door.

Grol stayed back with his shaman, preparing a strategy to get the door open. He watched as his horde of goblins swarmed around the big building, surrounding it on all sides and hooting and howling from their blood craze. He could almost smell the fear from the townspeople inside.

Grol knew his shaman would be the key to getting that massive, solid door opened, but he wanted to wait; he wanted to wait until his goblins were too hungry for blood to flee and the humans were too scared to act.

The mothers held their small children close, huddled in the back rooms, covering their ears from the death that was fast approaching. A few women had fainted, leaving their small children alone, crying and afraid.

Deli waited with as much fear as any other woman in the station but she would not let that fear paralyze her as it had so many others. She had felt that this day might come since the first day Alruin returned from his farm feeling uneasy. After he saw the footprint, she knew she had to come to the reality that, even if they returned behind the safety of Taris' walls, Alruin would likely have to fight.

If there was something she could do, she would do it. She knew if it came down to it, she would take up a sword herself against any goblins that entered to protect her children. She realized, though, that all would be lost if they ever got that far.

The yells and howls of the goblins sounded as if they were already inside the station, their voices filtering in through every slit and hole they could find. The guardsmen fired arrows through every slit where any unfortunate goblin happened to pass by. As often as the guardsmen, though, the goblins put their bows and crossbows right up to the slits and firing inside as well. It wasn't long before an arrow from a goblin finally found a target; the shoulder of a guard that was just passing by to shoot his own arrow out of the narrow slit. Pain coursed through his arm as the nasty, crude arrow-tip plunged deep into his shoulder, the tip breaking through the skin on the other side. The guard fell back against the wall, his face fast whitening from both the shock of the pain, and the fear that was quickly stealing over him.

Alruin grabbed the guard and dragged him back, out of the entrance room and into the hallway. Another guard squeezed in to take his place.

"Deli!" Alruin yelled for his wife.

Deli sat her two sons in the corner of the room, telling them not to move until she came back. They nodded and she left.

Deli entered the room and Alruin left, back to help out however she could. She led the guard back one of the tables and helped him lie down. She inspected the arrow, noticing that the arrow tip was protruding from the back of his shoulder.

"Madeline!" she called back to her neighbor.

Madeline, shaking but afoot, came in when she heard Deli's call.

"Grab a wet cloth and clear away the blood around the wound," Deli told her, "we need to see how bad the wound is."

"We need to get you on your side," Deli told the guard, holding his face in her hands. He was too heavy for her to move him alone and needed him to roll onto his side.

After Madeline had cleared away the blood, they could see arrowhead protruding partially from the back of the guard's shoulder.

Deli looked around until she found a wooden spoon and put it in the guards mouth. "Bite down on this," she told him.

The guard was almost unconscious and didn't realize what was going on until the pain in his shoulder exploded again as Deli pushed the arrow further through his shoulder until they could break the arrowhead off.

The guard swooned and nearly fainted.

Deli quickly took her wet cloth and cleaned all around the wound on both sides of his shoulder. She poured a little alcohol over the wound, which caused the guard to scream out. She grabbed a long, thin sheet and tore it into strips, bandaging the soldier.

Grol enjoyed watching the madness, the wild rage of the goblins, although they were, by his standards, as smart as vermin and almost as useless. He was an orc, a humanoid like the goblins, but unlike the smaller goblins, he was as tall as a human and built like a bull. He was chosen as a raid commander for that fact alone; a group of 5 goblins wouldn't attack Grol out of sheer fear and respect for his savagery and strength.

To his right stood his shaman; although the shaman was also a goblin, and therefore inferior to Grol in every way, he respected the shaman's discipline and intelligence. Very few goblins possessed the basic intelligence and discipline required to learn the ways of magic. A shaman was far inferior to a wizard, but still possessed unique magical abilities that were not open to wizards; being able to call upon not only the arcane, but also nature itself to do their will.

"Enough," Grol said calmly to the shaman. Despite his tenacious and savage appetite, Grol had an unusual characteristic for his kind; patience—although by the human's standards his patience was like that of a child, it was still more than what the goblins possessed.

The shaman immediately started for the guard station, straight for the door. He stopped about fifty feet from the door and the goblins, when they saw the shaman, moved apart to give him a clear view of the door.

The shaman's hands flew into motion as he pulled a small piece of root and a few drops of water from his pack. He began speaking in a high-pitched, monotone voice. As his voice began to crescendo, nearing the end of the spell, the root and water flew into the air, spinning around each other before connecting. The wet root shone slightly in the darkness before shooting off towards the door.

A few seconds went by and, since the door had no magical protection, it began to creak and pull inside the tight steel frame it was in. The door was thick, though, and it would take more than one warp wood spell from the goblin shaman to make it useless and breakable.

"What?" one of the guards at the door said when he heard the small pop of the magical spell hit the wooden door.

The guards closest to the door noticed the slight pulling and twisting of the door and the creaking of its twisting against the metal frame that held it.

"They are using magic!" another guard yelled out.

"What's going on?" Ryker said in a distressed tone, coming in from behind to get a closer look. He stopped before the door and examined it for a moment; until he saw its slightly warped features inside the metal frame. He stood there, staring at the door in fear, not willing to accept the fact that the hours or days he thought that they could last in the guard station could so quickly be turned to minutes or seconds. He knew the door was strong and could resist massive amounts of pounding, but how long could it last against magic?

Ryker knew he had to think of something; the door wouldn't last much longer against the magic.

"Again! Hit it again!" Grol yelled at the shaman.

The goblin was in motion even before Grol had finished yelling. Another piece of root and some water was in the air and a moment later flying towards the door. Again the guards on the other side of the door screamed out in fear, knowing that the only protection between them and the goblin horde just on the other side of the wall was the door and it wouldn't last long.

The shaman cast the spell one more time before exhausting his ability to cast that spell that day. He walked back to Grol, stopping in front of him.

Grol again smiled wickedly as the shaman began casting a spell on him.

Chanting slowly, the shaman brought his arms up, his fingers moving in fast, intricate patterns. Long, dark bull hairs fell from his hands as he began casting, which, instead of falling to the ground, were caught in the spell and flew straight at Grol.

Grol felt a familiar tingle start in his feet and work its way up his body. He had felt this before; many times before. It was the effect of the shaman's spell that gave him magical strength.

A few moments later, Grol found himself a foot taller and could feel the magical chords lining his muscles. His huge axe seemed a feather-weight now with his new strength, bringing an evil grin to his scarred face.

The goblins had again swarmed around the door, covering it from sight. Their blood craze was ripe with their howls and screams and the human's scent and fear, hiding inside a building, sent them into a frenzy.

One goblin didn't notice Grol's approach or that the other goblins had again cleared away from the area around the door and continued hopping around, caught up in the boisterous howling and yelping of the horde around him.

He stopped suddenly, caught in mid-air; a very weird and confused look came across his face. He had come down to the ground after every other jump, he thought, but this time he just hung there, and after another moment he started to feel tired, very tired.

His head now hung low and he saw blood dripping down to the ground from behind him. Curious, he pulled his head around at a weird angle and saw a pair of massive, armored legs standing directly behind him.

Grol.

Effortlessly, Grol raised the axe, with the goblins back still embedded around it, and kicked the goblin off. His eyes stayed open as he lay on the ground, twitching, though the look on his face was one more of curiosity than fear, he was already dead; he never had time to fear.

Grol dropped his freshly-bloodied axe to his side and turned to face the shaman that stood back where he just was and pointed at the door.

The shaman, almost paralyzed with fear, knew exactly what Grol wanted. He ran straight up to where the dead goblin was. It was his fear of Grol, not his loyalty, which allowed his legs to move him closer to Grol, for all he wanted to do in that moment was run; to run and never return to his merciless leader.

Taking only a second to steady his breath, he began chanting. His hands flew into his pouch and, with an audible sigh of relief, he drew out a piece of root and some water. His hands next went out wide, in an arching circle, to stop just before they crossed. About to utter his last chant and his hands already flying forward to send the spell to the door, he stopped suddenly; one of his arms was caught on something.

An arrow was protruding from his chest, its head buried deep within.

The shaman fell over, his body landing next to the other goblin, and he closed his eyes to the world.

Grol followed the arrows path to an arrow slit in the stations wall that was supposed to be covered. Grol had specifically commanded them to keep the arrow slits blocked with their shields when the shamans were casting.

Angrier than he had ever been, Grol ran over and grabbed the goblin who had taken his shield down for just a moment to watch the shaman cast. No matter how the goblin fought back or tried to break free, his strength was no match for Grol and his steel grip. He put the goblin onto his lowered shoulder and backed up in front of the door. Grol yelled, lowered his shoulder slightly, and run full-out for the door. He felt every bone in the small goblins back and chest break as the force of his shoulder was stopped by the door, with the small goblin's body in between.

The door shuttered and a crack ran off the larger warp in the wood that ran the height of the door. Grol smiled wickedly, both from breaking the small, useless goblin's body and from the crack he managed to put in the thick, warped wooden door.

"Nice shot!" one guard said, watching his comrades arrow hit its mark through another arrow slot. Everyone broke into cheers and a small amount of hope was returned to the people of Halsgrove.

Alruin and Ryker, though, were more reserved. They saw and heard what the massive orc had done to the door and still questioned how much more of a beating it could take. Alruin could see how badly the door had warped with the second spell, he could see how weakened it had become inside its metal frame.

Another loud thud hit the door, putting another crack in it and shaking the wall around it. The sudden noise took the smile from everyone's face. The guards at the door took a few precautionary steps back and glanced around, hoping that someone would have an answer or a suggestion of what they could do to save the door.

"Don't just stand there, barricade the door!" Ryker barked at the guards standing by the door.

The guards ran to the back of the station and grabbed the heaviest benches that were in the guard station common area and anything else they could use. They braced the benches against the door and the walls on either side, leaning against them for extra support.

"Here he comes again!" a guard from one of the side rooms yelled, watching Grol get ready to ram the door again. A few seconds later they heard, and felt, another tremendous blow hit the door; and another long crack found its way into the middle of the door.

Alruin, moving closer to examine the door, could see in how bad of shape the door was, and how only a few more hits from the giant orc outside would separate the wooden door from its metal frame, rendering it useless.

"If we want to survive we need to stop him. Two more hits like that and this door is going to be lying flat on the ground. Our wives and children depend on us!" Alruin was almost yelling to be heard above the noise of the frenzied goblins just a few feet away, though he kept his voice as calm as he could. He wanted to bolster the guards resolve and courage; he knew the goblins would get in before help arrived.

Chapter 5

Rising Smoke

Jarol was up before the sun rose over the Giants Steppes. He found little sleep that night; dreams of pain, fear, and cries constantly awoke him during the night. He roused the scouting party, none of whom were happy to be woken before sunrise; however, they knew the relationship that Jarol had with Captain Strongshield and none of them wanted to have to face him because they didn't want to wake up.

They rode at the same, fast pace as the previous two days. They would reach Halsgrove around night fall.

It was near sundown when Jarol and the other scouts saw it.

There, rising up as black as the night far off in the distance, was a swirling column of smoke. It was almost dark and Jarol knew they were still a hard ride from Halsgrove, but they spurred their horses on, hoping that they would not be too late.

The door was holding, or the make-shift brace that the guards had put up was holding. The door was almost knocked completely off its hinges by the giant orc's last battering, but it still stood, badly cracked and warped beyond repair.

Grol had to stop ramming the door when the spell from the shaman wore off, and he couldn't cast it again. Angrier than he had ever been, Grol ordered the goblins to cut down a tree and use it as a ram in his place. As thick as the door was, and despite the braces that had been put up by the guards, the goblins were making leeway.

Alruin and Ryker knew they didn't have much time, but they knew that there wasn't much that they could do confined in the guard station. They started prepping the entrance rooms opposite door. The entrance room had only two doors; the entrance and the inner door. It was a fairly small, rectangular room; the floor and walls were made of stone.

The only hope that Alruin and Ryker held was in blockading the inner door of the entrance room, in hopes of holding off the horde until help arrived; if help arrived.

A sudden, loud crack issued forth from the door, followed by a silence; an eerie silence that sent shivers down the spine of every villager in the guard station. Everyone understood that sound, everyone knew what that sound meant and everyone knew that the horrible death that was outside was much, much closer to reaching them. Another moment went by and the door burst open.

The goblin horde flew into an ecstatic frenzy, knowing that they would soon get the opportunity to taste human blood.

The guards cleared out of the entrance chamber and sealed off the room, blockading the inner door. This door was not, however, as think or strong as the outer door and the guards knew it. The only hope that they had was that the cramped space of the entry room would not allow them to bring in the ram that they had used to bring down the outer door.

"You three, brace the door!" Ryker yelled at the three closest guards to the door. "The rest of you, let's kill as many as we can through the arrow slits!" Ryker yelled to the rest of the guards and men that could bear arms.

They split into two groups; one group in each room on either side of the entrance room. The first few unfortunate goblins that entered the guard station thought that they would be running into a room filled with defenseless women and children, which threw them into an insane bloodthirsty rage that took all fear from them. What they met instead, though, was a two-sided trap; arrows flying out of both sides of the walls.

The guards had waited until the goblins had almost reached the door to start firing; each man firing at the goblin directly in front of him. Eight goblins fell in that room in the first few seconds, taking a bit of the frenzy out of the remaining goblins.

The goblins continued pouring in, though; two goblins filling every spot where one died. A few more seconds went by and a few more goblins fell; arrows found their marks, which resulted in a dead, or dying, goblin.

Soon enough, however, they began using the same tactic as they had outside; blocking the arrow slits with their shields.

This did not deter the guards and the men of Halsgrove, though, for they were, in every moment, spurred on by the cries of their women and children, knowing that if they failed their families would meet a horrible death.

The guards threw down their bows and pulled out their swords, axes and whatever other weapon they had. They searched for every hole in the goblin's attempts to block the arrow slits; looking for any hole in which they could stab their swords.

Many screams were heard from the goblins that had taken their attention off the arrow slits for even a split second, looking to see if the way was opened to enter the guard station. For that split second was all the guards needed to drive their swords into the unsuspecting goblins body anywhere they could.

The hallway behind the inner door was just wide enough for two men to stand shoulder to shoulder. At both ends of the hall were the guard's sleeping chambers. Since there were a limited number of men that could effectively be in the rooms on either side of the entrance hall, most of the men of Halsgrove waited in the guards sleeping chambers on either end of the hallway;

they were the last line of defense between their families and the goblins if they broke through.

Knowing that the narrow hallways were the only advantage the guards had when the goblins broke through the door, Ryker ran between the rooms explaining the plan. The men in each room would, when the goblins broke through, take up their shields and barricade the goblins in as close to the door as possible, eliminating a strong force from entering at one time and overpowering the guards.

Being the commanding guard in Jarol's absence, Ryker felt the responsibility fall completely over his shoulders. He wasn't very tall, but what he lacked in height he made up for with size. While off-duty he worked as a specialized blacksmith; an armor smith. His arms, though not as long as he would like, held his sword and heavy, double-plated shield with ease.

Ryker went out to the inner door, to where the three guards were bracing a very cracked and weakening door, "get your shields, we are the barricade now," he said.

Ryker took his place barely a foot from the door. Guards on either side of the door grabbed their shield and rushed out to stand by him.

"Nothing gets by us! We are the line!" he yelled to his men. "The lives of every woman and child here lie on our shoulders; no longer shall we fear, no longer shall we retreat. We are warriors of Taris! We shall not fail them!" he shouted when he finished, raising his sword high in the air and yelling as loud as he could. Every man in guard station took up the shout; a deafening cry for bravery and valor in the face of their enemy.

Ryker knew that even if help came and the townsfolk were saved he would die there, in that hallway, protecting his friends until death took him; he meant to make that death wait a bit longer before falling.

That thought brought a new feeling to Ryker, a feeling he had never felt. A very out-of-place smile broke through his recent doubtful expressions; acceptance of fate, acceptance of death. Fear was no longer playing on his emotions, but was completely replaced by an iron will of determination and vengeance. He knew many goblins would fall by his sword before he fell by one of theirs, and the thought caused him to laugh the most wild and barbaric laugh that any of the guards around him had ever heard. He almost stepped forward to take down the barricade and meet the horde head on. Almost.

He saw their faces start changing from fear and doubt to courage, determination and rage. Yes, rage! Ryker thought. He could only hope that their rage would flow as freely as his. He let it consume him; he let it completely take over his instincts. A fire burned deep within his eyes, a fire he welcomed completely with no resistance. It felt good, he realized, to give in to his most natural and basic instincts; to give himself over to the rage.

The guards formed up shoulder to shoulder, three sets deep on each side of the door. The guards standing behind the first held javelins and spears, ready to jab into the oncoming attackers over the shoulders of their allies.

A sudden ram against the door tore it from its hinges, knocking the door against the opposite wall in the hallway. In came the horde…

"Halsgrove!" the lead scout yelled, seeing in the distance the first sign of the small village; a tall, barren tree that marked the western edge of Halsgrove. The tree was massive, but had been burnt before anyone could remember; yet there it stood. No winter, storm, or fire had been able to bring its hulking trunk to the ground.

The town still lay much further down the road, but the sight of the tree spurred the scouts on.

"The townspeople will be in the guard station in the middle of town," Jarol yelled to the other scouts over the loud pounding of the horse's hooves on the dirt road leading to Halsgrove.

Jarol would ride on alone if he had to; he knew how dire his town's situation was if they were still alive and he would rather share that fate than live out the rest of his days in Taris knowing that he hadn't died beside his comrades.

"Most savage Grol," one of Grol's scouts ran up to him, "we have broken through the second door!" He knew his leader would be pleased to hear the news and wanted to be the goblin to share that news with Grol. He wasn't disappointed by Grol's reaction.

Grol smiled wickedly and raised his huge axe high into the air, once again showing off his chorded arm muscles.

"A hundred silver to whoever kills the most humans!" was his cry to the horde of goblins in front of him; the majority of the vast horde had not yet entered the guard station. He had no intention of giving even a copper to any of his useless fodder, but the offer, nonetheless, sent them deeper into their frenzy.

He stood back, relishing in the knowledge that he would soon be returning to Orgath, the kingdom of the savage orcs and goblins, with word of his victory over Halsgrove. The thought of climbing ranks and gaining more power compelled him to go forward, to personally see the victory through. He decided to wait; however, to let his fodder take care of what little resistance there might be upon entering the guard station.

With both his sword and shield bloodied with goblin blood, Ryker stood like an anchor against the waves of goblins entering his guard station. He had been hit several times and, though none of them were major wounds, his blood flowed freely in many places. He didn't even know that he had been hit. His mind had left pain behind and had given itself over to his most primal instincts.

He brought his shield straight up ahead of him in an arc, the bottom tip hitting the goblin directly in front of him on its chin, momentarily dazing it and causing its head to turn up. Its arms flew out wide to catch its balance, revealing the perfect opportunity.

Ryker thrust his sword straight forward, just below its rib cage and up into its heart. The goblin fell limply to the floor, but with so many goblins behind it trying to take its place he knew he couldn't block all the attacks.

Before he had time to lower his shield again, a wooden spear found its way from behind the dying goblin into Ryker's exposed left leg, puncturing his thigh. His shield came down in a flash, breaking the spearhead from the spear and ripped the spearhead from his thigh. This time he did feel the pain; his scream of pain from the spear turned into a yell of defiance and desperation. He would not give up and, though the guards behind him urged him to step back and let them take his spot, he would not retreat.

A sword came in low and Ryker dropped his shield arm, forcing the blade low and thrust his own sword forward, stabbing the goblin in the throat. As soon as his blade had cut through to the back of the things neck he pulled back his sword and brought his shield up just in time to block another spear, this time it came in high. The dying goblin in front of him fell to the floor.

The guards were too focused on the goblins and didn't see how the dead bodies weren't piling up around the door. They couldn't see the goblins on the other side dragging out the dead bodies to make room for more.

The guards opposite Ryker weren't fairing so well. One of the guards had already fallen and had been dragged back; his position being filled by the guard behind him.

Will was still up, the front guard opposite Ryker. He, like Ryker, had sustained many wounds, but he grunted the pain away. Thoughts of his wife and young daughter spurred him on despite the pain. Many goblins fell to Will's scimitar before he began losing strength from the loss of blood. He saw the overhead cut from the goblin in front of him and barely managed to raise his sword to knock it aside; it didn't miss by much. His vision starting fading and his reaction time was slowing, evidenced by the clumsy thrust of a spear that struck his side without finding any resistance.

There wasn't much power behind the thrust but the spear managed to wedge its head in between a crease in his armor and puncture his side. He suddenly felt as light as a feather and saw the ground coming up to meet him. The noise around him faded into the background as pictures and memories of his wife and daughter flooded his mind; their faces, their voices, their memories. He felt himself being dragged back by his foot, and then everything went black.

"Will! Will! Wake up!" Will heard a voice, though he was too far gone to recognize it as his wife's. He felt apart from the voice, as if it was only a whisper.

"Are they safe?" was all that he could manage to whisper. He had to know if he had done enough; if he had helped his family survive.

His wife, crouching over him, understood what Will needed to hear. She saw how courageously he must have fought; his entire body was bloodied with fresh scars and wounds. She saw all the wounds on his body that he had taken to buy more time. She knew she had to be strong and let him die in peace.

"Yes, Will. We are safe; you did it," she said, breaking into tears, holding Will's face close to her own as his eyes shut.

A sudden, slight smile pursed his lips as he passed; he died knowing that he had given his family a little longer. His eyes closed and his life passed away; his face peaceful.

Jarol, who wanted to ride straight for the host of goblins who were blocking the entrance to the guard station, almost didn't follow the scouts to the south entrance of Halsgrove; directly behind the enemy.

The scouting party was made up of only thirty riders; Jarol realized they were far outnumbered. They had been hand-chosen by Captain Strongshield for their courage and skill; each of them had been on many scouting missions and many of the older scouts had seen battle.

They formed up behind Jarol, who refused to take any other position but the spearhead. Five of the scouts stayed behind; Jarol didn't understand until he saw four of them take out their light composite bows, and the fifth, a greater surprise that raised his spirits even more, took off his jerkin and riding gear to reveal a robe; a wizard's robe.

Jarol knew his townspeople were still alive. The cries and yells of the goblin horde trying to get into the building was a clear sign to Jarol; the goblins knew there were people still inside. His villagers were making a stand. He could imagine how the guards had lasted so long; barricading the doors and using the narrow hallways to their advantage; but the thought of his guards falling in that building took all patience and strategy from Jarol's mind. He kicked his horse into a gallop, almost leaving the rest of the scouts behind. They caught up, though, and the goblins had only seconds to try to understand the sudden trembling in the ground coming from behind them; only seconds to turn and see what horrible death awaited them.

The wizard, Robilor, and the four ranger scouts, instead of heading directly for the mass of goblins, headed northeast, off the road and into the cover of the smoldering houses. They heard Jarol and the mounted scouts break into the ranks of the goblins, killing many under their trampling horses and sent many more scattering to get out of the way. They heard the cries of surprise and fear from the goblins.Robilor, after invoking a few simple defensive spells on himself, nodded to the rangers and they all stepped out from behind the smoldering house. They used caution, though they quickly found out that it was not needed. The whole of the goblins attention was focused on the new mounted scouts that were tearing through their ranks. They witnessed how complete their advantage was, both from being mounted and gaining the element of surprise, when the goblins began to scatter. The goblins, in all the confusion, couldn't see that those mounted riders were all the aid that the villagers had and that they outnumbered the riders at least five to one.

The four rangers picked their targets carefully, looking for either the biggest goblins to take down, or any that looked like they were trying to rally the others.

Robilor, however, only looked for groups of goblins that didn't have any of his mounted comrades nearby. Easily finding a group, both of his hands flew to two small pouches on either side of his belt, one pulling out a pinch of sulfur and the other a small seed. His hands flew forward and then up, tracing intricate, invisible arcane signs in front of him while he started a low, hum-like chant.

A moment later the seed, now glowing red and orange with fire, flew forward and hit a group of goblins nearest the door on the east side of the horde. As soon as the seed struck the the goblin near the center of the group Robilor had aimed for, it exploded into fire, enveloping and setting fire to all of them. The six goblins closest to the explosion where completely engulfed in flames and fell dying to the ground; the sudden explosion and fire, and the cries of the dying goblins, sent even more confusion into the rest of the already shaken horde.

Grol was halfway through the entrance room, his movement slowed by the mass of goblins trying to get in, when he stopped. He heard and felt the slight rumble in the earth and the sound of distant thunder; it took a few moments for him to realize what it was. He made it to the door when the mounted horsemen began tearing into his ranks of goblins. He thought this was the end, that an army had come. Standing a full foot over most of the goblins he could see no other forces coming to join the fight. He had only seconds to react before his force of goblins would completely disperse and run away in fear. The cowardice of the goblins angered him as much as the arrival of this new enemy.

Knowing he had only seconds, he jumped out from the doorway and raised his axe high overhead, calling the attention of all the goblins around him and rallying them to attack. Had it not been for Grol in that moment, the goblin horde would have broken apart and fled. With long strides and his head held a little low, knowing that his height would mark him as an easy target, he made his away over to where the riders would pass by. As the outer wing on the left side of the spearhead passed by just feet away he came up suddenly to his full height, yelling out to his god, Garamosh, and with his huge axe took the nearest rider from his horse; his axe embedding itself all the way to the spine of the unfortunate scout. He lifted the body up on his axe clear over his head and yelled, spurring his goblin horde to attack. The site of a dead scout on their leader's huge axe gave them courage and they turned back.

"Ryker!" the guard behind him yelled. He had seen all the hits that Ryker had taken and how he pressed on; never giving in until the end. Ryker's bravery and loyalty boosted his own resolve.

Ryker had taken a vicious hit to the chest; an attack from the goblin behind the one in front of him with a spear. The guard watched him double over from the pain and loss of blood.

As quickly as he could, he grabbed Ryker and pulled him back past the other guards, one of whom filled his spot as soon as it was open.

He dragged Ryker back to the room at the end of the hallway and set him down as gently as he could on the cold floor. Ryker was already gone. His expression was almost without emotion; he was gone.

The guard closed his eyes and said a quick prayer to their god, Valerum, that Ryker's courage, bravery and honor would not be forgotten or overlooked by the gods. His prayer was short as the sounds and cries of injured and dying goblins and men pulled him back to the fight. With one final look at his friend and leader, he grabbed up his shield and headed for the hallway. He arrived just in time to fill the hole of the fallen guard who had fought beside Ryker.

The goblins kept pouring in through the entrance room. The guards were nearly overrun; only two guards remained on either side of the entrance and they had been pushed back almost to the doors of the rooms on either side of the hall. If they were pushed through the doors the goblins would be able to fill the rooms in seconds. Most of the farmers didn't have weapons, and the weapons they did find they didn't know how to use. They waited in the rooms on either end of the hallway; without shields they knew they wouldn't last long.

There was an explosion outside that shook the guard station; momentarily stealing the attention of everyone inside. The guards had no way of knowing that the explosion was the fireball cast by Robilor, but they used the momentary surprise to their advantage; cutting down the few goblins directly in front of them that were caught off guard by the sudden explosion and had let their guard down.

"We must hold them!" one of the last guards yelled, just as much to himself as to the comrade at his side. They had to hold; if they fell, all the villagers would fall.

With all of the commotion and the mounted scout riders never stopping to engage one-on-one, the goblins hardly noticed the four ranger scouts picking them off left and right, usually taking out the goblins that tried to run away, not wanting to make it too obvious to the goblins that they were there.

The mounted scouts never slowed their pace and split into smaller groups of five to six men to run down the smaller groups of goblins left by their initial charge. Within the first two minutes of fighting, two dozen goblins lay dead or dying while only two guards had lost their lives; one to Grol and the other fell prey to a spear thrown by one of the goblin. Many of the guards had been hit, their horses also, but they shrugged off the pain and continued their assault.

Robilor was a bit older than the rest of the scouts. He had been a scout for many years and had accompanied Captain Strongshield himself on many of the scouting trips before the last war. He loved the thrill of battle; the excitement and danger of it pushed him on, forced him to hold nothing back. So, when a group of goblins broke off the main group and ran towards him he felt neither fear nor anxiety. A smile crossed his face when he realized, like so many times before, that he was alone and cornered against a wall; he did not dislike the odds.

The goblins knew he was a wizard and saw the fireball that had consumed a group bigger than their own. They quickly circled him, leaving only ten feet in between him and the goblins, forcing him to be consumed as well if he cast another fireball. A goblin jumped forward, its spear leading the way. The spear should have driven right through Robilor's back, but it just stopped. The goblin stood with a most puzzled look as the tip of its spear rested against the wizard's robe, as if it were a wall of stone.

Robilor let out a laugh; the goblins looked around at each other and each took a step back.

Before casting the fire ball, Robilor had placed a few different defensive spells on himself, one of which gave his skin the consistency of stone without changing his appearance. A certain number of hits would break the spell, he knew, but that didn't bother him too much; he knew these goblins wouldn't get a chance to hit him again.

He spun on his heel and faced the goblin that had struck him in the back. The goblin had never felt so much fear as he looked into the human's eyes; Robilor's face shaking slowly from left to right with a smile too calm for war. He closed his eyes and spoke a word in his mind to the ring on his left hand; 'shield'. Robilor felt a warmth course through his body the instant he spoke the word, the spell in his ring enacting to make him resistant to heat and flame. A split second later he opened his eyes and looked the goblin right in the eyes and sent another mental word to the ring on his right hand; 'suicide'. A flaming seed shot straight down from the ring to the ground at Robilor's feet.

He loved getting so close to the enemy that he had to use his rings; he loved the rush. Flames exploded from Robilor's feet and engulfed all five of the goblins that were around Robilor; their screams and cries of pain tore through the air, turning more than a few heads to see what happened. They would be dead before the flames died from off of their skin. Robilor felt as though a hot wind from the desert blew across his body, only slightly uncomfortable.

A few goblins that had watched the group surround the wizard stared in sheer horror as the goblin's spear stopped at Robilor's back. They expected him to be skewered, but instead they watched him turn slowly to the goblin that tried to kill him. Then they saw him drop a fireball at his own feet which engulfed the entire group. They could not understand why a wizard would drop a fireball at his own feet; it would just kill him too.

They were about to jump back into the horde of goblins and continue attacking until they saw their five comrades lying dead and dying in a circle around the still standing wizard, who looked around with a slight nod at the dead goblins, stretched out his back quick and turned right at them. That was too much. They howled in fear and dropped their weapons, all care for the battle and even fear of Grol himself flew from their minds when they saw the crazy human wizard look at them.

They ran; they didn't even know which direction they were running in but they didn't care. All they knew was that they had to get away from that powerful wizard.

A few minutes went by and two dozen more goblins lay dead and dying on the ground around the entrance to the guard station. More than half of the remaining goblin force had started to flee before any of the guards began entering the guard station. Grol, having killed three more scouts before he turned to flee, yelled for the goblins to follow him but he didn't wait to see if they were;

the more of them between him and the scouts the better chance he had of getting away. He needn't have feared, though, for the scouts were more intent on getting into the guard station than chasing down the goblins.

The four scouts, always moving and shooting on the run, had no problem staying out of melee combat. They, alone, had kept many of the mounted scouts alive, putting an arrow through any goblin that got too close to their backs. Almost another dozen goblins died while trying to flee behind Grol; goblins running away in a straight line were easy targets.

They each let off a few arrows straight into the entrance of the guard station before the mounted scouts got off their horses and went in.

What they found in the entrance chamber was a massacre; not of men but of goblins! At least three dozen goblins lie dead in the entrance chamber alone. They were more amazed when they entered the hallway through the inner entrance chamber door; a dozen goblins lie dead just entering the hallway, with maybe a dozen more stretched out along the hallway on either side.

Fortune did not shine on the goblins which were inside, though. All they could hear was the shouts and screams of battle outside and had no way of knowing that the rest of their force had retreated. In a matter of seconds they found themselves now surrounded by guards to their backs and armed villagers in front. No goblin that stepped foot into the guard station survived, besides Grol, who, from his longer and stronger legs, had far outdistanced the goblins behind him in their retreat into the forest.

Chapter 6

Massacre

The last guard fell and in came the goblins. The room was too big for Alruin and the other villagers to trap the goblins, so they bundled up in front of the door that led back to the women and children. Most of the villagers were able to take up the shields of the fallen guards but Alruin had only his personal sword that he used with both hands.

The room was wide enough where the Alruin and the villagers were to allow almost three goblins to every villager. The farmers had no prior experience with battle or weapons, except for Alruin, but they fought with such ferocity that there brute force and savagery made up for their lack of skill.

Every farmer defending the door had family on the other side and not a single one was going to let a single goblin pass while he still drew breath.

The goblins, despite the farmer's stone hard resolve, flooded the room and soon had the farmers backed up against the wall. A goblin fell for every step back a villager took, but there was always a goblin there to take its place. The bodies of the goblins began to pile up, but the farmer's had begun to fall. Just like the guards, the farmers had taken many hits and lost a lot of blood before being forced to the ground to die a brave man's death.

Alruin, seeing that the last few farmer's around him were about fall, made the hardest decision of his life; he felt that deserting those farmers in that moment would be considered cowardice but thoughts of Deli and Dryx and Weylor were more powerful. He jumped back into the room and waited close to the entrance.

The eyes of every woman and child were on him and no one said a word. His presence stole all hope from them; he was now the only thing between them and the goblins. But at the same time his body was bloodied and cut in many places, yet he looked like an anchor against the coming darkness, giving them a sliver of hope and a small sense of security. Those to his side could the resolve etched across his face; he would not die until the scouts outside were able to save those behind him. The goblins would come rushing in any second, yet he stood there poised and ready to give everything he had.

Alruin watched as the farmers fell and the goblins started for the door. For a moment it seemed as though the world had slowed down. Thoughts, memories, and images of his family raced through his mind. He knew Deli was behind him, holding his boys, and knew what the sacrifice he was about to make would do to Deli if she survived.

The first goblin came at him wildly, its crude sword held in both hands over its head.

Quicker than the goblin could react, Alruin side-stepped with the long blade of his sword following at an angle behind him, cutting a deep line the goblin's stomach. Just as quick, Alruin spun back towards the door, dropping to his knee as he went, his sword shooting straight through the stomach of the next goblin and into the belly of the goblin behind.

Alruin used the narrow entrance of the door to his advantage and was able to keep the goblins from swarming the rooms for a few minutes.

Eventually, though, the adrenaline began to fade and Alruin began to feel the pain from his many wounds. He felt weaker with his loss of blood and found it harder to breath with his massive loss of blood.

He resorted to shorter, quick bursts of speed with his sword to drop the last two goblins that entered before he fell to his knee, trying to keep himself up with his sword tip on the ground, pulling on the hilt for leverage.

He heard the sound of screaming goblins from near the entrance and knew the scouts were close. But he still had to hold the goblins off that were in front of him for another minute.

Deli watched as Alruin dropped to his knee. A moment later his sword fell down to the side and his hands fell to the stone floor. There, her husband, her love, her best friend, was defeated. No longer caring whether she lived or died, Deli thought only of her children. Just as she was turning to put herself in between the coming goblins and her sons, Alruin exploded up onto his feet.

Deli was couldn't look away; Alruin charged the door, grabbing the goblin in front of him around the waste and charged forward with every ounce of energy he had left. The momentum and extra weight of the goblin he held pushed the crowd backward, many of the goblins lost their balance and fell down.

Deli watched as, only a moment later, her love was swarmed by a dozen goblins, his body no longer visible. She turned around, covered her children's ears and dropped her head in defeat.

When Jarol and the Taris scouts finally made it into the guard station, they had to step over the bodies of the fallen guards; guards that Jarol knew personally and many of whom he considered his closest friends.

Jarol, his rage more fierce with every one of the guards he had to step over, cut his way through the line of goblins down the hall. He heard Alruin's yell and watched how the entire group of goblins in the room in front of him were pushed back. Jarol caught only a glimpse of Alruin before he was completely covered by goblins but that was all he needed; bounding forward, Jarol led the scouts into the room. His yell was a war cry to any god that would listen. Jarol, his tears now falling like drops from a waterfall, tore through the goblins with abandon. When the room was cleared of anything resembling a goblin, Jarol fell into a chair, his head in his hands crying like a child for his fallen friends.

There were no cheers or applause from the rescued women and children. This was no victory; every woman in that room had lost someone she loved.

Deli left the twins in the corner and slowly made her way into the room where Alruin had vanished. The guards, with respect and honor, cleared away the goblins from on top of him and Deli fell to her knees at his side. She took up his hand and his eyes opened enough for him to see her face one last time. She leaned down, telling Alruin she loved him as she did, and kissed his forehead.

"I love you," was all he was able to breathe out before his eyes closed again. Deli felt his grip loosen and held her face there against his, forehead to forehead, and cried. She felt as though her entire heart had been ripped from her chest in that moment. She couldn't move from his side; she sat there until the guards pulled her up gently, telling her it was time to go.

Jarol forced himself up from his chair and made his way around the guard station. He couldn't hold back his overwhelming emotions; both pride and grief coursed through him. There was not a single fallen guard with less than a dozen easily visible wounds.

He had to lean against the wall for support, more angry that he hadn't been there to share in the same fate with his friends than sorrow at their death. He knew what they fought and died for, and they accomplished their mission; the women and children were safe and the scouts had finished off the last of the goblins inside the guard station.

"I want four guards inside taking out the dead goblins and making a pile. The rest of you I want outside, form a perimeter. I want to know if those beasts mean to come back. Get the rangers to track the goblins and see which direction they are headed.

When all of the dead goblins are piled up, burn them," Veredus ordered to all the guards around him in the guard station. He didn't know if the goblins would regroup so he knew he had to act fast. The doors were broken and useless so the guard station wouldn't be a safe place to stay in.

"Have any of the guards from Halsgrove survived?" Veredus asked the guard beside him quietly.

"Eleven are dead and one is unconscious with serious wounds; we aren't sure if he'll make it. He's hurt pretty bad," the guard replied.

Veredus nodded his head, thinking quickly. "Go and see if any of the villagers have wagons we can still use. We need to leave here," he told the guard and the guard left.

He found the unconscious guard from Halsgrove lying on a bed, covered in blood and sweat. Some women from the village were trying to stop the bleeding and clean his wounds, but he was fading fast. Despite the pain he was in, a faint smile creased his face; he had done it. He had seen the villagers through to safety; he had held out long enough for help to arrive. He was young and, although selfish all his life, had given his life for his duty and to the people of Halsgrove, just like he promised to do when he was ordered to Halsgrove.

"What is his name?" Veredus asked one of the women cleaning his wounds.

"Dathon, sir," she replied through tear-filled sobs, her voice breaking.

"Dathon, I am Captain Veredus from Taris. Can you hear me?" he asked the guard on the bed.

Dathon couldn't open his eyes but heard the voice and responded by turning his head toward the voice and moving his fingers.

"You have done it, son. You held them off long enough. You have honored and protected your people," Veredus kept his tone the same, though tears started forming in his eyes. He saw the smile on Dathon's face become just a little bigger and heard him sigh out his last breath. He died feeling something he had never felt before: honor.

Veredus bowed his head to the young guard and crossed Dathon's hands over his shoulders.

Jarol was forced to come out of his shocked state when the villagers, people he knew personally, started thanking him with tears rolling down their faces.

They knew that he had been the one to go and get help, and that help had arrived just before it was too late.

He shook all of their hands, but he couldn't accept their thanks or praises; his guards lay dead on the ground. He could not forgive himself for not being there with his men to defend the guard station and for letting his guards die. He blamed himself for their deaths and didn't know what to do. He started walking back outside, to get away from the gruesome scene laid before him when he noticed a guard on his stomach in the room; he recognized the armor immediately. Ryker.

He rolled Ryker over, gently, onto his back. Dozens of wounds covered his body, from a cut on his shin to a long cut right across the left side of his head. Jarol remembered when Ryker made that shield of his, a beautiful, double-plated shield with not a single ding on it. Now, though, there was not an area on the shield that was untouched or not scratched.

Ryker had been Jarol's closest friend since Ryker came to Halsgrove four years earlier. Jarol wished he could have seen Ryker fight; he wished he could have seen how Ryker would grunt the pain away and keep fighting so that he could tell stories for years to come of Ryker's bravery and strength. Looking at his friends face, Jarol knew that it wasn't his fault; if he had sent Ryker in his place he wouldn't have blamed him for leaving. Jarol, as carefully as he could and out of love for his friend, picked up Ryker and placed him over his shoulder to get him to a wagon.

"Sir, on the west side of Halsgrove we were only able to get six wagons. The villager's horses have run off or were taken. The rest of the town is in flames; there are no other wagons or horses, sir," the guard who Veredus had told to search for the wagons reported.

"Harness our horses up to the wagons and get all of the women and children and the wounded loaded first. Robilor will lead the first wagon and put men from the village on the other wagons to lead them," he said to the guard, ordering him off to start preparing.

"Ledry, go and make sure the perimeter is set and get all of the women and children ready to leave immediately," he said to the other guard in the room with him.

"Yes sir," Ledry replied and left the room.

A few minutes later, after making sure that there were no bodies of any fallen guardsmen left behind, Veredus walked out. One of the wagons was filled with the dead; they wouldn't leave anyone behind. Everyone was crying from the sight of the wagon full of their dead family and friends. The other five wagons were filled with the wounded and the women and children. The few men that were able to get onto the wagons were the old and those that couldn't fight.

After harnessing the horses up to the wagons, only six remained.

Veredus walked over to the lead wagon beside Robilor, who would not take his eyes off of the tree line where the goblins had run away.

"Let one of the villagers lead this wagon, I would be of more use to you if I stayed," he said to Veredus as he walked up.

"It's for that reason that I want you with the villagers; if something happens I would rather have you protect them than us. We can take care of ourselves, they cannot," Veredus replied.

Robilor could not argue with that. He knew Veredus was right but still would rather stay with his comrades than leave them behind.

"The wagons are over-burdened as it is, Robilor. You cannot wait for us," Veredus said, guessing Robilor's next argument. "As soon as everyone is loaded and the wagons are ready, leave straight for Taris. Don't stop until you have to."

Robilor did not like the idea at all, but nodded his agreement and climbed up the wagon.

Veredus walked back to his guards watching the tree line. Two guards came out of the eastern tree line and jogged over to where Veredus was standing.

"We followed the tracks for half-a-mile, sir," one of the guards said breathing heavily. "None of them have turned around but they have slowed their retreat and seem to be grouping together again. If they mean to come again, sir, we don't know."

Veredus responded with only a nod to the guard who brought him the news. "How many more do we have out there?" he asked the guard.

"Four, sir. Two guards to the south and the other two rangers through the woods to the south-east," the guard replied.

Veredus turned around to his group of scouts awaiting his orders. "Six of you are going to mount up on the horses and ride with the caravan," Veredus told the guards. He motioned for Jarol to come over and told him that he would also ride his horse with the caravan. Jarol thanked him and left to ready the horses and tell his townsfolk the plan.

"Sir, are you not to ride with us? We will not leave you behind, let us stay and return with you or hunt down the foul beasts that have destroyed this town," one of the guards in the crowd said, the others nodding their heads in agreement.

"Your honor and bravery honor us all, but the villagers are our top priority now. I will leave none of you behind, so go and mount up. The rest of us will leave shortly after you, covering your retreat. We cannot take any chances," Veredus said.

"But sir, we will not leave…" the same guard began.

"You will do as you're told! Think not that you are leaving us behind. You must see those villagers to Taris, safely. That is your mission now," he replied. He didn't like talking to his guards like that, but he would not allow any delay. "Do not turn around no matter what happens. Get to Taris."

His guards nodded their agreement and saddled up.

The last of the villagers were loaded onto the wagons and they set off. Veredus watched them leave and breathed a small sigh of relief when they turned to the west and out of sight. A minute later two more guards came running back from the south, bringing the same news as those that had followed the goblins to the east.

"Pile up the remaining goblins and burn them; let us leave a sign for them if they should return," Veredus said to the remaining guards.

The fire and black smoke rose high before long. The stench of burning goblin flesh filled the air; the guards covered the noses and mouths with anything they could find. Not long after the fire had been set on the second pile of dead goblins the last two guards came running back through the tree line to the south-east.

"Sir," one of them started but had to wait for his breath.

"Catch your breath," Veredus said.

"Sir, the goblins have regrouped and have started coming back. They are still in scattered groups but we saw a lot of them heading back this way," the guard said through heavy breathing.

"Ok, time to go. If we don't make it, my friends, it was an honor to fight beside you," he said, then led them down the road to the west, towards Taris.

Chapter 7

New Beginnings

"A village has been burned, me king," the scout said to King Bourndrimiur.

The king looked towards the west, to where the rising smoke would come from although he knew that he was much too far away to see it.

After coming out of the tunnels a year earlier and deciding to make these mountains his new kingdom, King Bourndrimiur had sent scouts out to survey the areas roundabout and learn what inhabitants there were around him. He knew there was a small kingdom of humans to the west, and that one of their villages now burned due to goblins, most likely. Only goblins were stupid enough to let a whole kingdom know that they were there by burning the outermost villages, giving those they sought to raid time to prepare defenses and gather an army.

"It does not concern us. Keep yer scouting tight. I don't want anything sneaking up on me back," the king told the scout. "And find out what burned the village," he added in out of curiosity, though he would bet every gold piece he had that it was goblins.

The scout nodded and headed off back down the trail to the west, across the long mountain passes and down towards the forest at the base of the mountains.

He was King Bourndrimiur, king of the dwarves that came up from the underdark and settled the mountains to the north, close to The Calm Sea. He was short, at least by human standards, standing barely over four feet tall. But, like the rest of his race, his limbs were thick and solid; even the king worked in the mines and forges beside his workers. He wore a suit of armor that shined brilliantly in the sun; made of mithril, his armor shone like silver but was as hard as the rock beneath his feet. A giant, two-headed hammer hung from a hook off his belt and a round shield was strapped across his back. The shield was also made of mithril but was lined in gold around the outer edges; designs of runes and gods woven in thin lines around the entire shield.

The wind was cold up where the king stood; it bit at his protruding nose like small needles. He was getting used to it, though. After a year in the bone-chilling cold he began to see the benefits of settling his homeless clan high up in the ice capped mountains; there were no enemies near them, to his knowledge, affording them the solitude they so greatly desired.

The mountains around the dwarves were filled with forests; thick forests. There were plenty of animals to hunt and enough edible vegetation to keep his clan fed without having to leave the mountains in search of food.

The king, after another long look towards the west, turned around and headed back around the mountain, his personal guard both leading and trailing him. After half-an-hour of weaving back and forth and up and down through the small ridges and valleys they reached the opening of a small, narrow valley. The mountain's peaks were ice capped with the ice running from the peaks almost to the base of the valley. The back of the valley wall was solid rock behind the thick sheets of ice.

A hundred campfires littered the valley floor and the bustling of his clan was easy to see from his high perch on the mountain side. A cave at the bottom of the valley wall was the center of commotion; small figures moved in and out of the cave constantly, carrying out loads of rocks and moving in with tools.

"Me king," someone yelled, coming up the mountain trail towards the king and his guard.

Bornar, the king's mining leader and adviser, came running up the trail before the king and dropped into a low bow. His entire body was covered in dirt from head to toe. One would not have been able to tell that his beard, which ran down to his knees, was normally more gray than black; now it was as black as a young dwarf's beard. He wore no armor but a thin, leather vest that let bare his arms from shoulder to hand, showing off his muscular arms.

"What is it?" King Bourndrimiur asked, hoping this was good news that Bornar brought.

"Me king, we've hit a vein!" Bornar said with the biggest smile any of the clan had made since leaving the dwarves ancient kingdom of Brüevelden almost two years earlier. Bornar was one of the few dwarves that hadn't lost his optimism completely when the clan was forced to flee from its ancestral home.

"What kind of vein?" the king asked in his normal, even tone. He didn't want to get over excited and be let down; that seemed to be happening to him a lot lately.

"Mithril! The vein runs deep, me king, as thick as a tree!" Bornar said, his smile showing all of his square, yellow teeth as he brought out his hands, using his hands and fingers to show the size of the vein he had found.

"Well," the king said, "what're ye waiting for?"

"Yes, me king!" Bornar said, excited. He rubbed his hands together in anticipation and turned back down the mountain, running as fast as his short legs could carry him down the steep slope.

In their hasty flight from Brüevelden, King Bourndrimiur and his clan had no time to gather many supplies. Not a day went by that the king didn't think of that fateful day; a vicious battle with the evil drow. He yearned for revenge, but realized that even if he lived two hundred more years, his clan still wouldn't be prepared to fight those evil dark elves again.

King Bourndrimiur descended down the rest of trail to his camp. Four thousand dwarves, only a fifth of the number they boasted in their days living in Brüevelden, surrounded the king on all sides. Almost all the dwarf men were in, or around, the cave; clearing, mining, repairing, resting, and now working the new mithril they had just found. The dwarf women were cooking, tending to the injured, making clothing suitable to their new, cold environment from the hides of the beasts they had hunted, and keeping the children away from the busy miners and the cave.

He looked around and, after seeing that all was in order, picked up the nearest pick and headed for the cave.

"It's time, Deli," Arduus said to Deli. Arduus was the closest person that Deli had to family, besides her sons. He was one of the only people that had known Alruin's parents in Daley and it was he who had brought Alruin across the Calm Sea all those years before. Arduus was a goldsmith and had brought up Alruin as his apprentice, though Alruin had preferred to work with metals more suitable for weapons and tools; which is what he did when he opened his own blacksmith after his apprenticeship with Arduus.

Now, though, Arduus had found Deli in The Bough Inn after hearing about the attack on Halsgrove. After learning of Alruin's death, he took in Deli and the twins. He slept more at his goldsmith shop than at his house so he gave them the bigger of the rooms in his house. Deli cleaned and prepared the meals as payment; Arduus would accept nothing more.

Deli had found little sleep that night and was already dressed and awake when Arduus came to awaken her. She shook her head once, took a deep breath, and went and got Dryx and Weylor out of bed.

It was early, very early. The sun was just coming over the Giant's Steppes and a cool breeze greeted them at the doorstep. A wagon and two of the guard awaited them on the road in front of the house and they climbed in. It wasn't a far ride to the ceremony, but it was custom for the family members of the fallen to be picked up in a wagon and escorted by the king's guard to the courtyard.

Arduus watched Deli almost the whole way to the courtyard. She kept her face down and eyes closed. The dark color under her eyes proof of the sleepless night she had. Had Arduus watched her during the night, he would have seen that the little sleep she did find was full of her whining and turning in her bed; the memory of watching her husband disappear into darkness was the only dream she had.

Dryx and Weylor, sitting behind them, were awake but said nothing. No games, no smiles, no laughter accompanied them on their way to the funeral. The day before, they had gone to see their father for the last time in the temple of Valerum that lay to south-west where his body was being prepared for the ceremony. They were young but the death of their father had broken their young, innocent spirits almost completely.

Not many minutes went by before the wagon came to a halt, Arduus getting out first to help Deli and the twins out of the wagon. Deli wore a white dress, lined in gold. The hood was off and against her back. An image of the sun with a face in the middle had been weaved in in the middle of the dress; Valerum's sign. The dress had been given to Deli by the temple to wear to the ceremony; it was common for the wives of husbands killed in battle to wear the dress in hopes of appeasing their god, Valerum, to accept the dead into his paradise.

A tall pyre had been erected in middle of the courtyard, with the bodies of the fallen laid side by side on the very top. Many thick bundles of wood lie under them, the fuel for the fire. Many were already gathered together; the on-lookers were in the far back, family members were in front of them and the wives of the fallen were lined up in the front. All the women were in the same white dress. A small number of Taris' leaders were before the crowd, facing the wives, wearing their suits of armor and weapons in honor of their comrades who fell in battle.

After a few minutes, when everyone had been led to where they were supposed to be, the king came out of the keep and headed for the group of men in front of the widows. He wore a long, white cape that was only used for such occasions. He, like his advisers, wore his suit of armor with his sword sheathed at his side. He carried his helmet in his right hand and an unlit, ceremonial torch in his left. He stopped when he reached the group and put down his helmet and raised his right hand in the air to signal the beginning of the ceremony.

The ceremony was not long; the family members of the dead had already said their last goodbyes the day before so nobody would be climbing the pyre.

"My dear friends," he began. "It is truly a sad day. The bodies of the fallen that lay before us honor us with their sacrifice. Were it not for them, the entire village of Halsgrove would have been lost; but they stood strong! They gave their lives for you, but in doing so they have also saved the lives of many, many more. We now know what faces us because of their bravery and sacrifice. Let us say our last farewell to these courageous and honorable men!"

King Ironwill then took out a parchment and read the names of the guards and of Alruin and the other farmers that lost their lives in defense of their families. After finishing the list, he moved off to the side where a guard stood with a lit torch and lit the ceremonial torch. He moved to the foot of the pyre and, just before lighting the kindling that would set fire to the bodies, said in a loud voice that all could hear, "Valerum, god of light, bless these men that have given their lives for such a noble cause. Lead them to white fields in paradise where they can rest in peace.

Bless us to overcome the enemies that have taken their lives and destroy the darkness with your light!"

The king set fire to the bundles of sticks and almost immediately the whole pyre was up in flames. All the women brought the hoods of their dresses up and covered their heads. The only noise that followed the silence was the sobbing and sniffling of the crying widows and their families.

When the fire died down and nothing but smoke continued to rise, Deli and the twins returned to Arduus and the wagon and returned home. Deli entered first and went straight for her bed, thinking to cry herself to sleep in a silent somber but instead felt a peace, almost a light within her soul.

Valerum had noticed Alruin's sacrifice and granted him the one thing he desired; that Deli could have the strength to live on and prepare their two sons for what was coming.

Only a moment after feeling the peace, Deli felt a thought placed in her mind. 'Should the twins learn to be a light that stands against the coming darkness? Or will they fall prey to the cruelty of the world in innocence's weakness?'

She knew what she had to do; what Alruin had already decided. She remembered watching him at play in the backyard in Halsgrove just days before, and what he was preparing them for. They needed to be ready, she thought. Then she could be at peace.

"We've never had twins in the school before," Laedred said, the Master of the Fighter School. "Come to think of it, I've never actually seen twins before," he said to Arduus when he brought them to the school to be tested.

The test was simple; a rack with one of every kind of weapon sat in the middle of an emptied room and the student had to simply pick which weapon he liked best. There were, however, two special weapons; a completely ordinary looking, magical staff lie in middle of the weapon rack (a temporary gift from the mage school), and a one-handed mace hung by its handle from the end of the rack; it, too, was imbued with magical properties, but from the temple of Valerum.

"Well, we'll see if that changes," Arduus replied. He was very curious to see which weapons they would each pick. He didn't doubt that the twins were very much alike, but he noticed that their personalities were different enough that his excitement was peaked. He knew Weylor to be the more passive of the two twins, but he held his thoughts to himself.

"Dryx," Laedred looked back and beckoned Dryx forward, "go and choose whichever weapon you like best."

Dryx, not understanding the simple command and the way he was being watched, walked slowly over to the weapon rack. He moved slowly, examining each weapon as he passed, and stopped when he noticed two short swords hanging upside down on the rack. He grabbed them both, one in each hand, and pulled them off the rack. He misjudged their weight and they fell to the floor when they cleared the two, small wooden beams holding them up. Dryx quickly picked them up, though he was only able to hold them down at his side. He liked their length, though; just like the sticks he would break in half when he would play fight with Weylor. Not knowing what else to do, he looked up at Arduus, then at Laedred.

"A two-weapon fighting style, this will be interesting," Laedred said, more to himself than to Arduus. He nodded his head and motioned for Dryx to return the blades to their spots on the rack.

"Weylor, you're up. Just pick whichever weapon you like," Laedred said.

Weylor, never having really found a stick he really liked when he play fought with Dryx, took more time that Dryx. He walked up and down the rack, looking at each weapon, though he really didn't understand how there were so many different kinds.

He stopped when he noticed the staff in the middle of the rack. It was almost like a polished walking stick, he thought, that had a metal handle. He reached out and grabbed it; immediately he felt the energy, not in him but in the staff. He wasn't sure what it was but it felt, to him, like the staff was more powerful than it looked. He knew there was something different between the staff and the rest of the weapons; the other weapons, when he grabbed and touched them, felt like nothing more than cold metal and leather handles; but the staff, he felt that it possessed a power of its own. He grabbed the staff up in both hands and looked up at Arduus, just like Dryx did, and then at Laedred.

Arduus, a wide smile covering his face, had suspected as much. Laedred, on the other hand, looked sorely let down. He couldn't believe what he saw; he hadn't seen a student actually grab the staff, ever. Normally, the students in the Wizard School were family of the wizard teachers and were placed their without going through the test. He had been thinking how interesting it would be to see twins learn and fight together.

"Well, that's that, then," Laedred said. He looked at Arduus and walked out of the room. Dryx would enter the Fighter's School, and Weylor the Wizard's School.

Chapter 8

Icedome

Ten years had passed since the burning of Halsgrove. The goblin raids had increased on the outer villages and farms, and, in response, dozens of large scouting parties had been sent to the boundaries of the kingdom.

Taris had awoken from its slumber; the peace for the twenty years before the attack on Halsgrove had created a false sense of peace in the kingdom and its defenses lessened; children began staying with their families to farm instead of receiving military training and there were fewer guards on duty around the kingdom.

Now, though, every of-age male that had not received training was brought to Taris for training and placement in a scouting party. The population inside the walls of Taris had almost tripled with the influx of trainee's and the kingdom had to sacrifice luxuries for necessities.

The twins had begun their schooling at their respective schools, Dryx at the Fighter's School and Weylor at the Wizard's School.

Dryx was in the barrack's training room, preparing himself for the end-of-the-year duel with Rasit. For the past ten years, Rasit had been first in the class with Dryx coming in second behind him. They were both eighteen and about to start their last year in the Fighter's School. They began in the school at the same time but, almost from the beginning, there was a rivalry between them. Rasit preferred the sword and shield while Dryx had mastered two-weapon fighting with short swords. Now, though, they both had wooden weapons in their sheathes made to replicate their chosen weapons.

Dryx ran his fingers through his short, jet black hair; unlike most of the soldiers, he didn't like long hair because he felt that it got in the way. He stood just over six feet tall, slightly taller than the average person in Taris. He wore only a tight, leather jerkin over his chest; the chain mesh shirt wasn't necessary for this duel. His arms hung bare by his sides, his skin tight over his defined muscles. He let his facial hair grow out, though he had to keep it trimmed in the barracks.

"Calm down, brother." Dryx didn't look over to where his brother, Weylor, was standing; he as much expected his brother's voice though he hadn't heard him come in the room.

Weylor was standing only a few feet from Dryx, watching him. It was common for wizards to wear robes; armor got in the way of their spell-casting. But Weylor appeared to be in almost the same gear as Dryx. Dryx, however, knew better; Weylor's robes were enchanted to appear the same as the common guard, so as not to mark him as a spell caster in battle. Weylor wore his blond hair long but, unlike the rest of the guards, he let it fall over his shoulders in the front. His eyes shone a bright green, like leaves in mid-spring, and it appeared that he grew no facial hair at all; though Dryx knew that this also was the result of Weylor's magic. He was an inch shorter than Dryx and not as muscular; but his arms were nonetheless well formed from his work in Arduus' goldsmith shop. Both he and Dryx worked in the goldsmith to support themselves and their mother, who had long since moved out of Arduus' house and into a smaller one.

"You will not beat him unless you learn to adapt and change your tactics to his," Weylor said after a moment.

Dryx, knowing his brother was right but never willing to openly accept being wrong, turned and glared at Weylor for a moment before closing his eyes and taking another deep breath to calm himself.

"Every year he has won because he let you find an opening and you jumped for it. Be patient and let him make the first mistake," Weylor continued, then cocked his head to the side. "Or," he began, a smiling spreading across his face, "maybe he will find an opening in your defenses and jump at the chance." He let his words hang in his brother's ears for a moment before clapping him on the shoulder and walking out to take his spot by their mother to watch the match.

Dryx and Rasit were brought out into an open court in the middle of the Fighter's School; benches lined the walls and a cool breeze came in through the open roof. After a short introduction, Dryx and Rasit bowed and the match started.

Dryx started out strong, coming out in full force that had Rasit starting on his heels, backing up on the defensive right from the beginning. He was quick on his feet though, and was able to deflect Dryx's swings and keep his blades from finding their mark.

It wasn't long before Rasit found his footing and was able to stop Dryx's momentum. His older brothers, already graduated from the school, cheered him on from the side; each of them had graduated at the top of their class and Rasit was the last one.

Rasit's right arm swung out and came in suddenly, going for Dryx's side.

Dryx sent his left arm over, down and back, taking the sword harmlessly out wide and saw a hole to Rasit's chest as Rasit's left arm with his shield went out wide to catch his balance. Dryx didn't see that Rasit had subtly shifted his right foot back so that when he leaned back his balance had shifted to his right foot; his being off balance was to draw Dryx close in and take away his ability to use his swords. Dryx's body leaned forward as his right arm shot forward, his sword tip diving for the chest of Rasit as he fell back.

Reacting faster than Dryx expected, Rasit popped up, his left shield arm going over Dryx's right arm and across the bottom. Dryx's right arm was caught by his sword handle on Rasit shield and he couldn't get it free.

Dryx had been in close combat practice enough to know that he was at a disadvantage, even more so because he was unable to free his right arm. Rasit was shorter and thicker than Dryx; he knew he wouldn't be able to muscle his way out as he would have with almost any other opponent.

On pure instinct, Dryx dropped his sword from his right hand, a strategy he would never have considered before, which made it easier to free his right hand. In a sudden, quick burst of energy he leapt straight up into the air. Jumping put his right arm at an angle over Rasit's shield enough to be able to free it, and used his left leg to push of Rasit's shield, executing a desperate summersault, landing just out of reach of Rasit's strike.

"Lucky," Rasit said through gritted teeth, as surprised as anyone from Dryx's unusual tactic.

Dryx had never been known to take a step back when toe-to-toe with an opponent, and for that reason he had put himself in difficult situations time and time again.

Rasit knew he had the upper hand with Dryx in close, but now the odds were almost back to even; almost. Dryx only had one sword now.

Dryx glared at Rasit. Once again, just as Weylor had warned him, he had almost lost to one of Rasit's tricks. He would never admit it openly, but he knew he had to rethink his strategy. He was angrier that he had not seen the setup than for losing his sword; he could still beat Rasit with only one sword.

He tried circling around, to get Rasit to move, but he wouldn't while Dryx's sword laid at his feet. This was the only advantage that Rasit had and he wasn't going to give it up.

"I don't need it to beat you," Dryx said, an idea forming in his head. He came straight at Rasit with both hands on the hilt of his sword.

Rasit smiled; this was the mood he wanted Dryx in. When Dryx was angry he made mistakes; he got sloppy. He got down in his stance a little more, bracing to block the wild hit with his shield.

Dryx came in with a rage, or so it appeared. He waited until the last second, when Rasit had to raise his shield to block what looked like an over-the-head swing. When Rasit raised his shield, Dryx used the momentum and power of his swing to drop into a roll to his right and to Rasit's left. Rasit had swung his right arm out to hit Dryx's side as his shield would block the hit, but his sword arm found nothing but air and he felt no hit on his shield.

Dryx was only out of his view for a brief moment but that was enough. Rasit knew he had erred; Dryx had used Rasit's preconception of his fighting style and behavior to fake an attack that would put him at an advantage.

Rasit had no time to react as he felt the tip of Dryx's wooden sword press against his lower back; he was beaten.

A bell rang out twice, signaling that the match was over. Clapping and cheering erupted from the crowd as Dryx stood up behind Rasit, still holding his sword against Rasit's back.

All of the judges, nine teachers from the Fighter's School and three high-ranking city guards, stood up in applause. They knew this would be a very intense match; Rasit came from a very respected and skilled family, every member of his family had graduated at the head of his/her class, and they all knew of Dryx's popular yet barbaric fighting style with two swords and no shield.

Dryx sheathed his sword and retrieved the other. It was custom for the students to congratulate each other after a match, although that was a custom seldom followed by Dryx. This time, though, he waited. He knew how hard it would be for Rasit to turn around and congratulate him because every year before, when Rasit won, Dryx left immediately without even looking to the crowd, to his brother or his mother.

Rasit, not wanting to hurt his family's reputation, turned around and nodded to Dryx his congratulation. As quickly as he had nodded he turned and left.

Dryx looked, for the first time, to the crowd and found his mother and brother, each with big smiles still seated near the top corner of the benches.

Weylor smiled as Dryx, with a perceptive smile, nodded at him, silently thanking him for his advice before the match. Neither Weylor nor Dryx were the kind to stick around and socialize and revel in a victory. After winning, Dryx shook hands with the judges who, over excited, wanted him to stick around and enjoy the celebrations. He took his leave quietly and slipped out into the clear, star-filled night.

"Are ye sure that's where the smelly vermin are?" King Bourndrimiur asked the scout. The scout had just placed a map in front of the king of the entire mountain range that King Bourndrimiur and his people lived in. He had wanted it for a long time; he knew they weren't the only ones living in the mountains. Almost from the moment that they came to the surface they found out that goblins were in the area. Now, after ten years of carving out his kingdom, Icedome he had decided to call it, King Bourndrimiur was ready to look to their surroundings with more interest.

"Yes, me King. I saw 'em with my own eyes," the scout replied.

"How many are there?" the King asked.

"Thousands, me King. They've made some big, log buildings and it looks like they're getting ready for something. They wear a red, lizard claw mark on their chests, though I'm not for knowing what it means. Seems like they're after the humans with all the raids," the scout answered.

The King stared at the map for a long moment before looking back at the scout, "They a threat?"

"It was a five day journey through a lot of narrow mountain passes to get there. There are some good spots to set up defenses along the mountain, they wouldn't reach Icedome unless they flew," the scout said in a confident tone. He had spent that last month wandering through the mountains, with a few other experienced dwarves, at the order of the king.

King Bourndrimiur took in the news and turned again to stare at the map. He couldn't help but hope that the goblins did try and attack through the mountain passes; beating them back would raise the moral of his entire clan and bring back some of their pride.

"You, fetch me Bornar," the king said to one of the guards by the door. The scout standing guard at the door dipped into a quick, low bow and trotted off out the door and down the hall towards the entrance leading to the lower levels of Icedome.

The King looked up as he heard the familiar sound of heavy boots entering the room from the side. Danflorf, his only son, entered the room.

He wore a fine chain-linked shirt that covered his broad chest and down his arm to end in a peculiar design right above his elbows; the sleeves had been cut from shoulder to elbow in increments so that when Danflorf walked, strings or armor flowed about, clinking and flowing from side to side, but connected back at the elbow. His beard was normally such a deep shade of yellow that he gained the nickname "golden beard," although it appeared more black than yellow now from mining and working the furnaces.

"Father," Danflorf said when he walked in and saw the king. He dipped into the same quick, low bow as the scout that left had done only moments before.

"Dorf," the King said, using his own nickname for his son, "get a scouting party together. It's time we got to know our neighbors and see what they're about."

Danflorf's face went from a passive, tired demeanor to suddenly brighter than the king had seen him in a decade. Danflorf had always been strange among dwarves in that he preferred the outdoors to the near-lightless mountain tunnels. He enjoyed feeling the wind on his face and all the colors that the sun brought out in the trees and mountains. He couldn't believe his luck; for years he had been asking his father for permission to leave and make contact with the humans, though the king had always denied saying that they needed every dwarf for the tunnels and furnaces.

"Right away, father," Danflorf said dropping into a quick bow and scurrying away towards his private chambers. In his sudden change of mood, he completely forgot about why he had gone to see his father. *No matter,* he thought, *whatever it was, it would have to wait.*

"Are ye sure about that, me king? About sending your own son, I mean," the scout asked him. As soon as he saw the king's expression, though, he regretted questioning the king.

"You think you know better then, eh?" King Bourndrimiur said, looking over at him with a stare that would have stopped an ogre in its tracks.

The blood rushed form the scouts face and his eyes shot wide. He knew the king had a short temper with other dwarves questioning his decisions and wisely bowed and let himself out of the chamber; he didn't dare try to take his map.

An hour later a dozen dwarves were just outside the entrance of Icedome, fully armored and with huge packs on their backs. Danflorf wore an axe his own grandfather had forged three-hundred years before; the head of the axe held a long, vertical blade that curved out in the middle and back in at the top and bottom tips. On both sides of the smooth face of the blade there were engravings; on one side a hammer and anvil and on the other a mountain with a gem facet in it. Any dwarf in all the realms would instantly recognize the symbols as the two most revered and honored dwarven gods; Deramoin and Fargrinn. Over his right shoulder hung a beautifully crafted shield; the shield bowed out in the middle, giving Danflorf room to fit his arm in the latches to hold the shield. On the outside of the shield was the image of a hammer with sparks flying from it in all directions; not only a representation of their god, Deramoin, but also of their expertise in mining and blacksmithing. His shield had been the first item made from the mithril vein they found ten years earlier. His shield was the first relic of Icedome; being enchanted by Icedome's greatest weapon smith, his shield was nearly unbreakable, but only when held by Danflorf himself.

Enchanting items with such power was rare; it required a very experienced blacksmith and a powder of magical essence that was extremely rare. It was normally reserved for the king and his family, although many weapon and armor smiths enchanted their best items if they could acquire any extra of the magical powder.

"Here comes the king," one of the dwarves in the group said, recognizing the king's personal guards coming out from inside the entrance to Icedome.

The group formed up in a semi-circle and they all dipped into the same low, quick bow when he drew near. He carried nothing more than a piece of parchment in one hand.

"Yer job is simple; find out what the humans are about. If their fighting with the goblins, then we're already allies as far as I'm concerned. It may be hard trading with them, with the difficult paths through the mountains. If they're not for wanting our help, come back and don't tell them how to find us," King Bourndrimiur looked around at each of them until they each nodded that they understood his orders. "Two weeks. If ye ain't back in two weeks there'll be two thousand dwarves coming down these mountains looking fer blood and not going back till they get it." That last part was just to let them know that he didn't want them making any detours. He wanted to keep their presence a secret as long as possible, at least to the goblins.

Danflorf walked over to his father. "Ye come back to me now," the King said in a lowered voice.

"Bah!" Danflorf said in a loud voice and threw both hands up in the air while turning away and leading the rest of the group of dwarves down the path that would take them all the way to the forest at the foot of the mountains. "I'm fer coming back or I'm a blasted elf!" he yelled back.

The King chuckled; only elves, as far as dwarves were concerned or cared, left without a trace and never returned. The dwarves didn't hate elves, with the exception of the drow, but they looked down upon them for their fragile frames and strange, unfamiliar culture.

Fifty students of the Fighter's School were gathered in the main hall of the school. They were celebrating the end of their second-to-last and the beginning of their last year. Their last year of training was their graduation into the Taris Guard. They had been training for a decade and now they would only rarely see the inside of the Fighter's School. Their training now was hands-on; they would all be separated into already formed scouting parties and would be leaving the next day. Most of the students would not see many of their classmates for a long time, being in different areas of the kingdom.

Before, the scouting parties enjoyed spending every other week in Taris, not having much need or reason to leave. But now, with the return of the goblins from the mountains to the south east, Taris was maintaining a fairly large, mobile guard force in and around the villages closest to the Giant's Steppes.

Captain Strongshield looked over the students from his table at the head of the gathering. He knew they had trained hard and long and that their dedication was firm, but he knew that there weren't enough of them. By all accounts, thousands of goblins have been seen coming out of the mountains and, although they didn't seem to be gathering or uniting into one body, they had to prepare for the worst.

"It won't be long," Captain Strongshield began, "before you are no longer called students."

The laughter and conversations among the students died down, giving the Captain their full attention and respect.

"Many of you are already considered adept fighters and not to be underestimated. I can only hope that this be the case," he said and paused for a moment before he began again, his voice becoming more serious. "A darkness has begun casting its shadow on us from the mountains; a darkness that few remember and those that do, don't want to. The day has come to awake ourselves from our false sense of security and work to make that security a reality. All of you will be put into scouting parties; all of you will know what it is to shed the blood of beasts before long. This is the true test of a fighter," he said, his voice growing louder, "when you stare death in the face, will your courage and loyalty be enough to raise your weapon in defiance, or will you submit to the fear and give in? Some of you may not come back, that is the price we must pay to protect our families and friends." He paused and looked around at the faces of the students in front of him. "Now," he started, raising his cup, "to you!"

The students all yelled in one voice "to us!" and lifted their cups in unison. All drank deeply of the last wine they would taste in a long time; all but one. Dryx, although as excited as any other student, had only tasted wine one time before and did not like how it played with his senses. After all the cheering and farewells, each student returned home to find almost no sleep before the day they would leave Taris without knowing if they would return.

"Do you remember when we were younger? When we would run around fighting imaginary enemies with sticks and rocks?" Weylor asked Dryx, the memory putting a smile on both of their faces.

Dryx chuckled at the old childhood memories that came rushing back into his mind after so long; he hadn't recalled those days in a very long time.

"Back when our weapons were wooden and our enemies were fairy tales," Dryx replied. The reality of how fast things had changed caused them both to stop walking.

"It was our favorite game, was it not? Killing goblins, running from giants, and tricking dragons," Weylor said with a smile that came from his old, innocent childhood memories. "Now it seems fate has played that same trick on us; making our childhood games our present challenges," he added, the smile almost completely faded.

They walked in silence along the western cliff of Taris, the furthest they could get from the main street and reality. They enjoyed the solitude, and the cool, salty ocean breeze helped calm their nerves. They would both be leaving tomorrow, whether in the same scouting party or separate they did not know. And though they both hoped that they would remain together, neither would vocally say it. They shared a close bond, being twins, but they had never felt the need to come out and express it. They didn't need to; they both knew it and that was enough.

"It didn't surprise me the day we were tested," Dryx said to Weylor suddenly.

"What do you mean?" Weylor said, a confused look crossing his face, trying to think of anything unusual that happened that day.

"We entered the barrack's weapon room. I went first and went straight for the swords. I knew it before I went in that room. Remember?" Dryx said, chuckling. "When we would play-fight I would always break my stick in half. They just feel like extensions of my arms; I can wield these swords," he said, pulling out his swords in a quick, perfect movement, "as if they were part of my own body." He went through a quick, complex motion to demonstrate what he was talking about. As quickly as he started he stopped and his swords, an instant later, were in their sheaths. "But you," he continued, "I was curious which weapon would call to you. You never seemed to care what was in your hands, whether a stone or a stick. You walked up and down the rack, dragging your hands across the weapons. Then you stopped, your eyes fixed on the simplest looking stave that could possibly exist," he laughed at the last part, not even remembering that the staff was there when he chosen his weapons. "There is not a single fighter, student or guard, that I know that intimidates me, but you are the last person in this town I would ever wish to duel." He had stopped walking and looked Weylor straight in the eyes.

Weylor, thinking that Dryx had confessed this surprising news to calm his own fears about his safety, turned and said, in the most sarcastic tone he could, "and for good reason!"

His hand flew down to his side, snatching up a handful of small pebbles from some hidden fold or pocket that Dryx could not see, and threw them off the cliff. He waited a second before starting his chant, and a moment later each pebble exploded into a multicolored burst of energy. Though a single pebble was no louder than a stone hitting a floor, the handful together sounded as thunder on the walls of the cliff.

The explosion itself had lighted up the opposing cliff all the way to the water. A bird, flying in after hunting fish in the ocean, happened to fly right through the explosion and, being blinded by the sudden explosion of light, hit the cliff wall and nearly dropped into the water below.

Dryx stared out into the dark after Weylor's bright show of power had ended. More than ever he was happy that Weylor was his brother and not another rival to deal with. They both laughed at the exaggerated sarcasm of Weylor's magical prowess, but it served its purpose; it put Dryx's worry to rest about Weylor's safety and it also showed him that Weylor was as serious as he was about their duty.

They continued walking north; all the way until the cliff turned east and they could walk no further.

"Do you ever wonder what he would be like? How different things would be if he hadn't died?" Weylor asked Dryx, his tone somber and respectful.

They both flashed back to their father's murder those many years before. Their mother covered them with her own body but didn't manage to cover their eyes in time. They remember goblin after goblin falling before their father, who was taking almost as many hits as he was giving. They remember watching his last act of defiance as he charged into the goblins, pushing them back and away from the twins and their mother. That memory had become their drive to train and perfect their skills. They each knew that that was the true reason behind their discipline and their eagerness to go out and defend their home; they knew that what they had really trained so hard for was outside the walls of Taris and was growing like an unholy disease. Revenge was of their grasp, for the goblin that killed their father was lying dead beside him only moments later when Jarol and the scouting party from Taris arrived. But vengeance, that was still in their grasp. Not upon that one goblin, but upon its race.

"That question haunts my dreams," Dryx said, staring down at the ground as he spoke, his eyes unfocused as he thought back those many years. That memory had fueled his anger and taught him true discipline; whenever his training seemed to overwhelm him that thought drove him on to perfect his mastery over his body.

"Though we cannot change the past," Weylor said, "the goblins will know what destruction one of their own has brought upon them."

Dryx looked up and, when he saw his brother, was almost scared himself. Weylor had stood up, without Dryx noticing, and was looking out over the ocean with a look of complete confidence and determination. He would be the end of many goblins, Dryx knew, and the thought brought a smile to his face.

Chapter 9

Back to Halsgrove

Dawn. Light began to pour over Taris. A warm breeze let everyone know that winter was over and spring was in full force.

Now, with the warmth moving in, everything was coming back to life. The trees were turning greener and the shrubbery grew denser in the forest. More birds could be heard singing as they flew through the air, especially the brown seabirds that had long since taken the docks as their winter home.

Fisherman on the docks began to prepare their boats and schooners and fix their nets and poles; the fishing season was fast approaching. The waters would warm up faster closer to shore, bringing the fish within range of their small fishing boats.

The weapon and armor smiths had been hard at work all winter long. The black smiths had less work repairing and building wagons and wagon wheels and farm tools because there was less farming in the kingdom now.

That was the one road in Taris that had never closed; Anvil Road. The short, dead-end road, just north of the Fighter's School, was the life of Taris' defense. The clinging of hammer's on anvils and the scraping of metal and heat of fire was only silenced for the few hours while the smiths slept.

It was in the air; the anticipation of war. It had been for ten years, yet the people of Taris pressed on with their duties and chores, trusting in the guards that were out in the borders of the lands.

This day, though, was one of both joy and sorrow.

As the sun came over the peaks of the mountains to the east, fifty students were lined up in front of the city's gates. Twenty scout leaders were in front of them; they had come in from their patrols to receive their new recruits and would depart within the hour, wasting no time to get back out to their duties.

"When you have been called to your patrol," Captain Strongshield began, "say goodbye to any family and friends you have; this may be the last chance you get." His tone was serious but sympathetic, knowing the fear that both the students and their families were going through.

"Alek Thurmon, of Taris, you will patrol to the south with patrol leader Veredis." All eyes were on Alek as Captain Strongshield called his name. He walked over to his family and with only a short embrace, walked over and shook hands with his new patrol leader.

"Dryx and Weylor Stormcaller, of Halsgrove," the Captain paused to look over the twins, not surprised that they had been assigned together, "you will patrol to the east with patrol leader Thestian." The twins exchanged smiles and walked over to the only person that was there to see them off; their mother.

She wore a black scarf around her neck and a simple, white dress the reached to her feet. She was getting old, by Taris' standards, but felt no older than the girls around her. She hugged both of them, tears falling from her eyes.

"Your father would be proud," she said, her voice calm, not betraying her inner fears. "You come back to me, both of you, and look out for each other." She held a hand on either of their cheeks and with one last embrace they turned and headed to meet their new patrol leader.

Captain Strongshield continued to read off the names of the remaining recruits, but their names and positions were lost on

Deli as she watched her sons walk away. She knew she had done right, in sending them to their training schools; that is what Alruin would have done, that is what he had started doing when they were still young.

She stood there until the twins had mounted their horses and left through the city gate; back to the east.

Danflorf, the young though sturdy dwarven prince, was the second dwarf to ever set foot in Taris' kingdom; the first was Taffer, his scout.

They had been traveling at an easy pace, surveying and taking note of the land roundabout as they journeyed down the mountains they had come to call their home. The dwarves had their heading and had arrived at the forest at the base of the mountain the next morning. They knew that the forest was the only thing that stood in between them and the road that would hopefully lead them to a city.

When Danflorf and the other dwarves came over the last hill between them and the forest, they saw Taffer coming at them, and fast. In unison, as if they all received the same command at the same time, they all dropped their gear and had their weapons drawn and shields strapped to their arms. After a moment, though, when Taffer got closer to the group, they could see that no expression of fear was on his face; if was just red from running. They relaxed and replaced their weapons and shields, a few mumbling about how they wished there had been something to kill.

"Danflorf," Taffer huffed out, catching his breath as he bowed into a low bow before the son of the King.

"Oh don't ye be bowing down to me. What is it, Taffer?" Danflorf replied; he never liked being bowed down to, especially not by those he considered his closest friends, and also because he was not the king.

"I found," he started, taking one last breath to calm his breathing, "I found a path leading in from the south. I followed it a ways and it seems to be heading straight west. It's fresh; goblins." Goblins were one of the dwarves' most hated enemies, second only to the drow. Never would the dwarves forget the wicked slaughter that pushed them from their ancient home and the dark elves that were behind it.

Danflorf thought for a moment, turning to look at the woods where Taffer had just come from. "Well," he said at last, "there're only two things that we could find if we follow this trail. If the goblins are planning to attack whoever lives here then they'll have scouted out and know exactly where to go, so if we follow the trail it'll lead us to whoever that might be. Or," he went on, a smile creasing his lips, "it'll lead us to the goblins."

The dwarves looked around, smiling at each other; they could only hope to find some fun on their journey.

One of the dwarves in the party, an unusually skinny and bald dwarf, Cleff, smiled a wide smile and without missing a beat added in, "then let us pray to Deramoin that we find both!" There wasn't a dwarf in the group that didn't smile and shout his agreement.

"Well it's settled then. Keep yer shields ready and your weapons at yer side. With any luck they'll be painted before long!" A sincerely hopeful chuckle left his lips as he picked up his gear and led his party into the forest.

The forest was different than Danflorf and his party expected. Although they had been living on the surface now for many years and had scouted out nearly all of the mountains roundabout their new home, never had they come down into the forest at the foot of the mountains. From up high, the forest seems to be filled with tall trees, which made them think that there would be plenty of walking room in between the trees; but as they began following the path it quickly narrowed them into a single file line.

Thick undergrowth, nearly the same color as the vegetation on the ground, closed in around them. Within minutes of entering the forest their pace had slowed drastically and every dwarf was on alert. With the vegetation so thick around them, the sound of their movements seemed to eco off the wall-like bushes. The sound of every footstep seemed to reverberate off the trees and give away their position. They could only see as far ahead as the trail stayed straight; never in all their years above or below ground had they encountered a terrain that made them feel so vulnerable. Never had fear crept into their senses before even sensing an enemy was near.

Despite their uneasiness, the dwarves checked their fear and kept moving. Not a word was spoken for the first few hours, which seemed too long a time to not have found the other side of the forest. They each realized that the path they were following wound back and forth and did not keep a straight course and, of course, that in the dense foliage their pace had been slowed more than they would have liked. Many times they found small trails leading away from the main trail, but after close examination of the prints they decided that that the main group of goblins had continued on the main trail, so they decided to do the same.

After passing over a few more hills and winding back and forth for what seemed like hours, the dwarves came to a clearing. The sun was lowering itself in the sky and its light was fast retreating from the forest. They realized as they entered the clearing that the day was not as late as they had thought, for in the forest it was much darker than in the clearing; for the thickness of the canopy and foliage blocked the suns light.

"By me guess we've been heading more south-west than west. We'll make camp here for the night. Taffer, find out where the trail re-enters the forest to the west and take the first watch. The rest of you get some dinner and get some sleep, I have a feeling tomorrow might be an exciting day for us," Danflorf said.

The dwarves nodded their agreement but, although tired, they found little sleep in the clearing in the woods that night. It had been a long time since any of them had felt the thrill of adventure and they could hardly wait until morning.

Dryx and Weylor, along with their new captain, Captain Thestian, and a few other guards in their new scouting party, had traveled until the sun fell to the west behind them. In the past, while traveling east from Taris it was common to pass farmers and merchant wagons on the road, but now, with everything happening to the east, they passed only other scouting parties. They stopped for the night at the last, still-inhabited town before Halsgrove; Greensburrow.

Thestian awoke them at the first rays of sunlight that came through the windows of their inn. Not unfamiliar with little sleep, Dryx and Weylor were ready to go before the warmth of the sun shone through the window. They saddled their horses, checked their gear, and with only bread and cheese to fill their stomachs continued their ride to the east.

The chill air stung their exposed necks and cheeks, but was quickly replaced by the warm rays of the sun as it rose over the Giant's Steppes. Before long they reached a wide clearing around the road they traveled; a land mark all too familiar to the twins. A tall tree, long since dead and charred black, rose up in front of them, signaling the start of Halsgrove's limits.

The twins had not set foot in Halsgrove in ten years. The sight of the tree brought rushing back so many memories that neither Dryx nor Weylor were focused on their surroundings until they neared the village.

As they entered the western boundary of Halsgrove, the twins saw for the first time the destruction that the goblins had brought to their town. Of the dozens of houses that used to line the streets of the small farming village only two remained intact. Where the others used to stand were now piles off ash and burnt wood. The guard station had been repaired and was now the headquarters for all the scouting parties on the eastern edge of the kingdom. Dozens of tents lay scattered about Halsgrove, divided only by the banners of the different scouting parties.

"Welcome to New Halsgrove," Thestian said, turning to see the expression on his new scout's faces.

The twin's expressions were masked well by years of dealing with pain and sorrow. Though they hid their surprise well, they were still awed by the complete destruction of Halsgrove; the house they used to live in was now no more. There was literally nothing but in the lot they used to play in.

On instinct, both twin's eyes flew to the tree line, suddenly on edge by the scene and their memories of the night of the attack.

"As you have probably noted, we ride under the banner of the Silver Dragon," Captain Thestian said. A small pole had been attached to his horse with a white flag, the engraving of a silver dragon in the middle of it. "Every scouting party has a banner. Our tents lie on the eastern border of Taris, closest to the forest. Go find a place and set up your tents, I will see you shortly," Thestian told the twins, then turned his horse and headed to the guard station.

Dryx and Weylor unsaddled their horses and led them to the make shift barn where the other horses were kept. They noticed that all of the tents at their camp were full; they could hear snoring coming from all of them.

"Great," Dryx said, "the academy all over again." He hated snoring.

Weylor, as soon as he noted the snoring and Dryx's reaction, started laughing as he pulled out their tent.

"Don't worry, brother. You will be sleeping in my tent," he let the implications hang for a moment; the look on his brother's face was far too amusing to miss!

"How is yours any better than these?" Dryx asked, too fast to stop himself. He realized his mistake and chuckled away his embarrassment.

Weylor had laid his tent flat on the ground, no poles or ropes lay across or through the tent, and said "how is it better, you ask?" with a smug smile.

Dryx, although confused, thought better than to embarrass himself again and coughed back his question.

Weylor, watching his brother, chuckled at the fact that Dryx knew so little about his magic and how much he could actually do.

"Well, brother. It's a good thing that we were put into the same scouting party. Finally you'll see what it means to be a mage!" Weylor said to Dryx. He looked down at his tent and muttered a single command word.

The tent, obeying the voice of power from Weylor, took shape. In a matter of seconds it was done; a tent twice as wide as the others and as tall as a man.

Dryx, trying his hardest to hide his awe, grabbed his things and threw them insides, not caring to unpack or lay out his things.

Weylor laughed but didn't say a word. He had won this time and he knew it; they both knew it.

The rest of the day passed uneventfully. The other soldiers awoke and Dryx and Weylor were introduced to their new scouting party. Thirty men total made up the Silver Dragon scouting party, with Weylor being the new and only mage.

As night crept down the mountains and into Halsgrove, dozens of campfires sprung up all over the village. Stars spread across the sky like yellow marbles dumped out on a black floor. A cool breeze came down from the north, the scent of salt water filling the small town. Soldiers in one part of the camp began singing and as the song progressed others took up instruments to accompany them; soon the entire village was alive with music.

Dryx wondered if it was a good idea to be singing so loud while they were so close to the woods. He checked his suspicion, though. He knew they would not be so foolish as to leave the town unprotected. He knew there were likely many scouts out patrolling the outskirts of the town and knew that there was little chance for a goblin, let alone a group of goblins, to pass by the scouts without being seen.

As the night grew later, the singing grew quieter. By the time the moon shone found its way into the night sky the singing had faded. The only movement in the village was the silent glow of campfires dying down amidst the tents.

A sound rang out during the night, a whistle; first a short, high pitch then a longer, lower pitch. Most of the men awoke at the sound of the whistle but went right back asleep, recognizing the sound to be a call from a scout for the captains to meet in the guard station.

Dryx and Weylor, however, were unaccustomed to the noise and awoke thinking they were being attacked. Sleeping so close to the forest didn't help their jumpiness. Unlike those that went back to sleep upon recognizing the call, Dryx and Weylor couldn't fall back asleep. Obviously something was going on, something important enough to call the captains together.

"What is it?" Dryx asked when he left his tent just as Thestian left his, fully dressed.

"I don't know. That's what I'm going to find out. Don't worry, though, if it was more urgent they would have sounded the call to arms. There is no imminent danger." With the short explanation to Dryx, Thestian left his camp and ran over to the guard station.

Nine captains stood around the table in the guard station's war room; maps were strewn across the tables, markers dotting the locations of all the scouting parties to the east and of the last known locations of goblin raiding parties..

"There is a goblin force not far from New Halsgrove," the scout began, instantly gaining the undivided attention of every captain in the room. "My partner went to warn the other scouts in the area. We were not spotted, or if we were the goblins didn't care enough to even acknowledge us, so it's safe to assume, at least for the moment, that they don't yet know we know they are there. I counted their numbers around a hundred. They seem to have come up straight from the south along the base of the mountains."

"What were they doing when you spotted them," one of the captains asked.

"They made camp, sir," the scout replied. "It didn't take me that long to get from their camp back to here running," he ended, wanting to reiterate that the goblins weren't that far away.

"Thank you," Jarol said; he had been made captain of New Halsgrove and was in command over all the scouting parties residing in the village. He motioned for the scout to return to his duties.

"We have assignments from Taris for five of you and your scouts this day," Jarol stood up and said. "I will not leave New Halsgrove unprotected with fewer than two parties. Desperate times call for desperate measures, my friends, and we cannot leave this threat to grow so close to here. Thestian," he said, looking over to the captain of the Silver Dragon's, "you and your Silver Dragons, and Jeremy, you and your Guardians, will go take care of this threat. Thestian, make use of your new mage, he is the only one either of you have. Don't let any escape. Any questions?"

"No sir," Thestian and Jeremy replied together.

Jeremy followed Thestian to a different room in the guard station where a large table bore a map of the surrounding land.

"The scout said the goblins were camped not far to the east of here. We have a few hours until the sun rises, we should leave before dawn together, and split when the sun comes over the mountains. My men and I will go around to the south, you and your men to the north. If possible, we will drive them either up the mountains or back towards New Halsgrove, either way we have the advantage," Thestian told Jeremy.

Jeremy stood for a moment digesting the suggestion while staring at the map where the goblins supposedly were camped. "Agreed," he said at length.

Both Thestian and Jeremy returned to their camps and awoke their soldiers. In ten minutes both parties were ready to head out.

Chapter 10

Meeting in the Middle

Danflorf awakened his small company of dwarves as the first rays of sunshine made their way high in the sky above the mountains behind them. The dwarves knew they were camped right in the middle of an open clearing, and close to the path with fresh goblin tracks, but they got out their pots and pans anyway and made breakfast; it wasn't like dwarves to start off the day on an empty stomach!

The dwarves would take turns watching the trails as the others ate, but they finished quickly and readied their without a hint of any activity around them.

Finding the trail easily enough, Danflorf bent over and examined the footprints. There were a lot of goblins, he knew, and even if he and his dwarves could surprise the goblins, he wasn't sure if they could kill all of them. He wasn't about to put his small group in danger without knowing the circumstances.

"We'll follow them from a distance and see how many there are. We aren't to be attacking unless we know we can take 'em," he said.

Taffer took lead of the group and headed them off down the trail once more, following the fresh prints in the mud. The light of dawn would be creeping over the mountains very soon.

The first, feint signs of sunrise started to appear high in the sky, although it would still be a while before its light would be able to reach them in the dense forest. The Silver Dragons and the Guardians had traveled for almost an hour before the sun rose; they traveled slower through the heavier, denser parts of the forest to stay as hidden as possible. They reached the edge of a clearing and stopped.

Thestian got Jeremy's attention to his left and motioned his hand down to the ground, signaling for Jeremy to stop his men. He then pointed to one of his scouts, to his eyes and then to the clearing ahead of them.

With only a nod of acknowledgement, the scout passed Thestian and made his way through the trees to survey the land in front of them.

A few minutes passed by and the scout returned into Thestian's vision. He held up two fingers and then to their entire scouting force, both Thestian and Jeremy's groups included.

Thestian nodded his head, acknowledging to the scout that he received his message.

Captain Thestian motioned for Captain Jeremy to come to him.

"There are over a hundred, by my scout's guess," Captain Thestian said.

"Do you think we will ever get this kind of advantage again?" Captain Jeremy asked. "I don't want to put the lives of my men at risk any more than you, but we have to take care of this. There is no one else," he said.

It was true. There was no other force in that part of the kingdom to list help from that they knew about. Both captains knew that they had an advantage that they may not get again.

"There's no other choice, then," replied Captain Thestian. "We attack. I will take my men south and attack from below them. Take your men north and do the same. I don't think it will be difficult to time our attacks together; a goblin's dying scream will suffice," he said coldly. He let the thought of his wife and family fuel his resolve in the decision. He knew that he needed that drive to keep his mind free of fear and doubt.

So, they both set off. Captain Thestian led his men south and east, to come up from below the goblins, while Captain Jeremy led his men north and east, to effectively encircle them about.

It wasn't hard for either scouting party to find the goblin camp; like the scout had told them, dozens of campfires sent up enough smoke to see from a distance with the little light starting to peek over the Giant's Steppes, the smell of smoke also filling the dense air in the forest around them.

Captain Thestian signaled for his men to stop, just outside the range of the goblin scouts. He motioned for two of his best rangers to take out the scouts.

The two rangers nodded their heads. They crept off into thicker vegetation for better cover. They had to wait only a minute before two goblins came walking down a well-worn trail. They were tired and not overly-alert in the early morning hours just before sunrise, so they didn't notice the abnormal bulges behind the sides of two trees until an arrow pierced each of them right above the sternum of the rib cage and below the throat. Even if the arrows hadn't blocked their ability to scream out, the shock alone of seeing an arrow protruding from their chests would have been enough to silence them. They fell to their knees, but to them it seemed as if the earth came up to meet them.

A goblin scout, sheltered in a tree, had been watching the two goblin scouts walking their rounds on the ground. There was just enough light so this his natural night vision, his main vision in the lightless tunnels below ground in the mountains, was useless and just dark enough to where his normal vision, not that great already, could barely make out the walking figures.

"What you stop for? Sleeping on the job?" he said in a loud voice, laughing at the thought of catching patrols sleeping and the punishment that would be inflicted on them for it.

The two rangers, still hidden in the foliage, didn't understand the goblin gibberish from the tree, but they didn't have to understand it to realize that they were suddenly in a very dangerous spot.

If that scout called out a warning, all hope of surprise would be lost. They found him well hidden halfway up a tree at the camps edge. They both took aim and fired. One arrow pierced straight through the leather jerkin protecting the goblins stomach and stuck into the tree behind it, effectively nailing it to the tree.

The second arrow narrowly missed, digging into the tree a centimeter above the goblins head. Like the two before it, it found itself staring at the arrow suddenly protruding from its chest, then at the shaft above its head. It still didn't understand what had happened, and then it didn't understand anything at all as its head tilted down and to the side, staring down into the darkness without seeing a thing.

The two rangers waited only a few moments to make sure it was dead before they ran back to Captain Thestian.

As a whole, they moved right up to the edge of the camp, only feet away from the nearest tent. They could hear the sound of dozens of sleeping goblins; a beautiful sound to Captain Thestian. Less of his men would die; they had complete surprise.

After only a short while of walking, the dwarves came to a small, elevated hill. They could see the not-too-distant campfires in a clearing of trees at the end of the path they were following.

"If that's the goblin camp, then I'm thinking there should be some scouts around here somewhere" Danflorf said, motioning for his men to back down the hill.

"Taffer, you and Cleff go see if you can find them damned goblin scouts. Get close to the camp if you can. Let's see if there are enough goblins for all of us," he said, getting a chuckle from the dwarves close enough to hear him.

Taffer and Cleff set off, staying south of the clearing and heading west. Dwarves saw in low-light vision, which allowed them to be able to see with even the slightest bit of light. They were able to see, with the first rays of the sun, much better than the goblins with their night vision.

From a distance, Taffer and Cleff watched the two goblin scouts and then saw them fall, noiselessly, to the ground. They followed the direction of the arrows and saw the large group of humans crouched down not far from the goblin camp.

"Danflorf," Taffer said when they reached the others, "there's a group of humans, a scouting party it looked like, just to the south of the clearing. They took out the goblin scouts, it looks like they're meaning to attack."

Danflorf thought about the situation for a moment, stroking his long, golden beard as he thought. "I'm thinking there isn't a better way to meet the humans than in a battle with goblin vermin," he said, a fire starting in his eyes as the anticipation of a fight only moments away became reality in his mind.

Every dwarf smiled at Danflorf; they heard exactly what they wanted to hear, the chance to kill some ugly goblins.

Hiding their unnecessary gear around the small hill, the dwarves, led by Danflorf, crept toward the clearing. They got as close as they dared, not wanting to be spotted by the goblins or the humans until the attack started. They found an area of thick foliage twenty yards east of the camp and huddled together as low as they could get, waiting for the tell-tale sounds of war.

Captain Thestian almost hoped to be able to just sneak in and kill the beasts as they slept; as unorthodox as that seemed, he was willing to try to save as many of his men as possible. But he never had the opportunity, for there were still goblins awake around most of the campfires; some alone, some in small groups.

Captain Thestian turned around and nodded to the whole of his scouting party, the signal to make ready.

All of his men, thirty counting himself, lined up at the edge of the camp, where the light still hadn't illuminate them. He motioned for his men to follow after the rangers had made the first kills.

In a matter of seconds, the silence was broken by the war cries of the twenty Silver Dragon's that charged the camp; the rangers stayed quiet and stayed back to have a clear view of the battlefield and pick off stragglers.

Seconds after the sound of the Silver Dragon's war cries, the sound of twenty more men yelling the same war cry pierced the air from the north; Jeremy and his men had joined in the ambush.

The surprise was complete; the scouting parties dispatching the first line of tents before the goblins could wake and ready themselves for the ambush. An easy victory was hoped for in every man's heart, until the horde of recently sleeping goblins came scrambling out of their tents.

They would be dazed from the sudden attack for only a few seconds longer and both captains used those precious seconds to form the ranks in their parties.

A hundred yards separated the captains from each other, with well over a hundred goblins in between. On both sides they had killed nearly two dozen goblins in a matter of seconds, but their progress would slow drastically; goblins weren't as easy to kill awake as they were asleep.

Dryx felt no fear as his hatred for the small, ugly goblins fueled his rage. Dryx had taken a few of the sleeping goblins but searched for more of a challenge, going slightly further inside the camp than his fellow scouts. He smiled as he saw the horde of goblins come scurrying out of the tents; it was like picking off rats coming out of a hole when lit a fire in it.

His swords flew out, felling the first few dazed goblins that happened to come out of the tent next to him. Still more came, though, and Dryx soon found himself in a tight spot. He realized he had been too hasty in searching for a fight and was quickly on his heels. Still, he managed to spin and maneuver to block the simple attacks of the goblins.

Spinning in a complete circle, his arms out and blades facing the ground, Dryx blocked the thrusts of four different spears; they were fairly close together and came in at the same angle. He only had time to make an attack on one of the goblins, though, as the goblins were quick to continue their attack.

Weylor, already having put on himself a few defensive spells, stayed a small distance from the fray; magic was a ranged sport, after all. After years of practice and tutelage under one of the greatest known wizards in all the surrounding lands, Weylor fell into chanting.

An acorn, covered in sulfur and the power of Weylor's magic, sped toward a large group of goblins in the middle of the camp that hadn't yet entered combat. The seed exploded into a fiery ball, sending a few goblins flying through the air, burning and screaming, and killing a few from the explosion itself.

Goblins hated wizards and it wasn't long before many of the goblins that weren't fighting started off for the lone wizard. Few made it, though; the ranger's arrows falling almost a dozen of them as they separated themselves from the main group and became easy targets.

Those that weren't hit by the rangers arrows, though, met a barrage of exploding rocks; the explosion stung the goblins all over but wasn't meant to kills them, just distract them. The short burst of light blinded the goblins for only a few seconds. But that all the time Weylor needed. His hands flew out in front of him, this time no spell components were needed; muttering the short, simple incantation, magic missiles, the size of arrows, flew from his finger tips and dropped the four goblins in front of him.

The rangers watched as Weylor dazed the goblins and then as the powerful, blue magic missiles dropped all of the goblins at once. They decided they liked fighting with wizards; the lights and explosions were exciting and effective!

Dryx, slowly making his way back to his group, fell into a dizzying rhythm of parries and feints. The goblins couldn't follow the speed of his maneuvers and all of their attacks were stopped by the flurry of blades around him; but he was unable to attack in his new found defense. Gaining confidence, Dryx burst out of his double bladed defense and struck out at the two goblins in front of him, either blade finding the belly of the two goblins in front of him. In a flash, his defense was back up, just in time to block three more incoming attacks. This time, though, one of the attacks was low and came in from the side.

The goblin grinned as it felt its spear dig into the crazy human's left thigh; its glee was short-lived, though.

Dryx's left blade came down a second later and broke the spear head off from the shaft. He screamed out in pain and jumped back off his right foot. Still ten feet in front of the rest of the scouts, Dryx found it hard to maneuver with his hurt leg; putting any pressure at all on his left leg almost paralyzed him with pain. Dryx threw his swords out in front of him and blocked the two frontal attacks, but he knew a third was coming from his side again where he couldn't block. He tensed for the attack, but felt nothing.

Danflorf, having watched the first minute of the battle, thought the humans had done about as best as anyone could to surprise a group of goblins as big as this one. He wasn't about to let them have all the fun though, and helping them in this fight could be the key to making an alliance with them. Although that was his 'official' business with the humans, every dwarf in Icedome knew he yearned for travel and to meet the humans of the kingdom below the mountains and walk their streets out of curiosity and a desire to explore the world above.

"Look alive boys, let's show the humans we come in peace," he said, turning back and winking to his comrades. The only way to show the humans that they came in peace was to spill goblin blood alongside them, something they were more than eager to do.

Danflorf led the sprint towards the eastern side of the encampment and led the dwarves in their most ancient war song, a prayer to Deramoin, sang during battle. Coincidentally, the song laid out, in rhyming dwarfish, a glorious slaughter of goblins, specifically.

The dwarves hit the goblin ranks like a spearhead, effectively separating the goblin's ranks as Danflorf, the head of the dwarven spear, pushed further into the chaos. The dwarves fought together, shoulder to shoulder, with their shields out in front. Rarely did they attack the foe right in front of them; rather they would turn their shields out wide and attack the goblin on either side as it attacked the dwarf in front of it, not expecting a blow to come from the side. When one dwarf pulled his shield out to attack, both dwarves on either side would put their shields up to block.

With both sudden attacks from the humans, and the overall surprise of the ambush, the goblins morale was all but shattered; until they heard the dwarven battle song.

The goblins in the middle of the chaos heard the blood-curdling screams of its dying comrades at every side. The goblins on the outside, whether against the humans or the dwarves, tried to scramble back into some kind of formation, but the chaos was too much.

The dwarves, about the same height as the goblins, were just as happy being surround as they were being in ranks; they just wandered in the spearhead formation, following Danflorf, who followed the line of whichever goblins were unlucky enough to cross his path. With a turn here and a turn there, Danflorf could see they were headed toward the human ranks to the south; only a few dozen goblins stood between them.

Let's see what they make of us, Danflorf thought to himself, and turned almost straight south. He was going in no particular direction, just generally towards the humans; there was no rush as long as there were plenty of smelly goblins to kill.

Danflorf saw one human that stood out, though, and changed his direction slightly and increased his pace when he saw the human in a dangerous situation.

The human didn't have a shield, but Danflorf realized he almost didn't need one. He was weaving his swords in such a fast pattern that he blocked all of the goblins attacks; all but one, Danflorf saw. He watched the spear pierce the human's leg, and decided to take advantage of the situation and save the human.

"Forward, boys," he yelled out, going into almost a full sprint, his helmet lowered and his shield up. The sudden burst of the dwarves caused everyone, goblins and humans alike, to stop for a brief second and watch the triangle of armor, not taller than the goblins, burst through the camp and straight for Dryx.

Reaching the goblin to the side of the human just as it was raising its weapon for a fatal blow, Danflorf's right arm shot straight up and came down with enough force to severe the thing's arm from its torso. Without skipping a beat, Danflorf lowered his head and head-butted the goblin in the chest; it fell to the ground unable to breath, with an abnormal hole where his ribcage used to be. Straightening his helmet, Danflorf turned to the human, who stood staring as if he had seen a ghost, and smiled.

"What is that?" Captain Thestian said, turning his head as he heard a battle cry he was not familiar with, he knew it was neither of his men nor the goblins. Though a novice in knowledge of other races, Captain Thestian was no novice to war and recognized the song as a war song despite not understanding the words.

"What the..." he began but was cut off by an attack of a goblin that saw his momentary distraction as an opportunity. A goblin spear pierced his side. His armor stopped most of the spearhead, only the tip penetrating through to his skin. He slammed his shield down, tearing the spearhead out of his side and snapping the spear in two. His sword arm flew around and came down at an angle, taking off the right hand and entire left arm of the goblin who suddenly found itself weaponless and armless. Another quick strike to stomach and the goblin fell to the earth.

He looked to the north and, for a split second, thought that his eyes had played a trick on him; he saw dwarves! Then he heard the chanting again; they were inside the goblin ranks fighting!

They attacked the goblins? Captain Thestian thought to himself, perplexed.

With the arrival of the dwarves, it seemed like the 'belly of the beast' was collapsing; the overall confusion of the ambush on the goblins left them all but disoriented. No matter which way they ran they met resistance, they had nowhere to go. The goblins in the middle ran from the deadly dwarven formation that seemed to cut through their ranks like a ship parting the water over which it sails. Within only a few minutes of the dwarves joining the fight, many more dozen goblins had fallen.

Dryx couldn't believe his eyes; a dwarf, not five feet away, had just saved his life. The short, broad dwarf and his group had, in a matter of seconds, cleared the area around him of goblins and, after smiling at him, ran back into the fray.

The pain in his leg forced him to pay attention, once again, to his surrounding and hop back behind his comrades to safety.

Captain Thestian made his forward to try and get a better view of the dwarves. He called for his men to rank up with him and they fought their way forward; not so much fought as slaughtered. The goblins had lost all bravery for the fight and were now trying to escape in any direction they could, but there was no escape. Any goblin that did make it past the humans and the dwarves was picked off by the rangers and Weylor.

Only a few dozen goblins remained by the time Captain Thestian and his men found the dwarves. Captain Jeremy and his men had had the same success coming in from north and were now blocking the goblins in between the three parties; Captain Jeremy and his men to the north, Captain Thestian and his men to the south, the dwarves somewhat between them on the outskirts to the east, once again, and the rangers and Weylor to the west.

The goblins had circled up, the outer goblins trying to back into the middle of the group and the middle goblins trying to hide behind the rest, not letting the goblins in the front any room to back up. The goblins stood there, shaking, with their spears and axes and swords in hand; they knew they were dead.

Captain Thestian and Captain Jeremy both made their way, slowly, to the side where the dwarves waited.

Danflorf, seeing the two approaching men, realized they were most likely the leaders and dropped his axe and shield to his side.

Both captains stopped a dozen feet from the dwarf that had stepped forward. They didn't say a word, unsure if the dwarf would understand them if they did.

The dwarf looked from one to the other then, with a smile to both of them, raised his shield and sword and charged the group of goblins, his company right behind him, another battle song bursting into the air.

"Forward!" Captain Thestian yelled, his sword pointing to the goblins. The charge of the dwarves had given him courage and assurance that they were not enemies.

A dozen men lie dead on the ground; ten times that number were the bodies of the goblins around them.

There they stood, twenty-five men from the Silver Dragon's and twenty-three from The Guardians', in front of twelve of the most menacing things they had ever seen. They all knew that they were dwarves, but none of them had ever actually seen one.

The dwarf in the front of the group, after turning to his fellow dwarves and muttering something the humans couldn't hear, stepped forward. He hooked the handle of his axe over a notch on his belt at his side, slung his shield across his back and took off his helmet. With his right arm holding his helmet, he leaned forward into a deep bow, his left arm coming at in a gesture of peace.

"Ye speak common, I hope?" he asked, hoping that these humans were like the ones that they had known many decades before. They had had trade with a small kingdom of humans that lived on a mountain above the dwarf's ancient home.

"Yes, we speak common," Captain Thestian replied, also sheathing his weapon and taking a step forward to show that he was the leader. "I am Captain Thestian, of Taris. Who are you?" he asked with obvious curiosity.

"I am Danflorf, son of King Bourndrimiur, King of Icedome," Danflorf said, bowing low again.

"Icedome?" Captain Thestian asked curiously, "I have never heard of such a place, nor had I any knowledge that there were dwarves living in the area."

"Aye, that's because we didn't want no one knowing," Danflorf replied.

"So why are you here now? Why did you help us?" Captain Thestian asked eager to know the true reason why the dwarves had arrived.

"Me father, the king, sent us to meet yer king and propose an alliance," Danflorf answered.

Captain Thestian looked back to Dryx; the dwarves had saved his life for no obvious reason and had been a huge help in defeating the goblins before more of his men died.

"It's a five day journey to Taris by wagon, where the king is," Captain Thestian told Danflorf, letting him know that he would have to travel into the heart of their kingdom.

Danflorf, stroking his beard, nodded his head in agreement and with a smile the humans didn't understand; only the dwarves that were with him understood his excitement from being out of Icedome and the mountains. Danflorf, for ten years, had wanted to travel down to the villages and explore the kingdom and culture of the humans.

"Very well, Danflorf. We will lead you back to New Halsgrove, a scouting outpost, and from there we will ready a few wagons for you and your comrades to travel to Taris," Captain Thestian told Danflorf.

Captain Jeremy and his men stayed behind as the dwarves left with Captain Thestian; they retrieved the bodies of their fallen comrades and piled up the corpses of the goblins and burned it; they would leave the heaping, smoldering pile as a sign for any goblins that traveled that way in the future.

With the help of Weylor and another scout, Dryx was able to make it back to New Halsgrove without having to use his left leg. There was one cleric assigned to New Halsgrove, a young cleric by the name of Byron, and, after helping Dryx onto a table in the guard station, the scout went to find the cleric.

Captain Strongshield had sent some of his scouts to prepare three wagons for the dwarves and kept them company while they waited. He, now feeling completely comfortable around the short dwarves, had an unending stream of questions that Danflorf was more than happy to answer, asking just as many in return.

Byron found Dryx and Weylor and quickly cut his pants loose around the wound. The tip of the spear was still embedded in Dryx's leg and Weylor found him a rolled-up piece of cloth to bite down on as Byron yanked the spearhead free.

Instantly Byron began cleaning the wound. He pulled out various bottles of ointments and liquids, using some to clean the wound and some he poured inside the wound. When the cleaning was done, Byron took off the necklace around his neck and, holding his necklace in his right hand up in the air, he began chanting prayers to Valerum, the god of light and healing.

Dryx was no longer conscious; he had passed out when Byron tore the spearhead from his thigh.

"Well, that's all I can do out here," he said to Weylor and left.

"Captain Thestian," Byron said as he passed the captain on his way back to his own tent.

"Byron, what is it?" the captain replied.

Byron stood staring at the dwarves for a moment before composing himself and looking back to the captain. "I was able to help your scout but I can only do so much out here. I cleaned the wound of infection and disease, but he will need the help of the clerics in the temple to regain full use of his leg; the wound went deep"

"Thank you, Byron. Your service is always appreciated," the captain said, bowing slightly to show his respect to the cleric and his holy profession.

Captain Thestian made his way into the guard station to where Weylor stood next to his unconscious brother.

"It looks like you will be returning to Taris with your brother, Weylor," the captain sighed, sad to see the only wizard ever in his scouting party leave. "Byron said Dryx will need the cleric's help in the temple to heal his leg completely."

"Yes, Captain," Weylor replied, looking from the captain back down to his brother; Dryx's breathing had evened but he was sweating profusely.

"Can you steer a wagon?" Captain Thestian asked.

"Of course," Weylor replied.

"Good. I will have Dryx loaded into your wagon," the captain told him. "You will lead the dwarves back to Taris and then to see the king, understood?"

"Yes, Captain," Weylor replied, grateful to be staying with his brother. "Thank you, Captain," he added in appreciation.

"I will send a messenger by horse immediately, he will arrive before you and give them word of your coming," the captain said and left Weylor with his brother.

Chapter II

Alliances

Five days later the dwarven party, led by Weylor, finally came into view of the tall mage tower that marked the eastern edge of the city.

A salty breeze blew in from the north. It was a smell none of the dwarves took a liking to; none except one, Danflorf. That came as a surprise to no one.

"That tower marks the eastern edge of the city of Taris. It is the mage tower," Weylor called back to the dwarves.

"We are not strangers to the above world anymore," Danflorf said, still taking in the sight of the tower, "but we've never actually seen a human city. Things are different underground."

As the wagon drew closer, the dwarves grew wary; they knew they had nothing to fear from the humans, but the thought of being completely surrounded in a walled city by a people that were not yet their allies was disconcerting.

"Keep yer hands off yer weapons, boys," Danflorf said, putting a hand on Balarek's shoulder.

Balarek was perhaps the sourest of all the dwarves of Icedome and the most untrusting of other races, though a more loyal dwarf to his own king could not be found. "We don't want them thinking that we're here for a fight."

Danflorf spoke in a different tone as their wagon drew closer to the gates. He had longed for this moment a long time, and he knew how important it was to make a good impression and become allies with the humans. The dwarves of Icedome were fully capable of maintaining themselves in the mountains, but trade with the humans would allow them commodities and luxuries they didn't have.

"Halt!" came the expected call from the top of the wall as the caravan approached the gate. "Who are you and what business do you have in Taris?" The tone of the soldier was more inquisitive than threatening.

Weylor climbed down from the wagon and approached the gate. "I am Weylor Stormcaller of the Silver Dragon's scouting party. We are escorting our new allies to Taris to speak with King Ironwill. A messenger should have arrived with news of our coming," Weylor replied in a loud voice to the guard on top of the wall.

A moment later the guard called down to the inner court below the wall and the huge doors opened.

Weylor climbed back onto the wagon and led the party into Taris through the only gate that gave access into Taris, located in the southeastern wall of the city.

None of the dwarves in the party, not even Danflorf, had ever been this close to a human kingdom, let alone inside the walls of one of their cities. To Danflorf, the city seemed open and spacious; the houses stood alone and walled, almost exactly like the homes in Icedome except that in Icedome homes were carved out of the mountain, not built up. In the southwest corner of the city they could see a very thick grove of trees; they would have thought it an entire forest had they not been told that a cliff was just on the other side. Just to the north of the grove of trees was a very tall, very steep and narrow hill, topped by a tower.

As the caravan moved north through the city they realized that Taris was not as big as it looked from outside the gates. They could see that they were on the only main road in the whole city and that in a couple hundred yards it ended.

The dwarves admired the huge, wooden building to their right as they rode past; easily making it out to be a building for warriors by all the signs of weapons and armor and the students practicing inside.

The building that caught, and held, their attention the longest, though, was the keep. Situated in the center of Taris, the keep was made of solid stone. Huge doors, similar to those they had just crossed through, marked the entrance to the keep. The keep was twice as tall as the walls surrounding the city and dozens of inset windows dotted the face of the keep.

A small lake, or giant pond as the dwarves would call it, took up most of the keep's foreground. They had never seen a body of water so clear; below ground you could not see into the water of lakes and ponds, they were as black as the creatures that lived in them.

Weylor pulled the caravan off to the side of the road where the road split off to the west towards the keep.

A messenger was already waiting at the corner, waving them down as they neared, along with a smaller wagon and a few clerics.

Weylor stopped the wagon and approached the messenger, "I am Weylor Stormcaller, of the Silver Dragon's," he said, dipping into a quick bow.

"Well met, Weylor," the messenger said, also bending into a quick, low bow. "I am Halfein, messenger of Captain Strongshield. A messenger arrived yesterday and informed Captain Strongshield of your arrival. Rooms have already been prepared in The Traveler for our guests and dinner is waiting for them. After they eat, escort them to the keep," he said. "These clerics will take Dryx to the temple." With that he turned and strode off toward the city wall.

Weylor, after the clerics had transferred Dryx to the smaller wagon, led the party to The Traveler and the dwarves were more than happy to leave their packs in their rooms and sit down to a meal. All of the dwarves, even Balarek, were more than impressed with the food; they just kept eating!

The inn keeper had to bring out extra meat, bread, and cheese from the storage room and, by the end, an entire extra keg of ale from behind the bar; that made keg number six. The innkeeper didn't mind though; he was being recompensed handsomely for his taking care of the dwarves.

When all the dwarves were done eating, not that that really happens they more just take breaks than divide up the day by meals, Weylor stood up. "Master Danflorf, King Ironwill would see you now," he said.

Danflorf took a moment to concentrate now on his next task; not the easiest feat being full of food and ale. He stood up, along with the rest of the dwarves, stretched, and followed Weylor out into night.

Danflorf, when he saw the wagon being brought around to take them to the keep, looked from the wagon to his stomach, a nervous look crossing his face.

"Eh, if it's all the same, I'd prefer to walk; a bumpy wagon isn't the best thing for a belly full of food and ale," Danflorf said to Weylor.

The dwarves behind him agreed; they gazed warily at the approaching wagon as well.

"Very well," Weylor told him; he couldn't help but laugh a bit at their hesitation.

It took only a few minutes for the group to walk from The Traveler, situated on the corner of the street that led to the keep, to the keep.

As the party walked up the stone steps the giant doors swung open, granting them entrance.

The dwarves entered the entrance chamber of the keep and couldn't help but notice the fine craftsmanship and worked stone that was inside.

With a loud thud the door closed behind them. The dwarves, instinctively, had their hands on the handles of their weapons as soon as they heard the thud. There were two guards normally on duty at the doors, but with a company of twelve dwarves coming to the keep Captain Strongshield had ordered a few more; just in case. The guards, despite feeling very nervous and anxious at having twelve dwarves inside their keep, followed orders and kept their weapons sheathed.

A few moments passed and the dwarves' anxiety calmed, their hands leaving the hilts of their weapons.

"Greetings, master dwarves," one of the guards said, stepping forward and bowing. "It is an honor to have you in our keep. Which one of you is…" he said, forgetting the name of the son of the dwarven king and looking down at the parchment in his hands, "Danflorf, son of the King of Icedome?"

Danflorf stepped forward, trusting his gut which told him that he was in no danger. "I am Danflorf," he said, bowing slightly to the guard in respect.

The guard bowed when the dwarf prince stepped forward. "Well met. We ask that you take two of your guards, without your weapons, and proceed. The rest may wait in the next room," the guard said.

"How're we going to let the son of our king go with only two of us and no weapons?" Balarek argued, outraged. He wasn't about to let Danflorf trudge off with not a weapon on him.

"I am sorry, but we cannot allow all of you, armed, in to see the king. The rest of you may retain your weapons and wait in our waiting chamber. I can assure you that Danflorf will be completely safe," the guard said. He smiled and continued, "We, our king especially, are excited at the proposal of an alliance with you."

Balarek, not wanting to show that he let down at all, simply huffed and stomped his boot on the solid stone floor in protest.

"I haven't come all this way to not see the king, Balarek," Danflorf said. "You will come with me, and you too, Taffer. The rest of you, don't go startin' any trouble." His tone was as serious as ever; Danflorf had waited for this a long time.

Danflorf looked around, meeting the eyes of everyone one of his dwarves that wasn't going with him to see King Ironwill; none of them would start any trouble.

The guard led them over to a table to place their weapons, through a door and out of sight of the remaining dwarves. Restless as the dwarves were, they waited in the waiting chamber and talked with the guards, each asking questions, and soon they were all in the conversations, content.

Weylor left the keep and went to the temple. The clerics inside took him to where Dryx was; he was asleep and an older cleric was hovering over his exposed wound.

"May I enter?" Weylor asked, not wanting to interrupt the cleric.

"Of course," the old man responded, a smile on his face. "You must be his brother."

"Weylor," he replied, bowing to the sage-like man; the man was slender yet still stood straight. He was almost completely bald but his beard hung long and white as the snow.

"How is he?" he asked.

"The wound is deep," the old cleric said, "but he will heal and have full use of his leg again. The weapon was crude but non-magical; those are always the easiest to heal."

Weylor believed him; he noticed that the wound on Dryx's left thigh was almost closed completely and looked good, no hint of disease or infection.

"He should be able to leave in the morning," the old man said, looking up at Weylor and smiling.

Weylor smiled; it was a nice way for the old man to ask Weylor to leave and let Dryx sleep.

He got up and returned to the keep to await the dwarves and return with them to The Traveler.

Hours had passed before King Ironwill realized how late the night had grown. He had spent hours listening and following Clan Bourndrimiur's history from their ancient home, through their defeat to the evil drow, along the endless, lightless tunnels underground, and their eventual settling in the Giants Steppes.

The king was very disturbed to hear Orgath had been rebuilt and was now home, once again, to thousands of goblins; he knew they would be there but from what the dwarf scout described, the king's fears were a reality. He feared something was stirring with all the recent goblin activity away from their home in the mountains but had hoped that it wasn't turning into the same thing that happened those many years before.

King Ironwill was the most respectable man in the kingdom; he was actually named king by the people because of his courage and sacrifice for the people in defending Taris. He felt saddened at the story of the dwarves, but anxious and excited that they had found a new home, and one close enough to become allies with! He agreed to the alliance and promised to send the dwarves back with supplies and whatever else they wanted as a sign of trust and good faith.

Danflorf felt no hint of regret as he left the king's chambers and returned with his men to The Traveler. He had left the king with the map that his father had given him, a map that would show the humans how to get to Icedome. Trade would start as soon as a trail fit for wagons could be cleared from Halsgrove, through Ganders Forest, to the foot of the mountains.

Although Danflorf and King Ironwill both knew trade would be difficult because of the terrain, they both realized that, with time, each of their kingdoms would greatly benefit from each other.

Chapter 12

A Different Company

Weylor woke up as the light filtered in through the window. He made his way downstairs to make sure that breakfast would be ready before he awoke the dwarves.

Weylor woke up the dwarves and led them down to the mess hall for breakfast.

"I will be back shortly," Weylor said to Danflorf once breakfast had begun. "Dryx should be able to leave the temple this morning."

Danflorf nodded and might have considered accompanying his new friend, but the amount of new and delicious food in front of him kept him at the table; that and Weylor would be back shortly anyway.

Once again, a cleric near the entrance led Weylor to his brother inside the temple. Dryx was already awake on the bed, stretching out his leg when Weylor entered.

"How's the leg?" Weylor asked casually, hiding his concern.

"A bit stiff but good," Dryx replied, standing up slowly. He waited a moment, shifting some of his weight to his leg to test it, then put all his weight on his left leg.

"Wow," he said, a smile quickly forming, "I can't hardly feel a thing." He paced around the room, slowly at first then at a normal pace.

"You don't even have a limp," Weylor said, surprised.

"I should hope not," said a voice.

Weylor jumped, startled; he didn't hear anyone come to the doorway behind him. It was the same, old cleric as the night before.

"Here," he said, tossing a small vial with red liquid to Dryx. "That should take away any pain you still have. It looks like you healed up nicely," the cleric said, smiling.

Weylor thought his smile almost looked a little too smug.

"Thank you," Dryx replied, putting the small vial into his belt pouch as he donned his gear.

"So," Dryx said to Weylor as they left the temple and headed back towards the inn where the dwarves were, "what's happened?"

"You've been out a long time, Dryx," Weylor, hiding his smile, answered in a serious tone. "Orgath's been burned to the ground and the war is over. We're going back to farming now."

Dryx laughed loudly at the absurdity of his brother's reply. "Ah, and mother remarried too, then?"

Weylor had hoped for a better reaction, but it was hard lying when Dryx was his twin brother. "Danflorf spoke with the king and I assume we'll be returning to New Halsgrove with the dwarves."

The same messenger as the day before was, once again, was waiting for Weylor.

"Captain Strongshield sends for you," the guard said as the twins approached. "I informed the dwarves; they will await your return at the inn."

The twins followed the guard back to the keep and up to Captain Strongshield's room.

"Enter," came the expected call from outside Captain Strongshield's room.

Dryx and Weylor entered, ushered in by the guard outside the room.

"Please, sit down," Captain Strongshield said. He looked over the two young twins for a moment before continuing. "The king is very excited about our new alliance with the dwarves and seeing that you two are the ones that escorted them here and would have, if there is any, their confidence, the king has decided to send you two back to Icedome with the dwarves. You will become familiar with the trail that leads through Gander's Forest and then through the mountains to Icedome. We need to know how long it would take to cut a trail big enough for wagons to Icedome."

The twins looked at each other; even Dryx couldn't help but smile at their luck.

"Will it just be us two, Captain?" Weylor asked, beginning to see a potential problem with their new assignment; with the size of the goblin raid party they had destroyed just days before, traveling through Gander's Forest alone would be suicide.

"Yes," replied the Captain. "We cannot spare any more men at the moment. There are more goblins to the south east but they aren't attacking and that's not like goblins. There is something we aren't seeing."

"Is that to be our next assignment then?" Dryx asked.

"No, no. That will be an assignment for an army. With the amount of goblins down there it's too dangerous for just a few men. Weylor, you are one of very few mages that has come about in the last few years, that's the only reason the king decided to send only you two on this assignment. This is a big responsibility for you two," the Captain said. He understood, better than most, how potentially dangerous this could be, but he also knew that both of the twins were at the top of their class and very dependable.

Captain Strongshield let the twins think about the assignment. Even he had never seen an assignment this important be given to two students still not graduated.

"We will find the path and travel to Icedome, Captain," Weylor said. Dryx returned the smile that was beginning to crease both of their faces. "We will take care to stay as far north in the forest as possible to avoid any danger when we return. Are there any specific tasks in Icedome for us?"

King Ironwill hadn't given the Captain any specific responsibilities for the twins except to travel to Icedome and find the path that leads there.

"No, just gain the trust of the king; show him that he has nothing to fear from us. Danflorf was more than charismatic with us about the negotiations and alliance, but, from what I have heard of dwarves, very few are as…open…as he is," said the Captain, finding the best word to describe their neighbors.

"We will do whatever it takes, Captain," Weylor said.

Decades before, when Captain Strongshield was the same age as the twins, he was part of the army that pushed the goblins back into the mountain caves and burned the goblin city to the ground; but now it was being rebuilt. He understood the confidence behind Weylor's words; he had heard that same line over twenty years before by King Ironwill himself, then captain of the entire Taris army, when he led the siege against Orgath.

Two days passed before the twins and the dwarves started making preparations to return to Icedome. In fact, if it wasn't for the fact that Danflorf was so outnumbered by his kin, he might never have left; he had visited every corner of Taris, taking in the new scenery and experiences, and had no desire of returning to Icedome so soon. He loved being out of the mines of Icedome and in the open, fresh air below the mountains.

The worst of all the places he visited, for the rest of the dwarves, was the harbor. On the north end of Taris, down the long, steep staircase carved right out of the mountain, sat the harbor at the bottom of the cliff.

Danflorf had always wanted to see the huge ships that could carry a hundred men and stay afloat, but, in the underdark, all he knew were the small paddle boats for the rare, deep lakes that found their way underground.

"How big is the sea?" Danflorf asked a sailor walking by on the wharf.

"It takes almost a week with a good headwind to get to Daley, straight north of us," the sailor said, carrying a large crate of freshly caught fish.

Danflorf just stood there, staring out over the sea just a few feet away.

What adventures lay out there? he thought.

Danflorf would have jumped on the first ship leaving port had his comrades not been keeping a close eye on him; they knew he thought it was too soon to head back. They weren't opposed to staying longer, but they knew the king would be anxious for their return.

"Yer father will be worrying, Danflorf. We've been gone more than a week already and it'll be almost a week to return," Taffer said, joining Danflorf on the wharf. He knew that was the only thing keeping Danflorf from heading off in some random direction just to find a new adventure.

"Yeah, yeah," was all the dwarven prince responded. He knew it was true and couldn't deny that his father probably hadn't slept since they had left. After losing so many family members in the drow attack so many years before, King Bourndrimiur had never let a dwarf travel more than a few miles from where he was; especially not Danflorf, his only son.

Danflorf, regrettably, followed Taffer back up into the city and to the inn, to prepare for their departure the next day.

Once again, dawn's early light poured through the window, waking Dryx. And once again, like always, he awoke to Weylor finishing his morning meditation.

The silence of the morning lasted only a few minutes after Dryx awoke; dwarves, in all known history, had never been known as being silent by any interpretation of the word. By the time the dwarves had packed up and were ready to go, there wasn't a person in the entire inn still asleep.

Three caravans awaited the party as they filed out of the inn. One caravan was stocked with all the commodities that seemed to interest the dwarves; three full barrels of salted fish, two barrels of cheese and as many kegs of ale as could fit.

Danflorf was especially fond of the fish. He had tasted fish from the underdark, but the giant fish from the sea, now after having tasted them, made his mouth water at the thought.

King Ironwill himself was the first to say goodbye to the dwarves. His spirits had been raised considerably at the sudden arrival of the dwarves and the optimistically great news of a new alliance.

The trip back to New Halsgrove was easier than their trip to Taris; a storm had passed over most of the road and softened up the hardened road.

Upon arriving at New Halsgrove, the twins met shortly with Captain Thestian to let them know of their new assignment. He was not excited; he had one of the few mages in the region for less than a day before he was taken away. All the strategies and plans of how to maximize the use of a mage in a battle were useless to him now.

"Well, there's nothing to be done about it, then," Captain Thestian said a few moments after Weylor told him of their new assignment. "We cannot patrol all of Gander's Forest to assure you safe passage back, but you should be able to give a sign if you need any help?" he said, turning the statement into a question at the end to make sure that he was correct.

"Yes, that won't be a problem," Weylor responded, thinking on which exact spell he would use if he and Dryx were to need help; a fireball shot into the sky or perhaps a magical, whispered message that could travel long distances to someone the mage was familiar with.

It wasn't hard for the group to back-track their way to the small clearing where they had ambushed the goblins; large piles of ash were scattered around the clearing, the clear signs that everything had been burned, the goblin's dead bodies included.

From there, the dwarves found the trail that they had used to find the goblins that would lead them back to the small, narrow trail leading up into the mountains; the Giant's Steppes mountain range was vast and riddled with valleys and gorges, steep cliffs and high mountain peaks.

Nothing stirred in the forest as the group traveled in silence; there was good reason to be cautious. The silence made all of them feel uneasy; complete silence usually meant an ambush. But the darkness of night found them still climbing the ever-slowly sloping hills that made up the roots of the mountain.

Danflorf stopped the party for the night at a familiar spot where he and his dwarves had camped almost two weeks prior. The night was clear and the moon poured its light on the kingdom, illuminating whatever part of the ground was not shaded by trees.

The light seemed eerie to the twins; until the attack on the goblins they had never set foot in Gander's Forest. In Taris, where candles and torches were lit throughout the entire night, the light of the moon was less clear and brilliant, being somewhat distorted by the light of the fires. But on the sloping hills inside the forest there was no light to challenge the light of the moon. Tall shadows from the trees made the forest seem even more perilous; neither of the twins had ever seen shadows like this in the dark. It was unnatural, they thought. Color could still be differentiated, but hues were more difficult to distinguish, giving all the tall grass, shrubbery, and trees the same color and tone.

"In a different place," Weylor said to Dryx, both of them lying against a small log, staring out into the night, "perhaps this light would seem less devious, maybe even peaceful. Can you imagine looking over an entire valley at night from a mountain while it was illuminated like this?" The question was more to himself, more rhetorical, than to Dryx.

"Well, I'll bet you get your wish when we reach Icedome," Dryx replied casually.

Weylor turned to see his brother had already turned over to sleep.

His eyes, though, returned to the illuminated, eerie darkness for another few moments before he, too, turned over and feel asleep.

Chapter 13

Icedome

"We are meeting the expected resistance you told us about, master, but progress continues as you predicted," Chorzak said.

King Chorzak stood almost seven feet tall; tall even by orc standards. No hair covered his massive head; only scars were visible over his oily, green skin. He was different than the goblins that served him, almost twice their size, but more human-like, more intelligent.

"Good. It will require the death of many hundreds of goblins to blind the humans into thinking they are in control and that the goblins are scattered," came a voice from the darkness. The voice spoke in the orcs own language and with a perfect accent, yet Chorzak knew that whatever was speaking to him wasn't an orc. The voice was deep, yet smooth; even talking in a 'regular' tone, the voice seemed to boom, almost a power by itself.

Chorzak had never seen his "master," but in his dreams he had been shown the cave he was in not far up the mountain from his own quarters. Feelings of power, revenge and of being in control always accompanied the visions Chorzak received from his master. Chorzak was the king of Orgath, the goblin city. He was one of the few surviving orcs that had come up from the underdark decades before and survived the defeat by the humans.

"We have nearly cleared the eastern slope of trees; we will need to start cutting in the forest to south, where you told us," Chorzak said.

"Not yet, Chorzak. Send out more raiding parties to cut the humans off from going south; if they should uncover our plot, you will not be able to destroy Taris. Do not forget what happened last time..." the voice said.

When the voice mentioned their last defeat, Chorzak realized that his master had been here for a long time and had most likely had guided the last king. In the last battle with the humans, the goblin army was on the verge of destroying Taris when help came to them from two separate fronts; from the west and from the north across the sea. The goblins, at that time, had no knowledge of the other human cities and didn't anticipate Taris receiving help from any allies.

Chorzak knew that secrecy was the key to his victory and wouldn't allow any cracks in his plans. Any goblin that returned to Orgath with bad news or with failure to complete the task given by Chorzak was killed on the spot; not many goblins ever returned to Orgath with bad news.

Chorzak walked out of the cave, shielding his eyes from the bright sun. How he hated the light! He had grown used to it, nonetheless. It was bearable now, though he spent as much time in the tunnels and caves of Orgath as possible. It still took a few moments for his eyes to adjust to the brightness, but he was able to. It was nowhere near as painful as it had been for him decades before when he first came to the surface world; the light would leave him with headaches that lasted for hours and had even blinded him for two days the first time he looked directly at the sun.

As his eyes adjusted, he looked down over the valley that housed the rebuilt city of Orgath. To Chorzak, it seemed more like a hole dug right out of the mountain with only a small, steep-sided gorge that led out south to the plains. He envisioned the hordes of goblins that would soon be leaving through that small gorge and the havoc they would cause on the humans.

With a wicked smile he trudged off down the mountain, eager to keep his plans in motion.

After one more uneventful days of hiking, Dryx, Weylor, and the dwarves came over the last mountain pass before descending into the valley that housed Icedome, the dwarven kingdom. The group reached the lookout spot and was greeted by a dozen, fully-armored dwarves who, at the sight of Danflorf, bowed and ran to meet them.

"Yer back!" one of them yelled with a big smile.

"Yer father's been up here every day since ye left. He found Dolan, here, sleeping yesterday and just about kicked him down the mountain!" the other dwarf said, catching himself on his knees as he almost fell down laughing.

After a short greeting and discussion with the guards, Danflorf led the party down the final slope that led to the base of a huge, ice-capped mountain that dominated the panorama. The descent was steep, but a path had but cut into the mountain that almost seemed like stairs, except that each 'step' seemed to flow into the next so that there were no ledges or edges.

"How long has your clan been living here?" Dryx asked, a doubt coming into his mind.

"More than ten years now, since before the goblins started coming down out of their caves," Taffer replied, the closest dwarf to Dryx.

Dryx looked around in every direction after hearing the response. "Then where is your city? Danflorf said that there were thousands of dwarves here," Dryx said.

Taffer waited until they turned the last bend and then stopped dead in his tracks, a wide smile spread across his face. "There," was all Taffer responded, pointing to the face of a steep cliff on the south-east side of the huge, ice-capped mountain.

Dryx stopped when he saw what Taffer was pointing to. *Of course,* he thought, *these were dwarves...they lived underground.* He shook his head, embarrassed at forgetting that small detail of his short, stout companions.

An entrance opened up the base of the cliff. Not fit to be called a cave, the entrance was not circular; the stone had been worked into smooth, straight, symmetrical lines that showed the skill of the dwarves in working with stone. Two huge doors hugged the wall on either side of the cave entrance.

Many dwarves went about the outside of the cave entrance; some of them guards, some in aprons as dirty as the ground they walked on, others with packs and climbing gear. Trails met at the entrance to Icedome from all directions; one in particular was deeper and more used than the others. Two deep, solid lines lined the sides of the trail; wheel tracks.

The group continued on; the dwarves in the party saluting and greeting the many other dwarves as they passed.

As the group drew closer, the twins could see the details etched into the cliff face around the entrance and especially on the doors themselves. What at first appeared to be random lines in the stone, like those of termite trails in a log, now transformed into huge murals that stunned the ever-slowing twins.

"Go on," Danflorf said to the twins, seeing how captivated they were with the intricate and beautiful art. "This is our story; the history of Clan Bourndrimiur."

The whole cliff face around the door now seemed to be a picture, or a story, to Dryx and Weylor. At the bottom, where the ground met the wall, there was what looked like a massive city, but underground. Getting closer to take in all the detail, the twins noticed figures in the mural; dwarves. They lined the city walls, all armored and armed. Approaching the city was an army of taller, slender, dark figures with white hair.

As the twins glanced upward, where the mural continued, they saw devastation in the ranks of the dwarves. The dark evil drow had infiltrated the city and were slaughtering the dwarves; the drow's faces all seemed evil surrounded by hundreds of dead dwarves scattered throughout the city.

Above the city was a trail; it seemed an endless line of dwarves. The trail ended on the left-hand side of the entrance and continued on the right side of the entrance. The trail curved left and right, rose and fell. At one point the trail entered a huge chasm that made the trail of dwarves appear diminutive. The faint outlines of creatures that neither of the twins had ever heard of outlined the path, just outside the trail of the dwarves. The detail that the dwarves were able to put into the wall of stone itself was amazing; the story seemed to come alive to the twins as they followed the flight of the dwarves.

Writing also covered the wall. Dwarven letters followed the dwarves from their city, all the way to the top of the mural, above the doorway. Eventually the dwarves started their final ascent. They must have been deep in the earth when they started, because their trail on the wall was as long as the entire mural. They broke through the ground, up into the above world not far from where they were standing now.

Danflorf left Taffer behind to bring the twins in to the mountain when they finished.

The twins climbed a ladder that still stood against the wall a few feet away that had been used to etch in the mural high up above the door.

The dwarves caved in the trail that they had dug, to keep from being followed. They were safe but, from the intricate and amazing detail in the mural, the twins could see that there was not a single dwarf that looked happy.

At the top of the mural, by far the most intricate and important part of the whole story, was Icedome. Being carved in the stone nearly as big as the doorway, Icedome stood as an obvious sign of safety and solitude. Barren mountain ranges flowed out around Icedome in every direction with no signs of life on them. Two huge symbols, a hammer and an anvil, were etched in the base of the mountain, with an eye appearing in the peak of the mountain. The twins noted that dozens of small holes lined the sides of the mountains, and that the dwarven runes at the base had been carved into the mountain; as if something were to be placed inside of them.

The twins came down and back up to take in the whole story. Now understanding somewhat the story and seeing it all in one view, they noticed that the wall actually got lighter as the trail moved up the wall towards Icedome, and that Icedome was actually white compared to the very dark bottom of the beginning of the story.

A moment passed before the twins realized that only Taffer remained with them.

"Danflorf wanted you to finish," Taffer said when he saw the questions in their eyes. "Are you ready?" he said to the twins.

Both Dryx and Weylor, having a new appreciation for how far the dwarves had come, looked at each other and both nodded to Taffer.

Nothing could have prepared the twins for what they were about to experience; Icedome, the new dwarven kingdom in the Giant's Steppes, lived up to and exceeded all expectations and preconceptions that the twins had about the dwarves and about Icedome.

The entrance led them through a short, straight hallway which eventually led to stairs cut straight into the mountain; the entire complex seemed to be cut right out of the mountain. At the top of the stairs, once again, the twins stopped; they never imagined walking right into the middle of a mountain.

This was the King's Hall; the first chamber anyone would enter coming into Icedome. Massive pillars, as tall as trees, seemed to hold up the mountain from inside. As wide as four dwarves, a dozen pillars lined both sides of the marble stone that led straight up to the kings throne on the other side of the huge room. Torches lined the walls, illuminating murals and depictions as intricate and awe-inspiring as the one they had seen outside. Each pillar seemed to have been carved with the utmost care; they were all exactly identical.

The marble on the floor was a shiny white hue that had been laid perfectly into the floor and marked the way straight to the king's throne with a design that flowed through the stones. The throne was set many steps up above the floor and was the most decorated piece of furniture that the twins had ever seen. Made of pure gold and with many gems set into the its border, the throne itself was enough to make the twins feel intimidated; even without the king sitting on it.

Three passage ways led out of the king's chamber; one behind the throne to the west and one on either side of the chamber, north and south.

"This way," Taffer said, motioning for the twins to follow. "Danflorf will have found the king by now and he'll be wantin' to see you."

The twins followed Taffer back through the doorway behind the throne. The hallway led them straight a short ways before turning left. Another short walk brought them into another chamber.

"Ah, there you are," Danflorf said, getting up from a seat at a table across the room when Dryx, Weylor and Taffer entered the room.

Danflorf and another dwarf walked over to the twins. The twins had never seen this dwarf before but they immediately knew who it was; the king. Danflorf had told them enough about him on the journey to Icedome that it was easy to recognize him.

"Father, these are Dryx and Weylor Stormcaller, of Taris," Danflorf said to his father and, turning to the twins, "This is me father, the King of Icedome."

Both Dryx and Weylor dropped into a deep bow.

"We are at your service, King Bourndrimiur," Weylor said, still not quite able to pronounce the name like Danflorf tried to teach him.

"Well met," was all the king responded with a short nod of his huge head.

The king wore the finest armor of any dwarf that the twins had yet seen. A huge, two-headed battle axe was slung over his back. Three long scars marked his face; one across his forehead and one on either cheek. Both the hair on his head and his long beard were gray as much as they were black.

The king returned to the table where he had originally been seated and continued going over some parchment that was laid before him.

For the rest of that day, Taffer escorted the twins all over Icedome. The dwarven kingdom inside the mountain was much larger than they thought, even after having entered in the King's Hall. In a chamber far below the surface, down a very long, steep staircase, the twins saw Icedome come alive. The furnace room was gigantic; a dozen furnaces lined the middle of the room. The heat from the room caused the twins to start sweating even before they reached the floor. Each furnace was big enough to have a dozen dwarves working around it, putting in and taking out metals of all colors. Hundreds of dwarves worked over these metals, forming and beating them into various shapes and sizes. Carts were everywhere, some filled with unworked ore that still needed to be smelted, others full of finished items.

As the trio walked through the maze, the dwarves' eyes would open wide at seeing humans in their home; but as soon as they realized they were with Taffer and must be allies they returned to their work, focused as if they had never seen the twins.

Some dwarves worked a very dark substance that looked to be more like stone than metal into dishes and utensils; other dwarves worked gold and silver into fine jewelry and trinkets. But the majority of the dwarves were working with an ore common to the twins; iron. They were making all sorts of weapons and armor.

As the trio neared the end of the chamber, they came to a furnace that they could not see from the entrance. The furnace was built right into the wall and only a handful of dwarves worked it. It seemed that they were working more carefully and slowly with a metal that the twins hadn't seen in the main section of the furnace room. This metal appeared silver, but was shinier and had a slightly lighter hue to it.

"What metal is this?" Weylor asked Taffer.

"Ah," Taffer said. "This is mithril. It's the hardest metal that we know of, the best for weapons and armor. But it's very rare and very difficult to work."

The twins followed Taffer as he led them through passages in every direction, leading them both higher and lower at different times inside the mountain. The 'residential' section of Icedome was, by far, the most precarious of any construction the twins had ever seen.

Huge caverns, under the entrance chamber, had been completely renovated to make it livable for the dwarves. Caves had been carved out of the sides of the caverns and up the walls, forming many different levels. Tall stalactites and stalagmites were left unworked, forming natural pieces of art and giving the large cavern a different feeling than the rest of Icedome. Hundreds of dwarven women and children dotted the large cavern; the dwarven women cooking and cleaning while the children seemed to group up and try to imitate what they saw the older dwarves do; mining and fighting mainly, very few tried to mimic the cleaning of the dwarven women.

Chapter 14

An Unsettling Discovery

Balik and Tarek were sitting high on a mountainside northeast of Orgath; it was their week for spying on the goblin city. The night was clear and a cool breeze came over the mountains, the high mountains remained ice capped all year long.

The two dwarves found themselves a cozy, hidden spot to watch the city from a safe distance far up the mountain side, and not anywhere near where the goblins were logging on the mountain sides around the city. The goblin city was far enough away from Icedome that changing out lookouts daily was not possible, so each pair had to bring enough food and supplies to last.

"Looks like the goblins are on the move,"Tarek noted to Balik.

A long, winding line of fire started out of Orgath to the south, through the small narrow pass that served as the only entrance to the valley that housed the goblin city.

"A couple hundred, by me guess," Balik said. The end of the line of fire was seen just a few minutes after the front found the pass.

"More raiding parties," Tarek said, agreeing with Balik's estimation.

After a few minutes everything in the city went back to normal.

"Did you hear that?" Balik said suddenly to Tarek. On pure instinct, both dwarves jumped up, scooped up their shields and axes, and went into low crouches.

"Yea I heard it," Tarek said off-handedly; he was focused on the darkness around them. Even with their exceptional low-light vision, there was nothing around them that they could see; at least nothing close-by.

The dwarves couldn't see anything but they both felt uneasy, their instincts sending up the hair on the back of their necks.

"There!" Balik whispered, staring at a group of tall, thickly-leaved trees. "The shadows are wrong, out of place," he said.

Tarek backed up the few feet to Balik, making sure that there was nothing behind him, before he slowly started to turn to see what Balik was looking at. He turned slowly, examining the surrounding area and not wanting to appear too obvious if there was something watching. And he felt like there was something watching them.

The group of trees was too far away to see much detail, but the large shadows of the trees were obvious to the dwarves' vision.

"The shadows of the trees should fall the ground," Balik whispered, fear obvious in his shaky voice. "But they don't, they are high up. Something is there, something big."

Tarek could see the shadows; he could see that they were off, that there was something blocking them. *But what?* he thought. What was quiet enough to get this close to them making almost no noise and big enough to block the tall shadows of trees?

Balik noticed something high up in the trees. He looked up and, at first, couldn't make out what he was looking at. *Two small lights?* he thought. They weren't stars, and it obviously wasn't fire.

"Eyes!" The word barely left his mouth, fear all but paralyzing him.

As soon as the word left his mouth, though, it was all over. Faster than either of the dwarves could react, a huge form burst from the trees, snapping two of them, and came straight for them.

"Dr..." was all Balik was able to utter before his voice changed to a deafening scream of pain and agony as a massive flame leapt out at the from the huge, flying form. The fire stole the oxygen from the dwarves' lungs and their armor and shields were of no use; the fire consumed them both before either of them had time to move.

The twins spent most of the next week exploring the rest of Icedome, both inside and out. They eventually found the lowest levels of Icedome, many of which were natural caves already there before the dwarves ever settled the mountain. The dwarves had walled off many of the openings in the lower levels and built solid, steel doors into others; they didn't know how far back the caves went and how close they came to the underdark.

The underdark was the area below the surface of the earth where some of the most dark and evil of creatures dwelt. The dwarves were still wary of the underdark after their expulsion from their ancient home and so they made sure that there was no open connection from their new home to the underdark.

"There you are," came a voice from behind the twins as they returned to the main level of Icedome.

"Taffer," Weylor said with a wide smile. Both of the twins had come to appreciate and enjoy the company of dwarves, especially that of Taffer. The dwarves seemed to be less pessimistic and less worried about the menial things of life. The only complaint that the twins ever heard from the dwarves was about finding veins of precious minerals in the mountain, and, of course, about food.

"Yer summoned by the king in the entrance chamber," Taffer said, a hint of anticipation in his voice. Taffer waited only a moment before leading the twins through the upper halls and into the entrance chamber of Icedome.

"Looks like the king has found a use for us after all," Weylor said, noticing that Taffer was fully armored with his weapon;

a short, double-headed axe over his shoulder and his shield strapped across his back.

As the twins entered the main hall, a large group of battle-ready dwarves were gathered around the king. Taffer led the twins over to Danflorf, who was waiting just inside the passage that led out of the mountain.

"Our scouts haven't returned from their post watching the orc city. They're probably just late or got lost, but the king isn't taking any chances; he's as jumpy as a lothé in a basilisk den. He is sending out a scouting party to the pass that leads south to the orc city," Danflorf informed the twins.

He could see the twins' confusion on their role in a permanent scouting post with a few dozen dwarves. "Yer job is a little more… active," he said, letting on to a more mobile mission.

"Naturally," said Weylor, a small chuckle leaving his lips as he began to piece together the puzzle. "We have lived above ground our whole lives, so naturally we would be more suitable for an assignment like this."

"Exactly," Danflorf responded. "The king isn't asking you to do this, the potential risk is too much and our alliance only barely formed. He will accept your help and reward you, but only if you understand the risk."

Dryx normally left the talking in situations like this to his brother; he preferred reserving his opinion and learning as much as he could about his surroundings while remaining almost unnoticed. "How long do we have to decide?" he asked Danflorf.

"Until the king is done speaking to the scouting party," Danflorf replied.

"And who is to come with us to investigate?" Dryx asked, suspecting the answer before it left Danflorf's mouth.

"Just Taffer. The king isn't willing to send his men all the way to the orc city and risk a war. Besides, it's easier for a small group to hide and get close to the city; a big group would be too risky," Danflorf responded.

Dryx pulled Weylor over a few feet away from Danflorf and the other dwarves accompanying him.

"We have no idea what has happened or what to expect. This could be very dangerous and we haven't even graduated yet," Dryx said, letting the words sink into Weylor. "But," he added, his face just as serious as before, "this could be an opportunity to gain the trust of the king."

Weylor weighed both options in his mind. He knew that they would be well in over their heads by scouting out an orc city while they were still so inexperienced scouting, but the thought of gaining trust with the king of their new allies weighed just as heavily.

After a pause, both twins nodded at each other and returned to Danflorf.

"We will do it," Weylor said.

An hour later Taffer and the twins, accompanied by a sizeable scouting party of battle-ready dwarves, made their way out of Icedome and down the trail heading south to High Pass; the dwarves named the pass 'High Pass' because it was the narrowest and highest pass in all the mountains around Icedome. If the orcs did try to attack Icedome through the mountains they would have to travel through that pass, so that's where the permanent guard station would be placed.

Taffer and the twins left the dwarven scouting party at High Pass and continued south. The trail wasn't a difficult one, but progress was slow due to the potential danger lurking in the back of all their minds. Every canyon and crevice could be hiding enemies and they weren't taking any chances.

Taffer and the twins traveled for three more days without incident.

On the fourth night, Taffer found a small cave near the top of the last peak before the descent down to the valley that housed the orc city. The last rays of light could be seen high in the clear sky; the sun had already fallen under the mountains far to the west. The high altitude cooled the air in the mountains, but the thick forest on the mountain kept the wind out of their cave.

"I haven't seen any tracks leading back towards Icedome," Taffer said to the twins. "They haven't come back this way."

"Then they are still ahead of us," Dryx said, stating the logical answer with hope that it was true.

"Let's keep moving, then," Weylor said. "Danflorf said that Orgath was just on the other side of this last mountain," he said, pointing up to a large rocky outcropping just above them on the mountainside, illuminated by the last rays of the setting sun. "That marks the last mountain before the valley."

By the time the sun rose over the mountains to the east the next morning, the path had wound the group around the mountain to the other side overlooking Orgath, the orc city.

Taffer and the twins stood speechless as they took in the scene; the entire mountainside below them had been cleared of trees completely. A few moments passed before Taffer could pull his gaze away from the scene before them.

"They wouldn't have gone down the mountain at all; King's orders," Taffer told the twins. "And seeing how all the trees have been cut down on the mountainside, they would've looked for somewhere with cover…" he said, his voice stopping abruptly as he spotted a small group of tall trees with a few large boulders a short distance away.

The twins followed Taffer off the tail and up the mountainside to the east.

Taffer slowed down as they came around the bottom side of the group of trees and in better view of the boulders. Two massive trees had been snapped and had fallen towards the boulders.

Dryx hopped up onto one of the trees and ran down its trunk to the base. "The dwarves didn't fell this tree, Taffer. There aren't any axe marks, it just snapped," he said. "As did that one," he said, turning to see the other fallen tree.

Weylor couldn't imagine the trees having anything to do with the missing dwarves so he walked over to the boulders where he found Taffer on his knees, staring at an empty hole and a small bundle of burnt wood.

Weylor understood the obvious signs but didn't know why Taffer had gone down to his knees.

"They must have made a campfire here and..." his words died away in an instant. He had walked over to Taffer and saw the helmet; a single, dwarven helmet rested in the back of the hole. No other gear was visible.

"No," was all Taffer could say. He recognized Balik's helmet. He and Balik had been part of the rear guard for Clan Bourndrimiur on their expulsion from Brüevelden. He and Balik, along with only a handful of other dwarves, were the only survivors of the rear guard; the rest had given their lives to slow down both the drow in pursuit and the other dangers of the underdark.

He reached down and grabbed the helmet gingerly, as if it was brittle. He rubbed his giant palm across the face of the helmet, clearing the dirt away and revealing dozens of scratches, dinks and chips, evidence of a life of war. He brought the helmet up to meet his own, his forehead against the top of Balik's helmet, and then stowed it in his own bag.

He jumped up and, with axe in hand, starting looking for any signs of conflict, for any trace of tracks that would lead him to his friend's killer.

"How can there be no tracks?" Taffer thought out loud.

"It doesn't make any sense," Weylor said, walking up to where Taffer was standing, a confused look on his face. "I found Tarek and Balik's tracks leading up toward the rocks, but there aren't any tracks leading away from it."

Dryx was walking towards them from the small group of trees. He looked up to say something to Taffer and Weylor, and stopped in his tracks. He turned around, looked at the trees, then turned back around and gave a conspicuous stare at the boulders behind Taffer and Weylor.

Weylor was watching Dryx, watched him turn around and then back around, he saw the puzzled look on his face and watched him drop his head down in complete confusion. It was his next reaction, though, that made the hair on the back of his neck stand up. Dryx's head snapped up with a look of complete horror.

Instantly put into a state of fear and anxiety, Dryx ran over to Taffer and Weylor and pulled them behind the boulders.

"We need to get out of here, now," Dryx said, visibly shaken.

"What is it, Dryx?" Weylor said, now on edge because of his brother's uneasiness.

"Those trees were pushed over towards these boulders. There aren't any footprints around here and..." he paused for a moment, making sure he actually believed what he was about to say. "The boulders have been burned."

Taffer looked puzzled. He couldn't see how any of that information could have anything to do with the missing dwarves except for the footprints. "What're ye getting at?" he said impatiently.

"Dragon," Weylor breathed out, fear washing over him as he said the word.

The word froze Taffer in place. "It can't be," was all he was able to mutter. Nightmares of his exile with Clan Bourndrimiur into the monster-infested wilds of the underdark now rose back up when a new, very real danger similar to those of the underdark threatened his new home.

Without another word, the twins followed Taffer back down the small game trail to the pass that connected the mountains that housed Orgath to the mountains that led back to Icedome. Taffer set the pace at almost a run, wanting to get back to King Bourndrimiur as quickly as possible.

The trio took few breaks that day on their way back over the pass and through the winding mountain trails. Exhaustion eventually found them and forced them to stop for the night and rest, although none of them were able to find much sleep with their nerves so on edge.

They awoke early the next day, as soon as the sun's rays found their way into the eyes of the twins and dwarf. With perhaps the fastest breakfast that the dwarf had ever eaten they set off, once again, across the mountains heading north to Icedome.

The next day passed uneventful; hardly a word was spoken between any of the companions. They were all still on edge; the fear in the back of their minds that a dragon was following them kept them continuously on edge and alert. The sun rose, crossed the sky and set behind the mountains once again and Taffer and the twins were forced to stop for the night. None of the three could ever remember being more tired or ever having their legs so sore; but the situation called for a need to run through the tiredness and pain of fatigue. They had made much better progress on their way back to Icedome than on their way to Orgath. Taffer recognized the mountain off in the distance where the dwarven scouting party had started construction on a defensible lookout. *Tomorrow,* he thought to himself.

Taffer found even less sleep that night than he did their first night fleeing from Orgath. The news he brought for the king played through his mind in a hundred different ways. He tried thinking of the best words to describe what he had seen and how he would convey that message to the king. In the end, he knew the outcome would be the same despite the way in which he got the message across. He knew that even his paranoia would be nothing compared to the king's when he found out that there was a dragon in the same mountain range. Dragons coveted and hoarded treasure, gold above all.

Clan Bourndrimiur had, in their decade in Icedome, come to accumulate a sizeable amount of gold from the deep, underground roots of the mountain; but since they had no one to trade with until now, Taffer knew that their treasure would be known to no one.

Nightmares of dragons and the horrors of the underdark found their way into Taffer's already uneasy dreams that night, depriving him of the much needed sleep he sought. He would wake up with axe in hand screaming at the top of his lungs, the devilish nightmare fading as his eyes took in the real world around him.

Once again, the first rays of sunshine that found the party found them tired and sore but still alert and on edge. They set off, finishing their rations as they found their way up the mountain where the dwarven post waited just on the other side.

As the sun rose higher in the sky, Taffer and the twins rounded the last bend and came into sight of a structure blocking their path that had not been there when they left. A rock wall was being built across the path, going right up against a rock wall on the inside of the trail and over to the cliff on the outside of the trail. Dozens of dwarves were working on the wall, placing all sizes of stones in place and packing them in with mortar. More dwarves were high up on the mountain side, just in front of where the entrance would be, constructing a trap to completely close off the path to Icedome in an emergency.

Nearly all of the dwarves ran over as soon as Taffer and the twins came into view. Their smiles and cheers faded quickly with the news of the death of Tarek and Balik. Taffer decided not to mention the dragon; the king would decide whether or not to alert the entire clan.

Chapter 15

Deli's Secret

Same old routine, he thought. Cade sighed as he slipped his disguise on over his undergarments, turning himself into a beggar far older than he really was. His daggers were perfectly concealed by the layers of raggedy clothes that masked his identity. A professional make-up set put wrinkles on his face and dirt covered where his smooth, fair skin showed. He had mastered a limp in his right leg, so much so that he had to remember to not limp when he wasn't in disguise.

A man came into the room. He looked like a merchant; a dull, red robe covering his body from hands to feet and a round, dark-blue, cloth cap covering his head. To any normal person he would appear unremarkable but Cade knew better.

"Anything to look forward to?" Cade asked.

"A lot of new merchants from Viltress and Taris," he responded with a wry smile, pulling out a decent sized pouch of stolen coins from under his robes.

Cade put on the final touches of his disguise and left through the same door the man came in from. He wound his way through the underground hideout and up into the pantry of a fishing store. He let himself out of a window into a narrow alley, checked his disguise one more time, and limped out into the busy street.

So many people were in the street, paying attention only to the business they were conducting, that Cade could have come out screaming and no one would have turned a brow at the disguised beggar.

For the next six hours, Cade hobbled and limped up and down the busy, merchant-filled streets listening to the wealthier looking merchants for anything interesting.

Again and again Cade passed by unsuspecting merchants and traders, their full coin pouches easily within his reach and ability. Without realizing it, Cade would find himself playing out how he could steal the pouches that were so openly flaunted, but he found himself reserved; he no longer felt the thrill of it.

Before, when he first joined the secretive guild, he would spend hours pick-pocketing in the streets. He had lived for it; it was not only his job but also a competition, a way of showing the other rogues his prowess and skill and marking his place in the guild.

It was different now, though. There was no more fun in petty pick-pocketing, no more thrill for the competition. No one in the guild doubted his ability in the street, though; he became so popular that the other rogues would check their own purses whenever he passed by them.

On the south east stretch of the merchant highway that ran parallel with his hideout, Cade had found a small lookout, a hiding place. Hunched over like an elderly man on the side of the street, as if to cross the street, he waited for the bigger caravans to pass by, the ones pulled by horses and accompanied by many men. Cade took a step forward, right in front of the guards walking alongside the caravan. His limp over-emphasized, on came the expected guard's push against his back. Cade used the force of the push to send him in an exaggerated head-over-heals roll between the tires and underneath the caravan. The guard smirked, thinking of the people behind the caravan that were about to see the stupid old beggar sprawled out in the middle of the street for trying to cross in front of a caravan.

The street was so crowded that no one saw the guard push Cade down under the caravan, or how he rolled out perfectly under the caravan.

The guards on the other side of the caravan, between Cade and the entrance to his favorite spot in the small alleyway, never saw the agile figure fly out from between the wheels of the caravan and roll into the shadow of the alley. Cade made no more noise than a shadow would, although with the noise in the street it wouldn't have mattered. With the falling sun directly in front of them, the squinted eyes of the guards were focused on what was ahead of them rather on what was below them. Once in the shadows, Cade was completely in his element; not a guard in the city could have followed him once he reached the darkness in the alley.

Without looking back, Cade made his way down the alley and used a barrel to jump up and grab onto the roof of the building opposite the wall. Flipping himself onto the roof, Cade found his spot in the shadow of the second story roof. He perched himself on a support beam just under where the roof peaked, forming an upside-down 'V'.

There, laid out before him from the foot of the city to the horizon, was The Calm Sea. Dozens of ships lined the ports and wharves that made up the southern section of Daley. Merchant ships, fishing boats, and passenger vessels were all coming in for the night; rarely did anyone sail at night in The Calm Sea. Cade had heard talk of pirate ship sightings and huge sea monsters, but, as far as he knew, there hadn't been any incidents yet. He didn't care about that anyway; all he cared about was the freedom he saw.

Cade frequented this favorite spot of his as often as he could to stare out over the sea and imagine would kind of life he could lead across the sea. He saw freedom and adventure out in front of him, an endless world to explore and innumerable sights to see and experience.

Cade sighed when the sun dipped lower in the sky and the time came for him to return to his hideout and leave his view of freedom. He was young, still not twenty years old, but had already grown distant from the call of his rogue guild. He began to despise his way of life, and himself for living that way every day. He wanted to be able to walk among people without thinking of how to rob them; to have more meaning in his life than theft and no more need to hide in the shadows.

He jumped down to the alleyway and returned to the streets once more; back to his life of solitude and shame.

Taffer met with King Bourndrimiur as soon as they reached Icedome. The king was more than putout when Taffer told him of the evidence that a dragon had killed Tarek and Balik. There was very little he could do to protect his clan from a dragon. After thinking over the situation with his advisors, the king decided to keep the information from the rest of the clan and not cause panic when they were finally settled in to their new home.

King Bourndrimiur was determined that Icedome would be his last home and wouldn't budge, even for a dragon. Instead, he sent a small, permanent army to High Pass, to help with the construction of the guard's defenses and to keep the pass safe.

"Dryx, Weylor," Taffer said, finding the twins resting in their temporary sleeping quarters in Icedome. He tossed each of them a small coin purse full of gold. "A gift of thanks from Danflorf and the king," he said, smiling at the twins. His time with the twins had shown him that they were good; their drive came from wanting to protect their home and not out of pure hatred and malice, characteristics that Taffer respected.

The twins had never had money of their own before; growing up their mother and their respective schools had provided everything that the twins would need. "Give the king our thanks," Weylor said.

"Aye," Taffer said. "Tomorrow we'll escort you both to New Halsgrove at dawn."

The twins nodded their consent.

They were sad to say goodbye to Taffer when the time came for the dwarves to return to Icedome and for the twins to return to Taris.

The twins, by request of King Bourndrimiur, had told no one about what they experienced near Orgath and headed straight for the King's keep. King Bourndrimiur asked the twins to tell only the king and that he would send an emissary soon to King Ironwill.

Three hard thuds sounded inside the keep.

One of the big doors opened, bringing into view an armored guard.

"Dryx! Weylor!" the guard said, a smile spreading across his face.

"Trenton!" both of the twins said together. They had gone through the academy together and hadn't seen each other since the ceremony that separated all of the students into their new assignments.

"Enter, please," Trenton said to the twins, eager to see his old friends. "How are the outskirts? I've heard that there is a lot more goblin activity now, have you seen any combat?"

"It's getting more dangerous by the day. We ambushed a goblin scouting party just east of New Halsgrove when we arrived, a large one, too. But we are here to see the king; we have a message from King Bourndrimiur of the dwarves." Dryx said, pressing the point with the king a little to get the urgency across; he could tell that Trenton had more questions for him and his brother.

"Yes, of course. I'll go inform the king," Trenton said with another smile and a nod to the twins.

The twins recognized a few of the other guards in the room; two of them were a few years older and had been in the academy when Dryx and Weylor first entered. They looked bored and the twins could guess why.

Sure, Weylor thought, it would be an honor to be chosen to guard the king, but he knew that he would go crazy being kept in the same room day in and day out.

A few minutes passed by before Trenton returned. "The king will see you now. I'm going to need to take your weapons. Sorry, protocol," he said, taking the twin's weapons.

The twins made their way through the inner door and into the large, spacious room where the king often held audiences with the citizens of Taris. The king was known for his loyalty to and love for his people. Whenever possible, he would go through Taris and some of the outlying farm villages thanking the citizens for their hard work and dedication. There were very few, if any, citizens that did not approve of the king.

"Dryx, Weylor!" the king said, getting up from a table where he sat with some of his advisors and generals. He walked over and patted them both on the shoulder. "I've been anxious to hear about Icedome and the dwarves since you left!" he said, a wide, genuine smile on his face. "Come, tell us the message from King Bourndrimiur and then of Icedome and the dwarves." The king led the twins over to the table where he and a handful of other men were sitting. Two chairs had already been brought over, one on either side of the king.

The twins had decided to tell King Ironwill of the message from King Bourndrimiur last, letting the king put the pieces together to help him understand the story better.

When the twins finished there was not a single man around the table without a look of shock and fear across his face; even the king, a man known for being stalwart and unyieldingly brave, showed worry and doubt.

"King Bourndrimiur has not informed his people, not yet at least, of the dragon. Only Taffer and the king know. Whatever your decision, he is sending an emissary soon to discuss it," Dryx told the king.

The king was silent. He leaned back against his chair, both arms limp on either armrest. He stared forward, but his eyes were unfocused. The dragon was all that he could think about. Many minutes passed by before he came to and was able to again think clearly.

"Let us pray that if what killed the dwarven scouts was, in fact, a dragon, that it is not in league with the goblins," the king said at length. But he had his suspicions. *Why would a dragon not attack the goblin city and destroy it if it did live in the mountains?* he thought.

That statement sparked the worry and attention of all the members of the king's council sitting around the king. The news of a dragon was bad enough; the thought that the goblins had somehow gained the allegiance of a dragon was overwhelming.

"How could we defend against the goblins and a dragon?" one of the king's advisors asked. "Arrows can't pierce its scales and," he stopped when the king raised his hand, a sign for silence.

"We can't worry about that right now. This doesn't leave this room, understood?" the king's tone was as serious as any had ever heard it. "Our people are scared enough with the goblins, they don't need to worry about a dragon as well."

The king looked at the twins. "You two are not to speak to anyone. You did well with the dwarves; I have a feeling that our alliance with them is going to be more important to us than to them; especially if we go to war. Thank you."

Both twins nodded their heads in response to the king's remarks.

"You are dismissed. Report to Captain Strongshield tomorrow at sunrise," the king said, dismissing the twins.

"Yes sir," they said and left.

The twins returned to their home in Taris that night for the first time in over a month. They were more than happy to sit down to a nice, home-cooked meal with their mother and recount everything they had done and seen since they had left, editing out those details that would only worry her. They stayed up with their mother until all the light that shone was from the torches lining the city walls.

"Boys," Deli said to her twin sons, "it was a kind mercy by the gods that you returned to me this night."

The twins looked at each other, confused and suddenly worried. They could see worry and pain behind their mothers smile. Tears started to accumulate in her eyes.

"Mother, what's wrong?" Weylor asked, straightening up in his chair, as did Dryx.

Deli could see the worry in her son's eyes; she could see Alruin in them. She calmed down a little at the sight of their worrying, their love comforting her.

"I'm dying," she said at length, holding her now genuine smile. "I've been sick for some time now and the clerics at the temple say they can't cure me. I didn't notice it at first, but by the time I saw the cleric it was too late. They say I still have time but I don't know how much," she said. She knew how they were feeling; she had felt the same feeling right before seeing her husband die in front of her by the hands of goblins. But she wanted them to be strong, to be stronger than she had been.

"How? What?" Dryx began to say, but couldn't find the words to all the questions he wanted to ask.

"Shh," she said, putting her hand up to hold him. "You two have been my reason for living since your father," she stopped, the memories flooded back to her of that night he was murdered. "You are grown now and I spend all day worrying and twiddling my thumbs. There is nothing left for me, nothing except you," she smiled at her boys. How proud she was of them, and of all that they had accomplished!

"Mother, please. Let us go again to the temple in the morning and try," Weylor said, Deli again stopping him with an upraised hand.

"It's ok. I have raised you as far as I can, and your father would be proud of both of you," she couldn't stop the tears this time. She knew Alruin would be proud of them; she was proud of them.

It was not like Dryx or Weylor to cry, but the tears came anyway.

"I love you both. The priest in the temple says that your father will be there waiting for me," she smiled at the thought. She knew that if there was any chance of that being true, Alruin would make sure to be there. He had never let her down before.

"Don't worry for me, the time comes for all of us, sooner or later. After all, they say that it is a better life we go to, one filled with white fields and the only thing we will feel is peace," she smiled at them and stood up.

Dryx and Weylor hugged their mother before she lay down to sleep. They both told her they loved her and left out the door into the night. All thoughts of sleep and rest fled from both of them with the news of their mother's illness.

It was a nice night out; the air was cool and a soft wind blew. The twins went back to the cliff that they had so often visited growing up in Taris. The familiar, salty breeze cooled their exposed skin and the sound of waves crashing at the cliff base filled the air. They couldn't see the water, it was too dark, but they knew what the view would show them if there had been light. They didn't feel like sitting down; instead they closed their tear-filled eyes and let the pain well-up inside of them.

Now, more than ever, they needed each other. They didn't speak a word to each other, but consoled each other in silence with their presence. They both knew that they had to face the reality that their mother would soon be gone. They both came to realize, standing there over the sea in the darkness, that they couldn't let this pain cripple them. They realized they would likely have to face this pain many more times before they died. They couldn't avoid it. Their mother had dealt with that pain for a decade now with the loss of their father. The fact that she was in pain made it easier for them to accept that she didn't have much longer; her pain would cease and she would be at peace

Neither of them knew how long they had been there before they both turned around and headed home. The pain had not left, but they were able to bear it. They had had to learn to accept things they didn't like their entire life. They accepted their mother's fate and took comfort in knowing that she would be at peace. They had never been around the religious clerics and priests before, and knew very little of the gods, but they agreed to go to the temple in the morning, before reporting to Captain Strongshield, and pray to whatever god could help their mother.

Chapter 16

From Land to Sea

"Something's coming!" a goblin yelped, scared by the sudden noise coming from the darkness in the cave ahead of it.

Two dozen goblins scrambled about, donning their armor and readying their weapons for whatever was coming from the dark tunnel that led down into the underdark. They had been at the same post for almost a month without seeing another living creature besides the goblins that came from above to bring them provisions. They were the deepest, last post in the tunnel network that connected the underdark to the surface at Orgath. They had sealed off the cave entrance that led deeper underground so that nothing much bigger than an orc could pass through without hunching over, although there were plenty of predators just as deadly as the bigger ones that could easily maneuver through the space.

After another minute, the goblins could hear the shuffling of many feet and see the dim glow of torches coming down the passage. Another minute passed by and the figures with the torches came into clear view of the battle-ready goblins.

A group of orcs came out of the tunnel and stopped. One of the larger orcs in the group stepped forward, "I am Narz; we have returned!" the orc yelled, raising his torch as high as his arms could go.

All of the goblins and orcs, the handful with Narz and the two-dozen at the entrance, rose whatever they were holding into the air and yipped and yelled. They knew Narz and the mission he had been sent on and there was only one reason that he would return.

"Soon, soon revenge will be ours!" said Narz, listing more howls and screams from the goblins around him.

He made his way up the winding caverns and tunnels until he reached the surface. He looked out over Orgath, this time with revenge finally within grasp. He remembered the last war with the humans of Taris and how the humans had won and pushed them back underground and razed their city in fire.

Now, he thought to himself, *Taris wouldn't stand a chance against the thousands of goblins that Orgath housed.*

Their faces! He though. He howled to himself when the thought of how fear would disfigure the faces of the humans on their city walls watching thousands of goblins and orcs form up around their city and being completely cut-off from all sides.

He continued towards the city until he found the wide street that led up the mountain to the king's hall. He had passed hundreds of goblins, all busy at work, by the time he reached the king's hall. He smirked at how they would scramble to get out of his way; the biggest goblin in the whole city didn't even reach his shoulders. The doors to the hall were opened for him as soon as he came into sight of the goblins guarding the entrance.

"Narz," the goblins said together as he passed. Their faces showed confusion and then contorted into evil grins as they realized the meaning of his return. All the goblins in the city had heard that he had been sent to find the orcs deep in the underdark and every goblin knew that the penalty for Narz, if he were to fail in his mission, was death. No goblin or orc would return after having failed any assignment given by King Chorzak; they would take the chance and become rogues, wandering as far away from the king as possible. King Chorzak was known for caring more about his next meal than the life of anyone but himself.

Normally, whoever went in to see the king would wait for word to come back to the guards that the king was ready to hear them. Narz, however, paid no mind to the goblins telling him not to enter the room without permission of the king and threw open the doors into the kings chamber.

King Chorzak's head flew up in an instant, anger clear on his face from being disturbed without notice. Under any other circumstance he would have beheaded whoever it was before they could say a word, but at the sight of Narz the king howled with sinister glee.

"For your life your news better be good," the king told Narz, already knowing that Narz had succeeded; he wouldn't return unless he had succeeded.

"I found Uth'drek. The tribes fight each other for territory in the city. They have reverted back to the old ways but, with a little convincing," he chuckled, "they have made a treaty and will fight under Chorzak's flag!"

"Good, good," King Chorzak said, a wicked smile crossing his face. "How many?" he asked Narz.

"A hundred in the city; each tribe sent out scouts to find the rest wandering the underdark," Narz replied.

King Chorzak walked over to the table against the wall to his left. He eyed the open maps on the table with an eagerness for revenge and drew out a dagger and slammed it down on the table, right through the mark that was Taris and into the table underneath.

Thoughts and images were forced into his mind right then, forcing him to his knees. His hands flew to his head and his eyes were forced shut.

"King Chorzak!" Narz said in a worried tone, taking a step towards the kneeling king.

"No!" King Chorzak hissed at him. "Stay back, I'm fine," he said, his angry tone turning almost monotone as his head tilted up and his eyes opened. His gaze was unfocused and his face expressionless.

Many minutes passed by before the king came to. Narz, too scared to irritate the king, hadn't moved from his awkward standing position from when the king yelled for him to stop. The muscles in his legs complained at his uncomfortable stance.

For a moment after opening his eyes the king remained emotionless. But that changed in the blink of an eye.

"Dwarves!" the king screamed. "There have been dwarven scouts around our city!" He was fuming. He couldn't stop thinking about the vision that his master had just passed through his mind; two dwarves getting cozy by a little fire, looking down on Orgath.

"Dwarves? Here?" Narz asked, sounding skeptical. "I have never heard of dwarves living in this region."

The king turned toward him, fighting hard to control himself; he didn't want to lose an orc commander right before the war.

"Go find the raiding parties on the border with the humans. Find out if they have seen any signs of the dwarves," the king hissed.

Narz was smart enough to see the anger in the king's eyes and knew what was about to happen. With only a nod he ran out the doors towards the city. He was too focused on leaving to see all of the goblins guarding the door cowering in the corner at the sound of the king's screams. They were all too familiar with King Chorzak's rage.

Bornar had been in the lower levels of Icedome for two weeks straight without returning to surface. He and his team had followed a vein of silver deep into the base of the mountain on the northern end. Bornar couldn't believe how much silver there was; it seemed to go on forever. The vein was almost as wide as a dwarf and wound its way down into the base of the mountain.

"Hold," Bornar turned and said to the other dwarves behind him. He thought he felt a waft of cooler air when he chipped off a rather large piece of rock from the side of the silver vein. He ran his fingers across the stone until he found the small crack where the cool air came from.

He turned back to the talking dwarves and put his finger up to his mouth, signaling for complete silence. He put his ear up to the crack and pressed it against the flat stone. He could hear nothing a moment; then the faint sound of water and another barely noticeable waft of cool air hit his ear.

"An underground river?" he asked himself, puzzled.

"You hear water?" some of the dwarves asked.

Bornar took up his pick and went to work. It wasn't long before a gaping hole opened up into a large, hollow cavern.

"You two grab a torch and follow me," Bornar said to the two closest dwarves behind him. "The rest of you grab yer picks and open up this hole."

Bornar grabbed a torch and tossed it through the hole. The torch landed on the ground a dozen feet from the hole. Grabbing his pick-axe with both hands he stepped through the hole and into the cavern.

The ground was soft; it was not rock he stepped onto but a moist mixture of dirt and gravel. The walls and ceiling of the cavern were smooth and glistened in the torchlight. Green moss covered the rocks that littered the floor around the sides of the cavern. A cool breeze seemed to flow into the cavern at regular intervals, bringing the smell of salt.

Bornar had never seen nor smelt a sea or an ocean before, but he did know that they were often salt water. A dim glow came from the far end of the cavern, along with a low humming noise. Bornar looked back to the dwarves behind him, nodded and walked over to his torch. He could feel the cool, damp earth as his fingers closed around the torch and became very confused.

Rivers and streams were not uncommon underground in the underdark; but there were never breezes that carried the moisture of water around to areas where there was no water. *Here,* he thought, *everything was wet but there was no water near.*

Lifting his torch, Bornar saw that he was at the back end of the cave and that the sound was coming from the tunnel that led north out of the cavern.

"Egar," Bornar said, looking back at the hole that had half a dozen dwarven heads looking through it.

"Aye," Egar replied.

"Make yerself useful and get the king. I have a feeling he'd want to see this," Bornar told him.

"Aye," he replied to Bornar and started off up the winding passage to the upper levels.

Bornar, switching his torch and pick-axe so that his pick-axe was in the hand of his swinging arm, started off down the tunnel, followed closely by his two, just-as-confused comrades.

The tunnel wound gradually west, taking the trio out of sight of the dwarves left to mine the silver and open up a pathway into the cavern.

The low humming from where he entered the cavern had gotten louder with every footstep down the tunnel. After only a few minutes, the sound had grown much louder; the dwarves were unprepared for what they saw next.

A waterfall? All of them thought to themselves.

The three dwarves stood only a hundred yards from the inside of a waterfall. They figured the ceiling was at least forty feet up and the cavern was wide. A pool of water covered almost half of the huge cavern, leading to the waterfall and out the other side. The cavern wasn't bright, but enough sunlight came through the waterfall to make their torches seem less bright than before.

Bornar, after taking in the scene, realized that this could be a home to someone, or something, and that the cavern could potentially be dangerous. He told the others to look for any kind of tracks, of any size. For ten minutes they scoured the cave, looking for any signs of life but found none.

Feeling more safe and comfortable in this new environment, Bornar walked over to the edge of the water. He didn't have to crouch down and taste the water to know that it wasn't drinkable; the saltine smell was pungent. A sudden movement caught his eye in the water and he jumped back, letting go of his torch and took his pick-axe in both hands. He stared at the water for a long moment but didn't see anything else. He took a few slow, deliberate steps towards the water and froze again, staring into the water.

The two dwarves watching Bornar were put on edge by his yell and leap back from the water. So a moment later when he walked back over to the water and let his weapon swing down by his side they were scratching their heads in confusion.

Bornar let out a long laugh. "Fish!" he yelled looking back at them, "Big fish!"

A few hours passed before King Bourndrimiur was able to make his way down to the newly discovered cave. He and his personal guard found Bornar and his group of miners at the mouth of the hole that led from the mountain into the salty smelling cave. They had been opening up the entrance to the cave to permit easy passage and had begun making the modifications to the wall to allow a door to be placed to close off the passage from the cave.

"What is that smell?" the king asked as soon as he stepped foot into the cave.

"That, me king, is the smell of sea salt," Bornar told the king. "Not too far down the cave," Bornar pointed down the cave's long tunnel toward the ocean, "is the ocean. We've reached the northern edge of the mountains, me king."

"The ocean?" the king said to himself, looking very confused. He knew that there was an ocean to the north but the thought never crossed his mind that he would ever get anywhere close to it; dwarves had never lived so close to open water and had no idea how to build a ship and sail. "Show me," he said at last, more curious that anything.

Bornar led the king and his personal guard down the cave tunnel to the giant room that was curtained by the waterfall. Bornar and some of his miners had taken a few moments when they first reached the waterfall room to place torches at intervals along the wall to illuminate most of the large cavern, giving them an idea of its size. Bornar took the torch he was carrying and ran along the slick, moss-covered wall, lighting the torches as he passed them.

The king stood amazed at the openness of the spacious cave and the roar of the waterfall. He watched as Bornar ran along the wall, illuminating the cave. It was big even compared to most of the caverns in the underdark. The air was fresh and cool and the king took in deep breath when he realized how good it was to breathe such fresh air; the salty smell not unpleasant.

After lighting the last torch on the far end of the wall, Bornar ran back to the king. He tried speaking when he reached the king, but the soft sand under his heavy boots made running even harder than normal for the dwarf, and he couldn't catch his breath to speak.

The king didn't look down to the huffing dwarf; he never took his eyes off the waterfall. *So loud,* he thought to himself. He was captivated by its power, and the fact that he had never seen a waterfall before made him stare at it all the longer.

"There are fish, big fish, in the pools, me king," Bornar said after he caught his breath. He walked over to the edge of the nearest pool and pointed to the long, darting shapes weaving in and out of the rocks and foliage under the water.

"They for eating?" asked the king, not caring about fish unless he could somehow make use of them.

"I'm not for knowing, me king. Danflorf said they ate fish in Taris, that it was some of the best meat he'd ever eaten," Bornar replied.

"Well, what are we waiting for? Catch me a fish!"

Dawn came early to the twins; they had gone to bed only hours before the sun was to rise. They dressed in silence, not wanting to wake their mother. They knew her strength was weakening and could only watch in sadness, not being able to help at all. With gear in hand and clothes and armor donned, the twins stepped out of the house onto the still-quiet street.

The twins went west on the road, instead of east, deciding to take the path that would lead them by the temple. They passed the large, steep hill that served as the base to a tall light house; a beacon for ships during storms and at night. The hill had been built by the citizens of Taris decades before and was more of a tall, windowless building of dirt and stone that raised the light house on top high into the sky.

The twins stopped where the path to the temple left the main path. There, in front of them, was the Temple of Valerum, the god of light and strength. Student clerics and priests alike were beginning to arrive and enter through the huge, stone doors that had been bleached white, along with the entire outside of the temple, to shine in the dark with even the least amount of light.

There was a room dedicated to the citizens where they could come and pray to Valerum. The twins entered the temple and found the large room on the north side of the temple; wooden benches filled the room from side to side. The entire room was decorated in linens and draperies, lavished with golden thread throughout their designs depicting the sun and the triumph of light over darkness. In the front of the room, where one who sat on a bench would look, was a great tapestry covering the entire wall. Valerum himself was depicted as a golden sun, rays of sunshine leaving from all around the sun, spreading light and truth to the world below. Thick strands of gold had been woven in sacred patterns along the outside of the tapestry, which was bleached white to match the stone the temple was made of.

The twins sat on a bench close to the door and stared at the large tapestry in front of them. Silently both Dryx and Weylor prayed to Valerum in their minds, hoping that the gods would have compassion and mercy on them and grant them that thing they desired so much.

Leaving all of their hope for their mother's health with the temple, the twins left the temple and wound along the trail back towards the main street of Taris that would take them to the keep, to Captain Strongshield's office.

Déjà vu crept over both of the twins as they passed the guards and heard the familiar voice say the same words in the same tone as before when they visited the captain's office to receive their previous orders to accompany the dwarves back to Icedome.

"Enter," the voice said.

The twins entered the room. The same, almost-expressionless look was on the captain's face that had been there when they received their last orders from him.

"Dryx, Weylor," Captain Strongshield said, standing up and giving the twins a short, courteous nod of his head.

"The king is very pleased with you both. You have shown loyalty, bravery, and determination that has impressed the king and you are still students in your last year of training. I do not know why the king chose you two to accompany the dwarves back to Icedome and make an alliance with King Bourndrimiur but you exceeded his expectations in that assignment," he told them.

Saying 'thanks' did not seem fitting for such unusual and gracious compliments so the twins both bowed their heads instead, the unspoken and humble way of accepting and acknowledging the praise.

"That is why, I assume, he hand-picked you two, again, for another, potentially just as important, assignment. What I tell you next does not leave this room. Understood?" he asked, his tone turning slightly serious.

"Of course, Captain," Weylor said. Dryx nodded his head in agreement with Weylor's remark.

"The king, and all the council for that matter, believes something big is coming. The goblins are getting bolder and more numerous every day. They think another war is unavoidable and they want to be as prepared as possible. Here," Captain Strongshield said, pulling out a rolled up parchment, sealed with King Ironwill's own seal, and handed it to Weylor. "That is a letter from the king to King Linodus of Daley. Keep it safe, don't let anyone read it or even know that you have it if possible. You will be accompanying Captain Boran Terrell of The Mistress to Daley. Depending on the weather it should take anywhere from five days to a week and a half to get there. You shouldn't run into any trouble on the water but if you do, do what you can to help."

After being sent to be the first humans in Icedome, the twins weren't too surprised at the assignment. They had never traveled to Daley before and they were both excited to travel over the sea and visit their sister city.

"Sir," Dryx spoke up.

Captain Strongshield smiled; he could see the question in Dryx's face.

"What kind of trouble could we run into on the water?" Dryx asked. "I've never heard of any attacks on our ships before."

"That's because there haven't been any; not until recently. And they weren't our ships but Daley's ships. I've heard from some of the Captain's that travel regularly to Daley that there have been some boats gone missing and sightings of pirates and rumors of sea monsters. The incidents have all been isolated to the east of

Daley, far from the route you will take. The sea isn't land locked, it leads out for to the north east of Daley; there is no telling what may come in from the straight."

The twins looked at each other and just shrugged their shoulders and accepted the assignment. Weylor took the scroll for King Linodus and tucked it away into one of his many pockets inside his robe. Dryx knew he could probably never find the scroll if he searched his brother; Weylor had a way of making things disappear without a trace in that magical robe of his.

The twins found The Mistress at the far end of the docks, the last ship before the dock gave way to the open waters. The crew was already busy on the ship deck and dock, loading and unloading empty crates and crates full of food and supplies. Dryx and Weylor crossed the double-wide plank that served as the bridge to the ship and found Captain Terrell on the helm, overseeing his crew's work.

"You must be the twins, Dryx and Weylor," the captain said with a very charismatic smile.

The captain was a few inches taller than the twins and built like a soldier. He kept himself clean shaven and his hair short. He wore the common leather boots and baggy white pants that most of the other sailors wore; but from the waist up the twins would never have guessed that he was a sailor. Captain Terrell wore a long-sleeved, red shirt the twins would have only guessed someone in a king's court would wear. He also wore a large-brimmed, green hat that shielded his entire face from the sun. The hat's right-side brim was folded back and up against the center, giving the captain a very unique and unusual look. A rapier rested against his right hip and a sheathed dagger against his left.

"At your service, Captain," Weylor said.

"Tell me, have you ever sailed before?" the captain asked them.

"No, sir. Never," Dryx replied.

Captain Terrell let out a sincere laugh that gave both of them chills. "Well, you have chosen the best ship in Taris to experience it!" The captain laughed again and walked forward to the rail looking down on the deck where the workers were finishing the preparations for their voyage.

"Jack, how much longer?" the Captain called down to the man counting the crates and boxes being brought onto and being taken off of the ship.

"She's all yours, Captain. You're all set," Jack, the dockhand, replied. He waited for the last sailor to cross the plank onto The Mistress and pulled the plank off the ship and onto the docks.

"Mel, let's give our guests a warm welcome to the sea," Captain Terrell said to Mel, his second mate, and winked.

"Aye, sir," Mel replied, a smile spreading across his face. "Drop sails, men. The Mistress is late for an appointment!"

Chapter 17

To and Fro

The Calm Sea. The twins had never really thought about how different sailing might be than riding a horse or a wagon on a road. They figured that the balance wouldn't be too much different, what with all the dips and rocks on the roads. The Mistress had not set sail for more than an hour before both twins found themselves gripping the side railings for support as they heaved the contents of their previous meals into the sea.

Captain Terrell couldn't help but to grin at the scene. He didn't bother telling them about seasickness before they set sail; it wouldn't have helped in any case. He had gone over to them when they first ran to the rails to make sure they were okay, even though he knew exactly what was going on. Most sailors got seasick during their first voyages but it would fade with time and experience he knew.

"We have a fair tail wind," Mel said to the captain. "We might make the island before sundown."

Captain Terrell looked up at the sails on the closer and bigger of the two masts that the ship boasted. They were full with wind and it did seem like the Mistress was keeping a good speed.

"Our new guests may just get lucky and feel dry land again before we hit the deep sea," the captain replied with a chuckle.

He knew they would be anxious to rest a while on dry land after being sick for almost an entire day.

Mel shared in the amusement with a chuckle of his own; he also understood how uncomfortable they were feeling, having had seasickness himself when he first became a sailor on the Mistress.

Despite the dizziness and almost constant desire to heave overboard, the twins couldn't miss the new world around them. Eventually they made their way, with at least one hand on a rail at all time, up onto the helm where the captain stared pensively ahead along the front rail overlooking the deck.

Few clouds were visible in the sky and the sun was as bright as the twins had ever seen it. The constant glare of the sun off the water around the ship didn't help their queasiness.

"There is no land, anywhere," Weylor said in an exasperated tone, looking a little worried.

Dryx looked at his brother, who looked more than a bit pale, and guessed that the fact that there was no land in sight was not helping.

"No, there's not. We are sailing, Weylor. That means we left land," Dryx said in a sarcastic voice, thoroughly enjoying this advantage he had over his twin and ready to make it obvious. He was surprised that this bothered Weylor, not being able to see land. It didn't bother him at all. He couldn't hold back his sarcastic smile when Weylor glared at him with his blood-shot eyes.

"You'll regret that," Weylor replied under his breath. He wished he could think clearly to find a way to get back at his brother and even the score, but the to-and-fro motion of the boat and with no land in sight, he could barely focus enough to keep himself conscious.

Dryx laughed out loud now, not holding back his amusement at the situation. The twins had always been in competition over almost everything since they were big enough to walk. Dryx couldn't remember the last time either of them had a clear advantage over the other and couldn't help but think about how Weylor would retaliate.

Laughing, Dryx walked over to Weylor, "come on, I'll help you down below."

Weylor felt instantly better on his cot below deck; for some reason, the swaying of the cot was different than standing on the deck of the ship, it was more like swaying in the wind than standing on the boat. It didn't take long for him to fall asleep.

Dryx went back up onto the deck. He still stayed next to the rail; he had no desire to heave on the deck in front of all the sailors. His queasiness was not completely gone but he felt that he could manage.

It was a weird and different feeling, Dryx thought, being completely surrounded by water. He knew if anything happened, he could be stranded in the water with no land in sight and very little chance of being found before he drowned; he wasn't even sure how well he could swim. That realization made him a little anxious but he forced the thought out of his mind.

The sun was high in the sky now. He remembered the water near the shore was always too dark to see into, but out on the open sea he could see fish of all sizes in the clear blue water. Some were small, the kind of fish he was familiar with eating and seeing in the market place; other fish were huge compared to the smaller ones. He saw one that must have been almost half as long as the ship. *A shark,* he thought. He had heard of sharks, but had never seen one. They weren't big enough to be dangerous to ships the size he was on but he had heard rumors of bigger things in the sea; rare sea creatures as big as ships, but they were usually only seen from far off.

Hours passed by and the sun hung low in the sky, just over the western horizon. Dryx stayed on the deck as the day passed by, watching the sailors work the sails and all the different ropes and rigs. There were too many sails and ropes to remember all of their names but he was quick to pick up on the basic strategy of how to use the sails to catch the wind and maneuver in the water.

"Land!" a sailor in the crow's nest shouted.

Dryx remembered hearing that the route to Daley took about a week and didn't understand how land could be spotted at the end of the first day at sea. He ran, as fast he could while staying within easy reach of the rail, to the bow of the ship. There, not too far off in the distance, was a little island. A few massive rocks formed a semicircle around the northwestern side of the small island. The island itself was only a couple hundred feet long and about half as wide. Not a single piece of vegetation grew on the island; just a barren flat of sand in the middle of the sea.

"I've never heard of an island on the sea so close to Taris," Dryx remarked to the sailor next to him.

"We don't have a name for this island; I'm not sure it's big enough to merit one," said a sailor on the bow next to Dryx. "It's a common stop place for ships en route to Daley from Taris; lucky we found it when there was still light, it can be tricky maneuvering in the dark."

Dryx looked from the sailor back to the island. There really was nothing special about the island but he thought it would be a sight for his brother's sore eyes.

Dryx and Weylor, along with half a dozen other sailors from The Mistress, rowed the short distance from their ship to the island in a rowboat. Half a dozen more rowboats followed them after safely anchoring The Mistress a short way off the shore of the island. The sun had finally set under the western horizon and the moon was low but bright in the sky to the north. A few, low-hanging clouds still glided across the sky but the twins didn't notice; they were captivated at how clearly the stars shone. They had never seen so many stars before; hundreds of stars, some dim and some bright, littered the sky, scattered and bunched-up across the dark expanse above their heads.

The twins had fallen onto the ground as soon as the small rowboat made landfall on the island; they lay on their backs taking in the majesty of the sky. The stillness of the stars, while lying on dry ground, helped both of them to relax and clear the queasiness from their bodies; even Dryx, who was quickly growing used to sailing, felt better after relaxing from the constant sway of the ship at sail.

They didn't know how much time had passed before the sailors that had accompanied them to the island began to get back into the rowboat.

"What's happening?" Weylor asked with a slight hint of disappointment in his voice.

"The Mistress," one of the sailors replied, pointing back to the ship.

The twins sat up and looked back toward the ship; two torches were waving in the distance.

"We only stay on the island long enough to stretch our legs and let the other sailors search the ship to make sure there aren't any problems with the hull," the same sailor said.

Dryx laughed at the obviousness of the statement; of course they wouldn't stay the night on the island, they were in a boat, not a wagon. There was nothing to run into or any reason to stop for the night on the open sea.

Weylor fell back onto the sand, took a deep breath, exhaled a mumbled complaint and forced himself onto his now-balanced feet. Despite his sour mood, Weylor could feel the time spent on the island had helped calm him down; the short ride on the row boat was not as bad as the short, rowboat ride to the island, that was a good sign.

The next three days were much the same as the first. Few clouds roamed the sky and the sun began to take its toll on the twins who were unaccustomed to sailing. They wore long sleeve shirts and wrapped a towel around their heads to protect their now burnt skin from the sun; despite the intense heat they decided that putting on the extra clothes to keep from getting burned was better than being slightly cooler with less clothing. They tried spending more time below deck, but found that the heat was almost the same and that even a slight breeze on the helm with all their skin covered felt better than hiding from the sun below deck.

"How do we know where we are?" Dryx asked the captain on the fourth day. He couldn't figure out how the captain, or anyone else for that matter, could keep from getting lost on the water with no landmark signs to guide them.

"Experience, my young friend," Captain Terrell replied with a laugh. "We keep our bearing in the same general direction during the day and use the stars at night. Tomorrow we will be able to see the mountains far to the west of Daley and that's when we turn northeast until the mountains are directly portside. The sea isn't big enough to get lost for more than a couple days before seeing land, unless you're traveling to Viltress's port to the west; that's where things can get tricky."

Dryx thought about the logic of the captain's reply and decided he didn't know better anyway so he went with it.

Once again the sun rose higher into the sky with no clouds in sight to block its rays from The Mistress. As the ship made its way towards the northern shore of the Calm Sea, the size of the fish and sharks gradually declined. Sharks were seen less and the smaller, faster fish were more numerous. Sailors on both sides of the ship cast out nets, with the rope used to pull it in anchored to one of the masts. Half-a-dozen sailors had to pull the nets out of the water; the speed of the ship and the added weight of the caught fish and water made the nets too heavy for just a few men alone.

Dryx felt almost completely comfortable at sea by the fifth day. The to-and-fro motion of the ship on the waves became like a rhythm to him; Weylor, on the other hand, was almost the same as the first day they set off from Taris. He stayed by the rails and watched the fish and anything else underwater that he could see that took his mind off the swaying of the ship. His queasiness had partially subsided by keeping his sight and mind occupied on things other than the ship, but that lasted only until he tried to cross the deck of the ship to the other side. Midway, with no rail or rope to stabilize himself on, the sudden dip of the ship down an unusually high wave caused the already unstable Weylor to fall to his knees and heave all over the deck. The seasickness seemed to drain all the strength from his legs and he could barely keep himself from falling face first into his own vomit. He felt two strong hands on both of his shoulders and felt his body rise up off the deck. Dryx, now with the help of one of the sailors, carried Weylor back to his cot where he promptly fell into an uneasy sleep, pale as a ghost.

Dryx, back on the helm with the captain, felt embarrassed for his brother and himself and tried to apologize to the captain for taking so long to get accustomed to sailing.

The captain's first reaction was to laugh. It had taken some of his best sailors' weeks to get completely comfortable on the sea. "Nonsense," he replied to Dryx. "It's an easy clean up," he said and motioned for a nearby sailor to clean up Weylor's vomit on the deck.

The sailor grabbed a bucket in one hand and grabbed the rope attached to it in the other hand and threw it overboard. He dragged it back in and used the water to push the vomit towards the railing. There were spaced holes where the rail met the deck to allow water to drain off the deck when rain and waves washed over the side.

"It took most of the sailors on this ship at least a week to keep from vomiting on calm seas," said Captain Terrell.

"On calm seas?" asked Dryx.

"There are occasional storms that roll over our path and give us some trouble, but they are rare and we can avoid them sometimes."

"For my brother's sake let's hope we stay clear of any," Dryx said, trying to hide his own fear.

"You can't always tell when one is coming. You can wake up at dawn and not see a cloud in the sky and the next thing you know you can't see over the waves crashing onto the deck and the sky is a shade of black that just looks evil," the captain said.

Weylor met Dryx on the deck around noon, looking somewhat better than the previous days.

"We should be able to see land tomorrow, then one more day along the coast," Dryx said to Weylor.

"That's good news; I need to get off this ship," Weylor said.

The rest of the day, like all the days before, passed uneventfully. The twins passed the day, once again, watching the sea, learning how to help the sailors with the ropes and sails and helping check the cargo for rodents and bad food and water.

The twins awoke early the next morning to shouts of sailors from the deck.

"What's going on?" Weylor asked, on edge.

"I don't know," Dryx said, hurriedly putting on his clothes. He got up and ran down the hall and up the stairs that led to the deck while Weylor was still dressing.

It was just as dark on deck as it had been below deck. A storm, Dryx thought. His knees began to feel weak and the thought of being tossed overboard and left to die in the sea flew into his mind. Rain beat down on him like he had never experienced, he could hardly hear himself think over the noise.

Sailors were running in all directions; some were climbing up to the sails, others were pulling on ropes and others were trying to tie down everything that moved on the deck.

It took a minute for Dryx's eyes to adjust to the darkness outside, but when they did he could see how dire their situation was, at least to him. Huge waves tossed the ship around on the sea and crashed over the sides with great force. He saw the sails being drawn in to the mast and lowered; the fierce winds of the storm could tear the sales apart and drag the boat wherever it listed with the sails still up.

Weylor grabbed onto Dryx's shoulders for support when he made it to the deck. Surprisingly, his face wasn't pale and he didn't look queasy at all from the motion of the ship on the dangerous waters. Fear was all he could feel, it sharpened his senses and blocked his seasickness from clouding his mind.

"Man overboard!" came a shout from the bow of the ship.

The twins, knowing that they had to help out any way that they could, followed a sailor with a rope to the starboard side. Holding onto one end of the rope he threw the bulk of the rope out to the sailor swimming for his life. It was a good throw; the end of the rope landed a few feet away from the near-drowning sailor.

As soon as the sailor in the water grabbed the rope, the sailor on deck with the other end quickly wrapped it around his waist and tied it. The twins both grabbed on to the rope and began pulling with everything they had. The huge waves and direction of the moving ship made it almost impossible to pull the sailor. Another sailor on deck grabbed onto the rope and after a few moments, they began to pull the rope in. It was a slow process. The sailor in the water was an experienced sailor and pulled himself up the rope far enough to tie it around his waist; he knew either his grip would give out before reaching the ship or the sudden crash of a wave on him would tear him free of the rope.

Another sailor joined in on pulling the rope. The sailor in the back who threw the rope made his way, slowly, around the mast and promptly turned and put his right leg up against the mast. The friction of the rope around the wooden mast and the anchor-like strength of the sailor's leg against the mast insured that there would be no give in the rope.

After a few more minutes the sailor was pulled from the water and fell on the deck, completely drained of strength and energy.

"You two!" shouted Captain Terrell at the twins. "Quickly, get him below deck and stay there." The captain's expression was serious and the twins, each pulling an arm of the downed sailor over their shoulders, dragged him below deck.

The sound of the captain shouting orders to the other sailors on deck diminished as they made their way to the cabin below deck. They helped the man into dry clothes and wrapped him in warm blankets on his cot. They both changed also; the rain had drenched them both and they could feel the heat leaving their bodies in their cold, wet clothes.

"Look at your hands," Weylor said to Dryx, looking down at his own hands. A deep cut ran across the length of each hand where they had held the rope. They hadn't noticed the sting until they were calmed down but could now feel the sting of the salt water in their cuts.

Dryx stared at how deep the cuts were; blood was everywhere and the pain was growing with each passing minute. They tied cloth around their hands to control the bleeding. Dryx tried gripping the rail by his cot and pain shot up has hand like fire; he muffled his moan and laid down on his cot. If he couldn't grip the rail, he couldn't grip his swords, either; the thought was very annoying.

The storm lasted for another few hours. The twins made their way back up onto the deck when the swaying of the ship was back to its usual motion on the water.

The sailors were already busy cleaning off the deck and making repairs on the ship; a dozen sailors were up on the mast and out on the horizontal crossbeams sewing together small rips and tears in the sail and replacing rope where it had been snapped in the storm. The mast itself was seemed fine with no cracks or breaks in the wood.

The twins made their way up to the helm where the captain was overlooking the work on the ship. The captain smiled when he saw the twins. "Thank you both for helping rescue my sailor," the captain said with gratitude obvious in his eyes. "No one expected you two to come above deck and help, but we are all thankful that you did. I haven't lost a sailor yet," he said in a more serious tone, "and you helped me to be able to still say that."

"We did what we could," Weylor said, raising his hands to explain why they couldn't help more during the storm.

The captain looked down at their hands, wrapped in blood-stained cloth. The obvious selflessness of the twins struck the captain; he wasn't used to seeing people sacrifice so much to help a stranger. He didn't blame them for staying below deck; during the storm, he told them to take the sailor below deck both to help the sailor and get them off the deck to keep them safe.

The sailing was slow that day. The captain told them that the storm had delayed them a while due to damage from the storm. The damage was mostly minor but it would take the sailors some time before the sails were up and ready.

The mountains still lay in view to the north, the storm hadn't driven them too far off course. Dryx, staring out over the sea to the mountains, wished he had a horse that could run over water; he figured it would only take an hour to make land on a fast, galloping horse.

Enough of the repair work was finished by midafternoon, though, to allow The Mistress to continue sailing to Daley.

Chapter 18

Knowledge is Key

Growing up in Taris, the twins had learned about the other cities in the kingdom. They knew that Daley was much larger that Taris, both in size and population; but that didn't prepare them for their first sighting of the city. Dozens of large sailboats lined the ports, all much bigger than The Mistress. Dozens more were drifting or at anchor around the harbor. The twins couldn't count the number of smaller fishing boats that dotted the sea for miles around the port. Daley supplied most of the fish to both Taris and Viltress, the largest of the cities that lay far to the west.

Some of the ships, the massive cargo ships that lined the larger, outer docks of the port, had masts twice the size and height of those on The Mistress. Some held large amounts of timber and other large piles of rock and stone and dirt.

The city beyond the port was just as impressive to the twins. Daley, unlike Taris, was not surrounded by walls but lay open, buildings extending in every direction. The mountains that they had seen the day before had begun to grow smaller as the ship sailed east to the city leaving a large flat-land between the mountains and the city.

The sailors had to bring down many of the sails on The Mistress to navigate more slowly through the sea of other ships to reach the port; this was nothing new to the captain or the crew. It wouldn't take long to reach the port, though.

Marek made his way through the crowded, merchant-filled streets of Daley back towards the small fishing shop, The Wayfarer, which served as a front for his hideout. Marek was like every other citizen of Daley in only one aspect; he lived in Daley. The Daley Guard knew nothing of him or of his secret band of rogues. Despite the short sword and many daggers hidden on him, he looked completely ordinary to anyone that saw him and in public he had never done anything to draw attention to himself. He was a normal height and, clothed, seemed to have an average physique. He kept his facial hair trimmed except for below his chin and on his neck, which he kept clean shaven. His hair was coal black and trimmed.

He stepped into the shop and made his way to back door that led into the backroom. The clerk running the store gave only a nod to Marek; they benefited mutually from the partnership. The store was fully protected by the rogue group from any theft and, since the clerk was not part of the rogue band and knew very little of it, there was very little chance of suspicion and of anyone finding out the location of the rogue hideout should anyone ever learn of them. The clerk didn't even know Marek's name and didn't want to know; he was happy knowing nothing and thought the benefits of having them outweighed the slight possibility of being found out as their front.

Once in the back room, Marek made his way over to the far shelf. He reached around, carefully, to the back of the shelf and gently disabled the trap that would put a crossbow dart through his back should he try to open the secret doorway to the hideout. Marek then reached down, not far below where he disabled the trap, and pushed in a small lever concealed on the inside of the large, vertical support beam on the back wall behind the shelf.

A soft clicking sound was heard and a very well-concealed door opened in the wall to Marek's left. As quiet and as graceful as a shadow he opened and closed the door behind him as he entered the room. The hinges had been oily regularly to allow the door to open and close without sound. Once closed it would be hard to find the secret door by even an experienced rogue without prior knowledge to its whereabouts. Marek went to great lengths to insure the security of his band's hideout.

Avoiding a few more traps just inside the door, Marek made his way down a ladder and into the basement of the shop. The door through which he had just come had previously been the only entrance into the basement, but since the rogues had made the basement their hideout they had spent months digging tunnels and extending the basement as their band grew. They had tunnels leading out in all directions that led to different exits; both sewers and buildings. The rogues had even been able to dig right under an unsuspecting hotel. The trap door that led up into the hotel was as well concealed as the door in the shop above their hideout.

Marek entered the largest of the rooms in the basement that had been cleared out completely except for a large table filled with parchments and candles. Marek's top rogues, Ranin, Famir and Garel, and a handful of others, including Cade, were already in the room talking over the various maps and parchments that lined the table.

Upon his entry, everyone in the room, in one quick motion, bowed their heads in respect to the leader of the rogue band and silence followed.

Marek walked around to the open end of the table, his end, and glance at the maps in front of him.

"It's time," he said. He looked up, glancing around at his rogues. "We are outgrowing this small hideout and the petty theft and robbery that has brought us this far. It's time for a change."

The rogues held their silence, waiting for Marek to explain in more detail their orders and new responsibilities.

"Daley will come to fear and respect us," he said looking down and pulling out a larger map of the city and placing it on top of the others. "We are going to make our presence known to everyone. In time, merchants will pay us for protection or live in fear every day. We will soon be in the center of Daley and this hideout will serve other purposes. Does anyone know what the key to our success will be?" Marek asked, glancing at everyone in the room. He, himself, had thought long and hard about what the key would be to expanding his rogue band and reaching new heights of success and power.

"Fear," one of the rogues replied. "We will only have as much power as the people have fear of us."

"This may be true," Marek replied, "but there is still something far more important than fear. I can convince or kill anyone that fears me or not. No," he continued, "the key to our success is knowledge." He waited a moment to let them think; he wanted to see if they would come to the same conclusion that he had.

"Knowledge?" Garel asked.

"Yes, knowledge," Marek replied. "We cannot come out openly against the guard or the public; there aren't enough of us and that's not what we want. If we got rid of all of them, how would we profit from them? No, knowledge gives us leverage. We are going to infiltrate Daley where we can learn about everything and everyone. We need to know everything about everything; who we can use, who is dangerous to us, everything. I want to know what every ship is carrying into and from Daley, I want to know who is in charge in every guard station, I want to know everything about everyone."

"This will take a lot of time, Marek," Ranin said. "It will be difficult infiltrating the guard and even the port."

Marek stayed silent for a long moment, staring at Ranin directly across the table from him. Up until this point, it wasn't unusual to respectfully question certain things that the rogue band decided to do. But things were going to change, Marek decided.

Marek stood up straight and brought his hands to rest on his hips. He stared blankly at the table. "Yes, it will be difficult," he said in a tone barely louder than a whisper. Faster than any of the rogues could react, Marek pulled out a concealed dagger and threw it at Ranin. At first it seemed like Ranin had caught the dagger by the hilt, but after only a few seconds, and with a look of pain and disbelief, Ranin sank to the floor. The dagger was buried up to the hilt in Ranin's neck.

Marek had hoped that someone would speak up, questioning him. He was forcing change to his band of rogues and the more drastic his demonstration, the stronger the hold he had over his rogues.

The men around the table were stunned. The band had never killed anyone up until this point that they knew of; everything was based around robbery and theft. They looked from Ranin's dead body to Marek. He stood, cold as stone, his hands casually on his hips again; to the rogues this was an obvious sign of confidence.

Famir was the first to speak. "What do you need us to do?"

Marek's lips curved up slightly; he achieved his goal and solidified his position in the band. "We need more recruits, many more. We need eyes and ears everywhere; in the guard stations, the docks, the market place, everywhere. Tell the others there will be rewards for information," Marek said and decided to qualify his last statement. "Usable information," he rephrased.

The rogues needed no further prodding; they all left in different directions with different ideas. Marek knew that this was also important to grow his band; he had to trust each of them that they could make it happen without giving specific, direct orders individually.

He looked back down at the map in front of him. He eyed the small portion of the map where his hideout lay and the area of influence that his band covered. His band couldn't patrol even a quarter of the city; it was too big and his band was too small. *But that would change,* he thought. He stood up to see the entire city at once and imagined his men covering the entire map, hundreds of them on every street and infiltrated into every information-prone organization. He wanted to own the city from the shadows.

Cade made his way down the tunnel south, towards the harbor. He found the narrow ladder that led up into an old, abandoned workshop not far from The Wayfarer. He pressed his ear against the bottom of the trap door to make sure no one was inside the building, out of habit, before quickly exiting and closing the door behind him.

Cade grew up living on the street; he was orphaned when his parents never came back from a trade expedition to Viltress. He learned how to steal food and where to get clothes for the cold months and how to run away and lose himself in big crowds and where to hide. He had become proficient at his way of life and had never been caught. This is how Marek had recruited him. Cade had joined Marek's band of rogues when he was a teenager. He was quickly marked as one of the best thieves in the band and Marek rewarded him for his prowess.

The intense training of the rogue band honed Cade's skills and senses. He could sneak around before, rarely being seen or heard, but when he joined the band he learned how to use everything around him to his advantage; how to walk on old wooden floors without making them creak, how to run on the balls of his feet to not make a sound, how to move in the shadows and use the area in a person's peripheral vision to elude them. Cade also learned how to use daggers; the band trained intensely on hand to hand combat, but the skill with daggers helped them more cut purses loose of their owners and were helpful in so many other ways than combat.

Cade thrived on the intense training; he could lose himself in the thrill of sneaking around and not being seen. Before he joined the band he only stole what he needed to survive; but when he joined the band he learned how to steal much more than that. The rush had been unparalleled; being able to get close enough to people without them knowing and steal their purse from right under their nose. It wasn't until the last few weeks that stealing began to lose its thrill to Cade; he found himself more and more sneaking away to his secret place overlooking The Calm Sea and wishing he could see more of the world.

Tonight, witnessing Marek kill Ranin and the new direction the band was heading, Cade was on the verge of running away. But where would he go? He thought. He knew that Taris was too small for him; the population was mostly for farming and the actual city was small and surrounded by a high wall. There was nowhere to hide there, no way for him to make a living off of other people. Stealing was all he knew.

Marek had connections in Viltress and Cade wasn't sure how he felt about living in an even bigger, more populated city; he would have to survive in the same way he had survived in Daley for so long. *It would only be more of the same,* he thought.

So he decided to draw as little attention to himself in the guild as possible and stay as far away from the new, murderous side of the guild as possible.

"How long will we be here," Weylor asked the Captain.

"We will be here a few days. We have some trade cargo for the marketplace and some orders from Taris to fill. You should be able to see King Linodus in the morning and it will only take a day to get what we need to repair the ship," Captain Terrell replied. "I will accompany you personally to see the king; whatever message you have for him, according to King Strongshield, is of vital importance and we won't take any chances."

The twins then understood why the sailors had formed a protective circle around the twins as they made their way off the ship and down towards the marketplace. It was more a precautionary step than for any real threat.

The harbor was huge; the group had to use several different docks to even make it to shore. Once the wooden docks ended and the stone-laid streets of the city began, so did the bars. The entire port-side line of buildings was bars; the air was loud with shouts of drunkards and bouncers alike. The twins had witnessed men drunk in a bar before, but it was nothing compared to the sailors. The stench of alcohol permeated the air for an entire block. Two fights broke out in the time it took the twins to get from the dock to the city streets that lead to the market.

"It's always fun rounding up the men from the bars when it's time to go," the captain said with a chuckle. "That bar there," he pointed to a bar at the corner of the end of the block, "is where we will find most of them. The Drunken Sailor it's called," he said. "It's a fitting name."

The group followed the winding road into the city. They found one of the nicer, middle-class inns to rest for the rest of the day; they would go to the king the next day. Captain Terrell sent off one of his sailors with a piece of parchment sealed with the crest of King Strongshield to the palace; the twins would see the king the next day.

Famir watched the strange group of sailors make their way into the city. *How odd,* he thought; very few sailors ventured into the city even during long stays. They tended to stay in the bars and streets close to the port. What was odder to him was how they were obviously escorting the two young men in the middle, who obviously weren't sailors.

Famir, with the new direction of the rogue band still very fresh in his mind, along with Ranin's death, decided to find out why they were being escorted and followed them.

It was fairly easy to track someone in the city, at least for the experienced rogues. Very few people had caught on to the organized crime of the band in this area of the city and so very few people were wary and didn't make much of an effort to stay alert to theft. Even if someone had been watching him, Famir thought, the streets were filled with so many people traveling in every direction that it would be impossible to tell he was following the group.

He made his way out into the street from the alley where he had been hiding and watching. He figured he could walk around with both daggers out by his side and that no one would notice in the huge crowd; the thought amused him. He followed the group for a few blocks and watched them enter the inn.

One of the sailors, the last to enter, looked around before entering the inn.

Famir was now even more curious as to why the sailors were protecting those two young men. Holding himself back from investigating further, Famir decided to report to Marek and let him decide on how to continue with the situation; if there was anything worth finding out.

He stood there for a moment staring at the inn before disappearing back into the crowded street and towards The Wayfarer.

Famir found Marek in the same room they had met in in the morning. Famir entered the room and found another man in the room talking to Marek, a man he had never seen before.

"Marek," Famir said when he entered the room. "I have been out on the streets and I found something unusual."

Marek, not turning to look at Famir, raised a hand towards him to silence him while he spoke to the other man.

He spoke in a whisper that Famir couldn't hear, but the man Marek was speaking to smiled and shook his head.

"Very well," the man said, bowing slightly to Marek. The man wore a robe and was clean-shaven. He was very clean; his robe looked brand new. A dozen small bags and purses hung from various places on his belt and he leaned on a shiny, metal staff. It was obvious that this was a wizard.

"Famir," Marek said, turning to look at him. "Meet Avery, the newest addition to our band," he said, waving his hand toward Avery next to him. Avery turned to Famir and gave the same, short but courteous bow as he had to Marek.

Famir mirrored the bow, a little on edge at having a wizard in their hideout. He knew wizards were powerful; he had heard stories of the great wizards in Viltress that could blow apart entire buildings with a single spell.

Famir looked back to Marek, eager to share what he found and get away from the wizard; he wasn't used to being around wizards and didn't trust anything that he couldn't manipulate with his hands.

"What did you find, Famir?" Marek asked him.

"A group of sailors walking through the marketplace; they didn't stop at any bar but went to an inn. They were escorting two younger men who weren't sailors," Famir replied.

"How far did you follow them?" Marek questioned.

"All the way to the inn where they are staying," Famir said.

"Go to the docks and find out which ship they came on and why they are here," he said. He glanced over to Avery and a smile spread across his face as he thought of how he could put his new wizard to work. "Avery, I think we found your first target."

Avery smiled. He was from Viltress; an accomplished wizard that had grown bored with the same day-to-day life in the city as a teacher. He had come to Daley to find something new; he had no plans of making Daley his new home but when the opportunity found him, in the form of Marek, he couldn't pass up the offer for wealth and excitement.

"I will need a day to prepare myself and the spells I will need," Avery said to Marek.

"Good," Marek replied. "Tomorrow we will see what secrets these travelers have." Marek couldn't hold back his grin; he was ecstatic to expand his band and become a power in Daley, not just a group of low life thieves. The thrill of kidnapping the travelers without confronting the group of sailors and finding out why they were here took over Marek's mind. It wasn't so much that Marek thought they had valuable information as the thrill of becoming known and feared in his city.

Marek, with his wicked grin still showing, said, "Find out everything you can about them; tomorrow night we find out why they are so important."

The darkness of the night found Famir on the docks. He felt more comfortable in the darkness and even more so on the docks. Walking in and around the group of drunken sailors, both in and out of the bars, was easy and, using the shadows when possible, he drew very little attention to himself.

It didn't take long before he found a semi-sober, less volatile pirate to question about the group of sailors that made their way into the city. He was good at talking like a drunk; it helped when talking to sailors without wanting to seem like he was prying. This particular sailor was more than happy to agree with Famir on how strange it was for the group to escort the two men, who obviously weren't sailors, into the city.

"Aye," the sailor said. "They're from The Mistress. Good ship that. From Taris."

"Ah," Famir said, "No doubt bringing over a load of flour and meat." He turned his head casually to the side as he spoke, making it seem like he wasn't focused on the conversation and not caring too much for the ship.

"No, no," the sailor corrected him. "She ain't a cargo ship," he laughed; most sailors knew which ships were for cargo and passengers and fishing.

"The Mistress is captained by Captain Terrell," the sailor said, thinking the name should be obvious enough.

"Aye?" Famir said, feigning confusion. "And what's that mean?"

"What's that mean?" the sailor asked, now amused at the not-so-bright man in front of him. "Everyone knows he brings messages for the king from Taris," he raised a hand as he spoke and motioned all around him, demonstrating this was common knowledge.

"Oh Captain Terrell," Famir said. "Of course, I was thinking of a different lad."

The sailor looked confused; who could he have become mixed-up with? The sailor thought.

"Hey!" Famir shouted at the waitress walking around, "Another pint of your finest ale for my friend here!"

Shouts of agreement and raised glasses all around the room met Famir's request.

"Aye!" the sailor said loudly, a smile spread fast across his face.

Famir relaxed; the sailor, with a free pint of ale on the way, had already completely forgotten their entire conversation. Famir knew the sailor would have no recollection of him the next day. He got up while the sailor's head was back, chugging down his new ale, and left as quickly and quietly as a shadow, not drawing the attention of a single other soul in the inn.

Famir couldn't hold back his grin. He knew that he had found valuable information; he knew Marek would be pleased. He couldn't help but think of all of the opportunities to solidify his position in the band now; no more grunt work.

I should work the docks more often, he thought to himself. It was too easy to get information from the sailors.

Chapter 19

A Message for the King

The twins spent much of their first day in Daley walking around the huge marketplace; their escorts never too far away. Captain Terrell knew the twins' message was important and made sure an escort stayed with them at all times.

They had never seen such an assortment of goods; from food to weapons to strange trinkets and potions. They listened to traveler's and merchant's stories of their trips from Viltress both by land and by sea. They heard rumors of pirates, sea monsters, giants, marauders, and of large flying monsters called wyverns. These smaller cousins of the dragon lived high in the mountains above The Calm Sea and far to the west of Daley.

Travelers and merchants often banded together when taking the land route to Viltress, pulling together their resources and numbers and hiring guards in case of an attack from the untamed mountains by the many kinds of dangers that lurked in them.

There was one tent in particular caught Weylor's attention; a pair of merchants selling magical and enchanted equipment and trinkets. Weylor, casually pausing in between one of the sailors and his brother, closed his eyes and muttered a few arcane syllables, enacting a very simple and common spell of magical detection.

Weylor knew that his spell was not strong enough to detect strong magic cast by an advanced wizard who didn't want his magic detected; but truly magical equipment being sold in a market place would be no problem.

"Come, step up! Try out some of our gear; it's all magical and enchanted!" the merchant behind the table of items said, waving his arms in ways to exaggerate the words 'magical' and 'enchanted'.

Weylor, hiding his knowing smile, examined some of the items before him. He could feel a faint, weak aura on most of the items. He picked up a rope and held it as the tip wove itself in and out of knots and unkinked itself. Weylor could feel the magical aura of the rope, it was weak; Weylor guessed it was a temporary spell that would wear off in a day or two. Just long enough for the merchants to sell all they could and move to a new, unvisited spot.

"Ah yes!" the merchant said excitedly as Weylor examined the rope. "Magical rope can be very useful!"

Weylor just smiled; he knew better. He set the rope back on the table. There were a lot of items on the table, most of them resonating only a weak magical aura that led Weylor to believe that most, if not all the items before him had only temporary magical enchantments on them.

Despite the excitement of the huge marketplace, the twins returned to their inn as the sun began to fall and turned in for the night. They couldn't resist the opportunity to get in a full night's rest before they went to see the king; especially on beds that didn't sway with the waves on the sea.

Captain Terrell woke the twins shortly after the first rays of sunshine found their way into the windows in the inn the next morning. They ate a quick breakfast before leaving and found a wagon outside the inn waiting to take them to see the king.

The twins, riding through the winding streets of Daley, realized that they had not fully understood how big of a city Daley was from the sea; although the wagon was slow on the hard, winding stone roads of Daley, it took them half an hour to reach the section of the city that housed the government of

Daley. This section of the city was surrounded by a wall as tall as a building; guards patrolled the top of the wall on all sides.

The wagon stopped in front of the large gate that served as the entrance. The guards at the gate recognized Captain Terrell; he was the normal correspondent from Taris between the kings.

Captain Terrell pulled the wagon around to the biggest of all the buildings in the large, walled-off section of the city. The twins had never seen a more magnificent building; every inch of the building was polished and shiny. Tall columns supported the building, lining the entire outside of the building all the way around. Each column was unique and made of a different kind of stone or marble, varying in color from black to white and everything in between.

"I'll be waiting out here with the wagon," Captain Terrell said to the twins when the wagon stopped in front of the building.

The twins, familiar with the protocol to see a king, left their weapons with Captain Terrell on the wagon and followed one of the guards inside.

The king's court was bigger than any building the twins had ever seen. The entrance alone was huge, the roof reaching as high as Valerum's temple in Taris, and the at least twice as wide. The room boasted the same marble splendor as outside from roof to ceiling. The marble tiles in the middle of the room depicted the city of Daley sitting on the edge of The Calm Sea, ships dominating the sea around the port.

The twins were led into the king's throne room, a large hall just as ornately designed but smaller than the entrance hall.

A table had been moved into the hall and the king, along with most of his military and political advisors, were already seated at the table, talking amongst themselves when they twins entered. The guard led the twins to two seats in the middle of the long table.

"Weylor and Dryx Stormcaller of Taris," the guard said and turned back and walked out of the room.

"Please, be seated," a man said, who the twins presumed to be the king; he was seated at the head of the table.

The king wore a finely adorned robe held in place by a wide belt at his waste. The robe was striped in purple, gold, and black; the colors signifying royalty and importance. A sword hung from his hilt; Dryx guessed it was better suited for appearance than for battle with its gemmed hilt and thin blade. The man was average height, slightly shorter than Dryx, with a neat and trimmed beard. He was an older man, about the same age as King Strongshield of Taris, and slightly balding.

Weylor took out the scroll from the folds in his robe that King Strongshield had given him and motioned for it to be passed to the king. "A message from King Ironwill," he said.

"I understand, from Captain Terrell's message yesterday, that you bring very important and urgent news," the king said as he unraveled the scroll.

"Yes, King Linodus," Weylor replied.

There was silence in the hall for a short time while the king read the parchment. When he was done, his hands fell to the table but his eyes looked glazed over, unfocused as what was written took him back to the last war between Taris and the goblins from the mountains. Daley had sacrificed many men to help defend Taris. King Linodus knew that Daley depended heavily on many trade supplies that came from Taris; King Strongshield had been very generous in their negotiations. Despite those facts, the king felt it was his responsibility to help; Taris was Daley's neighbor and felt as though they were close friends.

The king motioned for a piece of parchment and a quill and wrote down his reply to be returned to King Strongshield.

He sealed the scroll himself and passed it down to Weylor. Weylor bowed his head to the king and place the scroll in the folds of his robes where the previous scroll had been.

"Tell me about what you saw on the mountain overlooking Orgath," the king said. "I want to hear it in your own words."

Weylor looked to Dryx, who nodded at his brother and began from how the twins first met the dwarves and their journey to Icedome. He told the king of how King Bourndrimiur worried at the absence of the two dwarven scouts that were late in returning and their journey to where the scouts should have been and then what they found.

Everyone around the table was silent. The king called the guard over that had escorted the twins in, writing down a quick message on a piece of parchment and sending the guard off to Captain Terrell.

"Thank you," he said to both of them, looking at each of them in turn and curtly bowing his head in respect.

The twins, according to King Ironwill, were vitally important because of their important connection with the dwarves; the dwarves would be the key to defeating the goblins again if they were really being commanded by a dragon. King Linodus couldn't see how there could be a connection between the presence of a dragon and the sudden uprising of the goblins, but it was obvious that there was more there than he understood.

"Make sure that scroll gets to King Strongshield," the king told the twins as the guard returned to the room to escort the twins from the room.

Captain Terrell was waiting on the wagon. The twins climbed in and headed off back towards the port.

"It looks like we'll be cutting our stay short here in Daley; whatever message you have from King Linodus to King Strongshield, it's of utmost importance," Captain Terrell said, folding up the message the guard had given him.

"Yes, it is," Weylor replied.

"We'll go to the docks and round up the sailors; we leave at first light tomorrow morning."

Famir watched as Captain Terrell's wagon went by. He had followed the group that morning and waited a safe distance from the entrance to the king's hall, outside the walls to that part of the city. He found a nice, discreet spot a short ways down an alley of tall buildings, giving him darker shadows to wait in.

The expressions on the faces of the captain and the two young men with him hadn't changed much from the day before; Famir couldn't make any assumptions on how their visit affected him. Normally, people would wear an expression indicative of how their meeting went with someone so important as a king; but these men wore the same, serious expression as when they had arrived.

Famir, traveling by foot, ran down backstreets and alleys, keeping in the shadows as much as he could and avoided areas with more people. Famir knew the city well and by taking his shortcuts on foot, running, he was able to make it to the inn where the group stayed just as they were arriving; they climbed out of the wagon and entered the inn.

Finding the same place where he had hidden before while the group was in the inn, Famir settled in. Only a few minutes had passed, though, when Captain Terrell came back outside with a few of the sailors that had been escorting the twins the previous day.

Famir decided to follow the captain. *The two young non-sailors wouldn't leave without their escort,* he thought. It wasn't long before Famir understood what was going on; they were leaving very soon. He watched the captain send out the sailors in all directions to the various pubs and inns; they were rounding up the other sailors. Famir, grabbing a casting net from a nearby pile of supplies in an alley, inconspicuously followed the captain down the rows of docks in the port to his ship.

The Mistress, Famir muttered to himself, memorizing the name of the ship and how it looked. A life-size picture of a woman standing bare-foot on the sea colored the bottom left corner of the large sail on the forward mast.

When the captain boarded his ship, Famir dropped the casting net in the water when no one was looking and made his way back to his guild's hideout. Famir didn't know what had happened to make the captain leave so abruptly but he knew it had to be important, especially because he knew that Captain Terrell was the spokesman between Daley and Taris.

Famir made his way through the busy streets. He couldn't remember ever being this excited; petty theft was not nearly as fun to him as the new direction that the guild was going in. He felt as though he had been stalking prey for the last two days, his senses always alert; it was the feeling of beating his prey's senses that was the ultimate feeling of success for Famir. That is what every rogue strives toward; to be nothing more than a shadow. Famir found Marek in the same room where they had spoken the previous day, but now looking very busy and very irritable.

Marek was in the hideout far more often now than ever before. Rogues were now coming in and out of the hideout at regular intervals, making it seem like the guild was much larger than it actually was. Marek was trying to organize all of the new information coming into to him on pieces of parchment placed on different maps covering different parts of the city.

"If it's not important, write it down and place it on the pile," Marek said to Famir without looking at him.

"Those two boys I've been following, the ones with Captain Terrell, they are leaving in a hurry. They went and spoke with the king today. The captain left the twins at the inn and left to gather his sailors and prepare their ship," Famir said, confident that his information was important enough to interrupt Marek's current organizing agenda.

Marek looked up at him; he stared for a moment at Famir then leaned back in his chair, pensive.

"Avery!" Marek called out.

The mid-age, lanky man entered the room. He wore the same, new-looking robe that Famir had seen the other day. His beard was black with a few grays hairs starting to show up. It was neat, combed down and tied with a small metal band a few inches below his chin.

"Yes, pasha?" Avery said to Marek.

Pasha? Famir thought. He had only heard that term used rarely and only in books to signify a character of high standing and leadership in big organizations.

"I have too much to do here," Marek began. "Go with Famir and see what you can find out about our young friends that make them important enough to see the king."

Avery bowed to Marek before following Famir out of the room.

Famir led Avery down the hallway leading away from Marek's room and towards the quarters where he could recruit a few more rogues. The quarter's room was also the weapons and kitchen room. It was the largest room in the hideout. When he entered the quarters, though, there were only two people in the room; Tracey and Kade.

Tracey was the only female in the rogue guild. She was average height for her age and when fully clothed she seemed of average build, also. Her long, black hair was tied back behind her head, falling down over her spine. She was quite attractive, too. Her skin, unlike most other men and women in Daley, was not tanned from the sun but was a very light shade. Her complexion was perfectly clear and her teeth pearly white.

Famir, though, knew better than to underestimate her. She was one of the most feared rogues in the guild; people seemed to disappear from Daley after crossing her. She spent endless hours in the training rooms, honing her skills and her muscles to perfection.

Kade was also a very familiar rogue to Famir; he was one of the first when Marek formed the rogue band. Famir respected Kade's reputation; Kade seemed to move like the shadows themselves, never making a sound, and people's money bags seemed to just fall from their belts when he passed.

"It's your lucky day," Famir said to both of them. Kade was lying on a cot, his eyes only opening when Famir spoke. Tracey was over by the weapons rack, sharpening her daggers.

"Is it now," Tracey said in a less than enthusiastic tone. Everyone knew Famir was higher up, even without an organized hierarchy, but Tracey only took orders from Marek.

"Even you wouldn't pass up this opportunity, Tracey," Famir said in a non-threatening tone.

Tracey, flipping her daggers casually in between her fingers and from hand to hand, sheathed three of them as quickly as Famir had seen anyone sheath a dagger without looking. "And why is that, Famir?" she asked.

"Two young boys came on a ship from Taris and were escorted to see the king. Now they're in a hurry to set sail again; tomorrow morning," Famir said. "I want to know why."

Kade sat up; he was more intrigued at what their job was than the information they were trying to get.

"Finally," Tracey said, "something fun."

The twins had never been so bored in their entire lives; Captain Terrell had them stay in the inn while he and his sailors prepared The Mistress to set sail the next morning. They exhausted everything that could take up their time in just a couple of hours. The twins, since they were old enough to walk, had practiced fighting with anything they could get their hands on. Weylor, although a wizard, was particularly skilled with daggers thanks to Dryx. Out of both boredom and their drive to reach their maximum potential, the twins, growing up in Taris, would practice hand-to-hand combat at night after returning from school. Dryx always held the edge; he was, after all, the one trained in hand-to-hand combat.

Dryx, his sword resting on Weylor's shoulder, backed up smiling. "You would have been the best fighter Taris has ever seen!" Dryx said to Weylor, both of them breathing heavily. Being Weylor's brother was the only reason Dryx was not surprised at his skill with his daggers; anyone else that knew Weylor was a wizard would have unconsciously underestimated his hand-to-hand competence.

Weylor sheathed his daggers with a slight smile from the compliment. Since Weylor didn't have any of his books to study from, besides his personal spell book, he and Dryx would pass their time on the ship and in the inn by dueling.

Weylor walked over to the window, "the sun is setting. Might as well sleep now, I think we'll be sailing before it rises tomorrow."

"Nothing else to do anyway," Dryx said, truly never having felt more bored than he did spending all day in the inn.

"I'll find out what room they're in," Tracey said. She headed back down the dark alley that they had come down, away from the inn. A block away Tracey hopped out into the street and headed back towards the inn on the main road, walking casually but with an obvious purpose. A slight smile on her face and a little more sway in her step, she didn't pass a single man that didn't stare.

As she walked into the inn, she unbuttoned the top button of her tight shirt; just the top button. Her daggers were still easily accessible but well hidden.

The first floor of the inn was a pub, just like every other inn in the city. She walked into the inn, filled with drunken men and men fast becoming drunk. She smiled wider; it would be so easy to have her way with any man in this bar. A little flirting and they would never notice the loss of the coin purse.

She didn't know what the two men looked like she was after but she figured they wouldn't be in the pub; she looked around anyway to seem casual. She noticed the bartender was young and very busy; too easy, she thought.

"You look like you could use a break," she said to the bartender, knowing he couldn't; he was the only bartender there. She loved playing these little games with men, each one was as predictable as the next.

The bartender couldn't help but stare for a moment before remembering he had a dozen other men to serve. *Damn my luck,* he thought.

He looked back at the men waiting for their ale and then back at Tracey.

"Oh well, another time then," she said with a wink. "Two men told me to meet them here," she said and added in "not sailors. Would you happen to know them?"

The bartender thought for a moment, then remembered the group that had come in the night before. "Yes, second floor, last door on the right," he told her.

She held his gaze for another moment then smiled and winked as she walked back outside.

Shouts of impatient, thirsty men brought the bartender back to reality. He looked back at the door one more time then returned to his duties.

Tracey walked back the way she had come, buttoned back up her top button and slipped back into the dark alleyway like a shadow.

"Second floor, back right room," she said to Famir and the others.

Avery looked at her with more respect than he had before. He had never really given a thought to women as anything more than servants, but he looked at Tracey with admiration at her prowess. Her confidence seemed to radiate from her; he would take care to not get on her bad side.

The group made their way, keeping to the shadows in the alleyways, to the back side of the inn. The only other person behind the inn was a passed-out drunkard; he wouldn't be a problem.

Avery, having prepared special spells for tonight's endeavors, simply levitated up to the second floor in the darkness as the others climbed up, not making any more noise than Avery.

"Avery, you're up," Famir said to the wizard.

Avery, still levitating in the air, began casting a variety of spells. He touched each of the rogues on the forehead, each of them tensing up as he did. Their eyes glowed a light hue of blue and they saw as clearly in the dark as they did during the day.

Again Avery began casting, this time towards the window. The group saw no difference but Famir knew which spell was cast. He pulled out a rock from his pocket and held it out in front of him. Looking at Avery he opened his hand and let the rock fall to the roof. Both Cade and Tracey flinched at the noise that would surely come, but they heard nothing as they watched the rock hit the roof and roll down. Famir smiled; Avery was fast growing on him.

Famir nodded his head at Avery then moved in front of the window. He could see both Weylor and Dryx asleep in their beds. Not needing to worry about making a sound, Famir pushed on the window; locked. He smiled and used his elbow to break the glass closest to the handle on the inside. Again both Tracey and Cade flinched but no sound came when the glass shattered. Famir reached in and unlocked the window.

Even with the spell negating all sound in the area, Famir, Tracey, and Cade all entered as they would if there were sound. No spell could break that habit for the rogues.

"Well, this was too easy," Famir said, but heard nothing. He started laughing when he remembered that even his voice would have no sound. Tracey and Cade both watched as Famir laughed with no sound, it made both of them feel uncomfortable. They had never worked with a wizard before and the thought of Avery turning on them was more than unsettling.

Famir pulled out a short, wooden blowgun and two slender darts from one of his pockets and shot both of the twins. The darts were tipped with a simple, sleep-inducing poison; nothing would awake them for at least a few hours.

Famir looked back at Avery again and nodded.

Avery waved a hand through the air, dispelling his spell of silence. Avery, again using a very simple and common spell, caused both of the twins to levitate; it was easier to move them when they weighed nothing more than a feather.

Even with the spell gone, the group made no more noise than a slight breeze. As quickly and quietly as they had entered they left. It wasn't hard staying hidden in the dark alleyways, especially since the rogues knew the city better at night than anyone in the city, so it wasn't long before they were back in their hideout, safe underground.

Famir led the group, and the unconscious twins, into one of the unused rooms and tied them each to a chair.

"Now, let's see what is so important," Famir said and pulling out a flask that held a liquid that would wake the unconscious men with a single whiff.

Chapter 20

Tied and Bound

A sudden, repugnant smell jolted the twins awake. Each of them felt a thumping, deep pain when the darts had hit them. It took their eyes a minute to adjust; one of the side effects of the poison.

Dryx tried to raise his hands to rub his eyes but they were restrained. He looked down to his side and saw the rope tying his hands to the chair he was in. He pulled as hard as he could but the ropes wouldn't give.

"Weylor!" Dryx called out, turning his head to the other side. Weylor's head twitched at the sound, then shot up when he, too, found his hands retrained behind him.

"What's going on?" Weylor said, his voice anxious and confused.

"We've been kidnapped," Dryx said, his voice equally anxious.

Still confused, they looked around the empty room. The room was small and smelled musty. Nothing was in the room besides the twins and the chairs they were tied to.

"Agh!" Dryx yelled, again trying to break loose of the rope restraining him. He pulled as hard as he could, the veins in his neck coming out as he pulled, and his face flushed red with the sudden rush of blood through his excited body. Again to no avail.

Weylor watched his brother. He noticed the small hole in his brother's neck, red and swollen. The pain in his own neck seemed to match what he saw on his brother's; a dart, he concluded.

Not being able to see his own ropes he looked over at the ropes restraining Dryx; they were a light shade of yellow and perfectly smooth. Not a single strand in the entire rope was frayed; a magical rope. Weylor knew that rope would never break, it was a common item back in the Taris' wizard school.

"That rope won't break, stop trying," Weylor said.

Dryx looked over to his brother, who was scrutinizing every detail in the room that he was able to see. He knew better than to question his brother in this kind of situation; he wouldn't make a claim he didn't know for certain.

"Do you feel drowsy? Or groggy?" Weylor asked Dryx.

Dryx stopped looking around and glanced at his brother, then down at the ground in front of him. He closed his eyes and tried to focus on what he was feeling physically.

"Yes," he said. "There's a sharp pain in my neck and I feel sick in my stomach."

"I feel the same," Weylor replied. "I can see the small hole in your neck, I think we were poisoned. That would explain the grogginess and upset stomach," Weylor said. He had learned about the basic poisons in school as had Dryx, but Weylor paid more attention than Dryx had.

"The ropes tying us are magical, so there is probably a wizard involved," Weylor said, now feeling even more uneasy as the words left his mouth.

"Why us?" Dryx asked, more rhetorically than directly.

"I don't know," Weylor responded, not having any idea why they would be kidnapped.

The door opened suddenly and both the twin's heads snapped up at the sound.

A man walked in. His coal black hair was trimmed along with his beard. He looked normal, except for his apparel. All of his clothes were dark but well kept, straps tying different places together along his body. A short sword was sheathed on his right hip and a dagger on his left.

"How are we feeling this morning?" Marek asked the twins, sarcasm heavy in his tone.

"Who are you? What are we doing here?" Dryx asked, his voice raising.

Marek grabbed a torch from the hall outside and placed in on the wall next to the door inside the room.

"I'll be asking the questions. Now," he said but paused. "What have we got here?" he said and chuckled. "Twins! Even better," his smiled wickedly.

Weylor tried his best to hide his fear but he knew the man in front of him could see it. Dryx, on the other hand, glared at the man. The hidden threat replaced his fear with anger.

Marek chuckled again at Dryx's stare. "Now, what are you doing here in Daley?" The man's tone was serious, no hint of sarcasm. He looked from one to the other.

Weylor was confused at the question; why would it matter why they were in Daley. "We brought an urgent message from Taris to your king," Weylor said. *There really was nothing to hide about why they were there,* he thought. "The goblin threat to Taris is increasing," Weylor said, thinking that even the people of Daley would find this as common knowledge.

"Yes, we know about the goblin uprising. But you two are not sailors, and must have had a more important message for the king than that," Marek said.

Weylor realized what the message must have contained; the king could have sent any messenger to Daley but only he and Dryx knew about the dragon and the details of their new alliance with the dwarves. Still, Weylor thought, there must be some reason the king doesn't want those things to be known by everyone.

"That's it," Weylor said.

"You're lying," Marek said, impatiently. It was one of his gifts to tell when someone was lying, one of the gifts that helped him retain control of his guild.

Weylor clenched his teeth together; he wasn't going to say anymore.

Marek stared at him for a moment, then looked over to Dryx who was still glaring at him.

"You know what he won't say, don't you," Marek said to Dryx. "Of course you do, you're brothers, after all."

Dryx, his rage having pushed all common sense from his mind, tried again to break the ropes to jump up and strangle the man in front of him. Again his attempts were thwarted by the unbreakable magical rope.

"You will talk," Marek said and left the room, closing the door behind him.

Marek, still busy with many other important matters to attend to, made his way to the sleeping quarters.

Famir, Cade and Tracey jumped up when Marek walked in.

Marek thought for a moment then motioned for Tracey to follow him. A wicked smile spread across her face and she followed Marek back to his room on the opposite side of the hideout than where the twins were held.

Tracey closed the door behind her and stood silent, waiting for Marek to turn the men over to her.

Marek sat down behind his desk and his hand came up to stroke the hair on his cheeks.

"The twins are messengers from Taris," he began.

Twins, Tracey thought; her smile got even bigger.

"They say they were sent by Taris to tell the king that the goblin attacks have increased, but there's something else. That, itself, wouldn't merit an escort to the king. Find out what they are hiding," he said to Tracey. If anyone could pry out whatever the twins were hiding, it would be her, Marek knew.

"With pleasure," Tracey replied. She waited another moment to make sure there was nothing else then left the room and headed towards the twin's room.

Again, the twin's heads jolted up when the door opened. This time, though, a female entered, an attractive female.

"Hello boys," Tracey said, her voice soft and inviting.

Neither Dryx nor Weylor replied.

Tracey closed the door softly behind her and flipped her hair as she turned; her casualness sent chills down both of the twin's backs.

"Now," she said, looking from one to the other, "we can do this the easy way," she paused and smiled, "or the hard way."

Dryx already hated this woman more than the man before. Her confidence scared him; her attractiveness made her seem harmless and weak, but he knew this only made her more dangerous.

Again, neither of the twins answered.

"What was so important that your king sent you two with an escort to King Linodus?" she asked again.

The twins made no reply.

"So you want the hard way, then?" Tracey said. She took a few steps forward and leaned down next to Dryx's ear and whispered "perfect".

Dryx shot his forehead forward as fast and hard as he could, hoping to make contact with that pretty little nose right next to him.

Tracey, underestimating Dryx but nonetheless with perfectly honed reflexes, shot backward at the same time, but not before Dryx's forehead made contact with the tip of her nose.

Tracey couldn't hold in the short gasp of pain that escaped from her lips when she felt the tip of her nose break. Her body shot up and her fingers gingerly went to her nose.

"You broke my nose," she said as she looked at the drops of blood on her fingers. She could see her nose was now black and the pain started swelling.

In a flash that not even Dryx was prepared for, Tracey spun a circle with her right leg extended, her heel making contact with Dryx's nose at its base. They all heard the snap as his nose broke.

Dryx let out a sigh of pain but looked back up to stare at this woman he now hated more than anyone he had ever met. He could feel the warm blood flowing freely now from his nose.

"No!" Weylor yelled as he watched, helpless.

All sarcasm and playfulness gone, Tracey turned to Weylor. "Don't worry, I haven't even started yet, you'll get a turn."

Captain Terrell knocked on the twin's door in the inn. No answer. He knocked again, this time louder but still no answer.

"Dryx, Weylor. It's time to go," he said in a calm voice, not wanting to wake anyone else in the rooms next to theirs.

Captain Terrell put his ear to the door and could still hear nothing. He tried the handle but it was locked from the inside. Confused, the captain turned around and opened the not-locked door of the sailors left to guard the twins while the captain readied the ship the night before.

The sailors were already up, dressing and packing up the room.

"Have Dryx and Weylor come out?" he asked them, a little anxious.

"No, Captain," one of the sailors replied. "One of us was awake all night; they never opened the door."

Captain Terrell, thinking they had to just be sleeping in, went downstairs to see if there was an extra key to the room. The captain returned a moment later with the owner of the inn.

"Let's see," the owner of the inn said, searching through the many keys hanging on his key chain. "Here it is," he said and unlocked the door and stepped to the side.

Captain Terrell opened the door and stepped in. "It's time to," his voice cutoff when he saw the two empty beds. As soon as he noticed the empty beds, he caught sight of the broken window. He looked around the room and found both of the twin's gear still under the beds.

"Oh no," Captain Terrell breathed out, now suddenly anxious and scared.

The sailors walked in also and examined the room.

"The window is broken and unlocked," he said, picking up a piece of shattered glass and staring at it. "They've been taken," he said slowly, confused at his own words; besides in the caravans that travel between Daley and Viltress, he had never heard of any kidnapping's in the city.

"Retrieve their belongings and return to The Mistress," Captain Terrell told the sailors. "I'm going to go inform the king; the twins carry an important message to Taris. Stay alert," he said and left the room in a hurry.

An hour later there were dozens of guards at the inn. Captain Dantre, Taris' captain of the guard, sent them out in pairs in every direction from the inn.

Tracey left the twins crumpled in their chairs and on the edge of consciousness. Her fists were trembling and her knuckles sore and bleeding. Sweat beaded down her forehead and matted her hair to her face. She took out a handkerchief and covered her nose before going back to the general quarters.

"What happened to you?" Famir asked. It was easy to see she was hiding her nose, and it wasn't hard to assume why.

"Mind your own business," she hissed, her hands still shaking visibly. She walked over and grabbed her personal bag and left.

Cade's interest was now peaked. It was obvious that she had spent the last hour beating the two men in the other room. *What could be so important?* he thought. The fact that they were now kidnapping and torturing people unsettled Cade. He didn't mind the kidnapping for information so much; he had never had a moral guide in his entire life to tell him otherwise. But torture, that seemed wrong to him.

His heart started pounding. *Why?* he thought. He thought about his last few months in the rogue guild and how he would go up to his secret place and look out across The Calm Sea, secretly wishing to explore and leave Daley behind. He realized that he had lost his care for petty theft and stealing was no longer a rush for him. He could almost taste the bitterness he now felt knowing that he was part of a fast-changing group that now used torture to get what they want.

"I'll take the next shift with them," Cade said as he got up and walked towards the door. He took out a dagger and flipped it through the area, catching it as it came back down and repeating the motion. The dagger flipping, in Cade's mind, made his statement seem more sinister, as if he was also going to go torture the men to get answers.

What am I doing? he thought, now very anxious. He knew that if he entered that room he would likely be committing suicide. He had no intention of harming the men, or even asking why they were in Taris. He had never made such a bold decision in his life but his body seemed to follow his deeper desires; if he went into that room, it would be to find a way out of Taris. He surprised himself at this realization; he had dreamed of leaving and exploring for so long, but the thought of turning against his guild of rogues had never crossed his mind. The more he thought about it, the more he realized how much he had ignored. Each step towards that room that held, perhaps, his only escape strengthened his resolve. He didn't know how he was going to do it, but it was too late to turn back.

His hand reached down and opened the door. He walked in and closed the door behind him. *Well,* he thought, *here goes nothing.*

Dryx, barely able to see through his puffed-up and black eyes, moaned when he saw Cade enter. He couldn't take anymore; he slumped over in defeat, wishing death would find him before that female returned.

Weylor was completely unconscious. He, too, had badly bruised black eyes. His right cheek was raw where Tracey had mercilessly beat him. He sat slumped forward in his chair, only the rope held him up.

Cade looked at the sad sight in front of him and grimaced. The stinging pain of vomit found its way up his throat and onto his tongue, though he held back from throwing up.

Cade took out two small vials from a pouch on his belt and walked over to Weylor first. He popped the small cork off the vial and leaned Weylor's head back.

"What are you doing to him?" Dryx mumbled, forcing words slurring through fattened lips and exhaustion.

"It's a healing potion," he said as he held Weylor's nose closed and pour the potion into his mouth. Weylor was instantly awake and, with his nose held closed, he was forced to choke down the rest of the liquid. He felt better almost instantly. His energy and vitality returned, and enough of the swelling around his eyes went away for him to be able to see. Still, there was too much damage for the small potion to cure all of it, but he was awake enough.

As soon as the vial was empty he walked over to Dryx. "Open your mouth," he said.

"It's poison," he spit out the words with difficulty.

"No, it's not. Drink it, Dryx," Weylor said, his voice sounded almost as good as ever.

Dryx, still hesitant, tilted his head back and opened his mouth. Cade poured the contents of the potion into his mouth and stepped back.

Dryx instantly felt the effects of the potion; his swelling went down and most of the pain subsided; although, like Weylor, there was too much damage for the small potion to cure all of it.

"Why?" Weylor asked, looking up at Cade. He noticed that this rogue wore a different expression on his face, not one of anger or malice, but of grief and inner struggle.

"We must move very quickly," Cade said. "There isn't time for me to explain everything right now. I'm going to free you two, and you're going to take me with you back to Taris."

The twins, with no other options and no other hope of escape, nodded their agreement.

"If you attack me when I untie you, you will not leave this place. Even if you got by me, you would not make it out," Cade said, wanting to clear up any ideas the twins might have.

Magical rope would not break from being pulled on or from holding too much weight, but it was just as vulnerable to being cut as any other ordinary rope. Cade cut the rope the tied the twin's hands and feet and moved back to the door, still hesitant of an attack.

The twins stood up, rubbing their wrists and lightly rubbing their still aching heads.

"What do we do?" Dryx asked, ready to leave the place as fast as possible.

"Do exactly as I say," Cade replied. "Wait here."

Cade opened the door slowly, careful not to let the door squeak. He poked his head out and looked both ways down the hall; clear.

"Follow me, quickly," he told the twins and headed south down the hallway, away from the sleeping quarters and away from Marek's room.

Light shone in from an open door down the hall and Cade froze; other rogue's were returning.

There was nowhere to go; the next hallway was at the end, where the rogues were about to enter from and there were no exits between them and that hallway. Cade wouldn't turn back towards Marek's office.

"Keep your heads up, don't make eye contact," he said, then added in, "and try to act like rogues."

There was nothing else to do than hope that whoever was coming in hadn't heard about the twins yet.

Cade started walking again, the twins on his heels.

Two rogues entered the hallway; they seemed to be in disagreement about something. The rogue in front recognized Cade and nodded slightly. Cade nodded back and kept walking.

The twins kept their gaze forward as they passed the rogues in the tight hallway.

"Cade, who are they?" One of the rogues said. He had stopped and was turned around, facing the twins.

"New recruits," Cade said without hesitating. "I'm taking them out to see what they're made of."

The other rogue had also turned around and walked back to the other, now also curious about the two unfamiliar men with Cade.

"Is that so," one of them said, thinking hard about something, his gaze never leaving the twins.

Cade's nerves were about to break. His right hand had already drawn out a throwing dagger and his left was inching towards the main dagger on his belt.

Only seconds went by before he spoke again, but to Cade and the twins they seemed like hours.

"You should take them to the Old Trade Circle, a lot of merchants from Viltress there setting up shop since it's too packed out down the main street," he said.

"We'll see if they're up to it," Cade said, forcing a slight smile and a feint nod of his head.

With another short nod from the rogue, the two set off back down the way Cade and the twins had come.

Cade quietly breathed out a sigh of relief; the twins felt as though their hearts would pound right out of their chests.

Cade led the twins down the next hallway and up a ladder into an abandoned building. Once they were all inside and had closed the door, Cade motioned for them to be quiet and stay where they were. Cade knew that there was a guard posted at all times at all the entrances to the hideout. He thought about what day it was and who would be guarding the entrance to the building. *Finally,* he thought, *some luck.* A new rogue was on duty, Cade didn't know his real name but knew his nickname 'Dice'; he gambled on everything. He wasn't the brightest rogue in the guild, nor was he known for being the best at hiding. That wouldn't have mattered anyway; Cade knew where he would be.

Climbing up to the second floor, Cade carefully opened a window and vanished outside. It was still the early morning; the sun hadn't started its ascent in the sky yet. Cade welcomed the chill, cool breeze outside; it was the feeling of freedom.

He carefully made his way on the roof around to the east end of the building, staying in the shadows. When he made it to the lip of the roof, he looked down at the place where Dice normally hid disguised as a beggar. There was no one there. Growing anxious, Cade decided to get a closer inspection. He moved over to the corner of the roof and used the wall beams and boxes along the base of the building to get down, making no more noise than a fish swimming through water.

Staying in the shadows, Cade made his way over to Dice's hideout. He stopped for a moment to let his eyes adjust as much as possible to the darkness, then peaked around the corner. There was no one. Cade's heart began to race; where is he? Cade thought.

Just then, Cade heard footsteps behind him. Instinctively, Cade dropped down to a crouch, his daggers already in his hands. There, coming down the alleyway, was Dice. He didn't notice Cade as he passed the crouching figure only an arm's length away in the shadows.

As soon as Dice had passed, Cade rose up behind him and hit him in the back of his head with the hilt of his dagger as hard as he could. He quickly caught Dice's falling body and dragged it into the shadows. He looked around, waited a moment to make sure the coast was clear, and went to the door of the building the twins were still waiting in.

With quick, experienced fingers, Cade disarmed the few traps around the door and opened it. He stepped in and found the twins right we he had left them.

Cade hurried over and forced some small, wooden wedges in between the trap door and the sides, making it harder to open the door.

"That won't hold them for long," Cade said. "Hurry, let's go."

Chapter 21

A New Life

Marek, never one to be taken by surprise, barely made it out of the hideout when dozens of guards swarmed the place. Every rogue in the place was apprehended and everything was taken. Marek watched from the shadows a safe distance away, noting every rogue taken out in shackles. When the guards were finally done, Marek realized that Avery was nowhere to be seen and neither were Tracey and Cade, or the twins that they had kidnapped.

Anger and confusion welled up inside of Marek; his entire life's work, gone.

How did they find us? Marek thought. He watched the guards until they left, his rogues chained together, off to prison.

Avery, Marek thought. Like a shadow Marek was off to pay his new accomplice a visit. He realized that Avery would be waiting for him had he been the one to turn his back on the guild, but Marek could think of no one else capable of doing it. Avery was the newest member to the guild and, in Marek's mind, the most likely to turn away.

"Come in, Marek," Marek heard as he neared the door to Avery's house.

Cautiously, Marek opened the door to Avery's house. The outside of his house looked plain and normal, like every other house on the street, but inside the house seemed to have the splendor of a palace. Large, colorful tapestries and paintings lined the walls, thick carpets covered the floors and the finest furniture that Marek had ever seen filled the large greeting room.

Still hesitant, Marek took a step inside, his eyes searching quickly for traps.

"Don't be shy," Avery said, turning the corner with a tray of liquor and two cups.

"How did you know I was here," Marek asked, unsettled by being tracked so easily.

"I'm a wizard, Marek. I know everything that happens around my house," he said, waving one arm out towards all the fine things in his home. "It wasn't easy to come by all of this. To what do I owe the pleasure?"

Marek closed the door behind him. "You don't know?" Marek asked, he couldn't tell if Avery was lying, or bluffing, but he was a wizard, after all.

Avery's head tilted slightly to one side and puzzled look spread across his face; it had to be something important if Marek himself sought him out.

"The hideout's been ransacked; somebody talked," Marek said, eyeing Avery suspiciously; his right hand was gripping the handle of a dagger hidden up his sleeve.

Avery, confident that even if Marek attacked he would be sufficiently safe, set the tray down on the small table beside him and turned back to Marek.

"It wasn't me, Marek," Avery said in a calm tone, his eyes staring back at Marek's. "I wouldn't hang around so that you could pay me a visit."

Marek, as much as he wanted to snap his right arm forward and send his dagger into Marek's chest, believed him. Avery was, Marek knew, too smart to stick around and give an entire rogue guild the chance at revenge.

"I know where every rogue lives that wasn't in the hideout tonight. I want to know today who it was. Everything was taken, everything," Marek said, his voice turning angrier with each word.

Avery noticed the whiteness on Marek's knuckles as his fists clenched tighter and tighter.

"Tracey and Cade weren't taken, either," Marek added.

"I left when Tracey did, Marek," Avery said. "It wasn't her. She was with the twins for an hour and left with a broken noise and, no doubt, a few broken knuckles. She was angry, but I imagine it was at whichever twin it was that managed to somehow break her nose," he said, holding in a chuckle; it would do him no good to make light of the current situation.

"I watched Famir be taken, so that means…" Marek broke off mid-sentence. "No, it can't be, it doesn't make any sense," he said. "Cade freed them?" he asked out loud, "he has been in the guild almost ten years, he was one of the best. Why..?"

"I may be able to help," Avery said and went into one of his back rooms. He returned only a moment later with a large, glass ball.

A scrying ball, Marek realized. He had never seen one but he had heard about them from travelers from Viltress.

"I am not too familiar with Cade but if he is still in the city it shouldn't be too hard to find him," Avery said. He closed his eyes and thought of every detail he knew about Cade, every physical feature about him, even the way he moved and the sound of his voice.

Marek watched as a white mist began swirling around inside the globe.

Avery's eyes opened when he sensed a person close to his mental description and the mist in the globe dissipated to show a man surrounded by sailors on a ship. The view slowly turned, bringing the face of the man to appear in front of Avery and Marek.

"Cade," Marek said, though uncertain of what was going on.

Cade was disarmed and surrounded by sailors on the deck of a ship.

"What ship is that?" Marek asked Avery.

Avery closed his eyes again and focused mentally on the spell. The view in the globe slowly turned, giving Marek a clearer view of the ship. There, on the sail above the men, was the insignia of a woman standing on the waves of the sea.

"The Mistress," he said. "That's the twin's ship!" he said angrily.

Avery opened his eyes again and the view in the globe went back to Cade. Two more figures had appeared; the twins. Avery and Marek couldn't hear what was going on but they watched as one of the twins spoke and the sailors seemed to relax.

Marek, more angry and full of hate than he had ever been, couldn't speak. His eyes were reddening from the sudden surge of blood and emotion and his hands began to tremble. Without saying a word Marek got up and left.

Avery, too, realized that he couldn't stay in that house. If Cade was the traitor then the guard would know about everything, him included. With an annoyed yawn, Marek cast a few defensive spells on his house that would give him a brief head-start if his house was also raided and started to pack.

Not caring about staying hidden as he moved, Marek ran full out towards the southern end of the port. Curious glances followed him as he ran past groups of people down the streets towards the harbor. He only slowed as he reached the open harbor. He paused only a moment to catch his breath and walked, as casually as his surging energy allowed him, down one of the docks not far from the dock where The Mistress was. With most of the sailors around him focused on their own work, Marek watched The Mistress half-hidden behind a tall pile boxes and nets.

Two dozen sailors were on the deck alone, each one alert and engaged on what was happening. Marek noticed that a dozen city guards were at the base of the dock, guarding entrance to it, checking everyone who entered that part of the docks.

He watched as Captain Dante, along with another man and surrounded by guards, walked down the dock and board the ship. Captain Dantre shook hands with Cade and turned to speak a moment with the unfamiliar man that had accompanied him down the deck; when the captain and his guards disembarked the boat he realized that man must be the captain of The Mistress.

"Traitor," Marek mumbled angrily under his breath. He watched, helpless, as Cade sailed away. "Your day will come." Marek made his way back into the city; he had a lot of work to do.

Cade had a lot to think about; the only way he got out of going to prison, despite having rescued the twins, was to trade his freedom for information on the rogue guild. Captain Dantre made the deal with Cade, but only after he raided the supposed hideout and saw it with his own eyes. The captain had never even heard rumors of such a guild, but after finding the hideout and arresting almost a dozen rogues, he was convinced. According to Cade's information, though, Captain Dantre knew they hadn't captured the leader, Marek, or the wizard, Avery, along with about two dozen other rogues that weren't in the hideout.

Captain Terrell had Cade checked and relieved of all of his weapons; he wouldn't need them on the ship anyway. Cade wasn't shackled but he felt like he might as well have been; only the twins looked at him with thanks, the rest eyes him suspiciously and warily.

The twins, still exhausted from the night's ordeal, slept until the sun began to sink over the clear blue sky. The swaying of the ship on the sea didn't bother the twins at all; they fell asleep to the soft swaying of the cots soon after lying down.

Cade, though, could find no rest. His body was exhausted by the time the light of day began to fade; the rush of freeing the twins took its toll once the adrenaline wore off. But the constant fear of Marek's retribution kept him looking over his shoulder, always expecting to see another sail off in the distance. Captain Dantre had assured Cade that his guards would remain on the docks but Cade knew that if Marek really wanted to board a ship, he could.

He took a deep breath and decided that, if Marek was coming, he would enjoy the expedition across The Calm Sea like he had always dreamed. With his hands on the rails, Cade closed his eyes and exhaled deeply, taking in the cool breeze and salty air, basking in his freedom.

Cade's eyes shot open when he felt two people on either side of him.

"Calm down, it's us," Weylor said, looking at Cade.

Cade exhaled and dropped his head when he realized he had over reacted.

"We never got the chance to properly thank you," Dryx said. "I am Dryx and this is my brother, Weylor," he said, waving his hand toward Weylor.

Cade knew this conversation was unavoidable; he would much rather have disappeared after freeing them but, on a ship, that wasn't really possible. "Cade," he said and nodded.

"Why did you save us?" Weylor asked. The question had bothered both he and his brother and they were both too curious about it to let it go.

"I have been part of that guild for a long time," Cade began. "It used to be different; pick-pocketing and petty theft was all. Marek, the leader, changed that. He wanted to be bolder and change the guild into a force to be reckoned with." Cade paused for a moment before continuing, knowing that what he said next might change how the twins felt. "I was assigned to accompany the other rogues that kidnapped you," Cade looked up at Dryx as he spoke, guessing that Dryx would be the first to annoy. Dryx, though, just waited. "Avery, the wizard, cast a spell that silenced everything, that's why you didn't hear the window break. Famir used a poison to make sure you didn't wake up."

Both twin's hands went to their necks where they could still feel the slight bump where the darts had hit them.

"We brought you back and, well, you know the rest. When I saw Tracey, after she left your room, I realized what had happened; it was too much. Torture," Cade paused, "that's just too much. I couldn't be a part of it any longer. When she left I decided that my only way out were you two," he said.

Dryx's face stiffened and his expression turned angry when he heard Tracey's name.

"We are in your debt, Cade," Weylor said after a moment. "But," he began, another question coming to his mind, "why didn't you just leave?"

Cade looked up at Weylor, surprised that he could so quickly overlook his past of robbery and theft.

"Every day I would look out over The Calm Sea, wishing I could see what lies beyond. Life in the guild, life in Daley, grew monotonous and tedious. Surely there has to be something more out there than that kind of life," Cade said, now staring out over the sea, imagining what kinds of new adventures might possibly await him. "Marek will expand to Viltress; besides, a city of that size could only offer someone like me the same kind of life. Across the sea was the only way."

Dryx was still angry; he wouldn't oppose returning to Taris to hunt down that devil of a woman. But, he realized, he really did owe his life, and that of his brother, to Cade, who was also risking his own life.

"Well," Dryx started. Both Cade and Weylor were anxious to hear what Dryx would say. "There is a war coming to Taris. Dwarves have moved into the mountains and goblins are pouring out of them by the thousands," he said and looked at Cade, "you won't be able to find more adventure and excitement than that anywhere else right now."

Cade looked at him, surprised at the possibly-hinted invitation, then stared pensively out to see about staying in Taris and fighting; surely he would have plenty of opportunities to scout out and see more of the world like he always wanted.

Cade's heart raced at the possibility of actually reaching Taris and starting a new life, one full of adventure and freedom where he didn't have to live in fear or off of other people. He smiled at the thought and put his fear of Marek behind him; if he did come, Cade knew he wouldn't have to face him alone. In fact, Cade thought, Dryx would probably invite the opportunity to get back at Marek.

"Then I will stay and help in any way that I can," Cade replied. "No matter what happens, it will be better than what I am leaving behind."

Marek stayed on the docks until The Mistress was out of sight. He knew how easy it would be to stow-away, unknown, on any ship leaving for Taris, but his ultimate goal kept him there on the docks. He still had many rogues in Daley that had not been captured. It would take time and would be even more difficult now that Daley was searching for him and probably many of his rogues, but Marek was set on restoring his guild in the city.

Reluctantly, Marek made his way back into the city. It was no challenge for him to bypass the guards; he picked up a fishing pole, opened his cloaked to appear as nothing more than a fisherman, and walked right in between the group of guards at the dock's entrance.

He set off to find his rogues and rebuild his home; but Cade never left his mind.

Soon, Marek thought.

Chapter 22

Narz's Discovery

Narz, knowing that the king would be waiting for him and any news of the dwarves, had set out with only a small group; he took only the fastest runners with him. They found the closest raiding parties to Orgath and worked their way north, following the forest at the foot of the mountains.

None of the goblins had seen a single dwarf, or even any evidence of one.

Narz reached the furthest raiding party to the north and was met with the same news; no news of any dwarves.

"You're the last one?" Narz said to the orc leading the goblin band.

"Yes," the orc replied. "There was another, but we haven't heard from them in weeks."

"Did you send scouts? What happened!?" Narz said, annoyed at the orc's lack of knowledge.

"No, we've been busy with the humans," the orc said, not knowing what else say. He saw the anger in Narz's eyes and began to fear for his own life.

Not wanting to waste any time, though, Narz set off north to find out what had happened. It wasn't long before he and the other orcs with him had to retreat deeper into the forest to remain undetected. The further north they went, there were more human scouting parties making regular sweeps of the area.

Forced almost to the eastern edge of the forest, where the ground started sloping up towards the mountains, Narz and his small group of orcs managed to slip by the humans.

It wasn't hard, after a few days, to find the trail of the goblin scouting party. It was old, and unused, but still evident enough to follow. They found the rotting, burnt pile of goblin corpses but the bodies were too far rotted and burnt to make any marks that might hint to dwarven weapons.

"Over here," one of the orcs called out to Narz. He was bent over on the eastern edge of the camp examining the ground.

"What is it?" Narz said as he approached.

"The human came in from the west; these prints are on the wrong side and are not human. They are too big," the orc said, pointing out the width of the boot prints and how deep they went.

"Heavier, too," Narz said. "Is there a trail?"

"It's too old; I could only follow it a short way then it was lost," the orc replied.

Narz knew he could not return to Narz with only a boot print; he knew he had to either not mention it at all or stay until he found the answer.

"If these are dwarves, then they came from the mountains," Narz said, "and if they came from the mountains, there has to be a way up the mountains; a trail."

The other orcs looked around anxiously; none of them, not even Narz, were overly excited about looking for dwarves with such a small number. But each of them, especially Narz, knew the consequences would be worse should they return without having searched.

They set off towards the mountains and worked their way, slowly, back south. It wasn't long before one of the orcs found a small game trail leading up, appearing to lead into the mountains.

"Do we follow it?" the orc asked when Narz and the others neared.

Narz, not responding to the stupid question, set off down the trail at a quick pace; the sooner he knew what was going on the sooner he could return to Orgath.

They followed the game trail as it wound its way through the forest towards the mountains. They came to a small clearing, just before a particularly rocky section of the lower mountain.

Narz walked towards the mountain, until the grass stopped and the ground was just dirt and rocks.

"What do these look like to you?" Narz said, noticing some very subtle changes in the ground.

"I can't make out anything; they could be foot prints but they would be very old. There is no way of knowing if they are," the orc said; the same one that found the footprints before.

Narz found himself in an even worse situation than before; not only had he found what could be more foot prints, but this time he would have to journey up into the mountains on a very narrow trail where scouts could be hiding behind any rock and in any crevice.

"We wait until dark, and then we follow the trail," Narz said.

Night time came and the orcs, leaving their packs any everything else that might weigh them down behind, made their way up the trail. The trail was narrow and the orcs made slow progress. The moved slowly and stopped to listen for any kind of movement every few minutes. Nearing the top of the pass that their trail led to, Narz decided to stop the group and find a vantage point overlooking the pass. There weren't any good trees to climb; they were all too small and misshapen, often growing more horizontal than vertical.

Narz left the other orcs to hide along the trail as he left the trial and made his way up the steepest part of the mountain, very slowly. It wasn't long before his eyes, more accustomed to the lightless underdark, found hints of light off in the distance down the trail; probably torches or small camp fires, he thought. He was too far away to make out any shapes until something moved in front of the fire. The figure, for a moment, completely blocked the light of the fire and the light behind the figure made a nice outline of a short, plump, thing. Narz, positive that it was not a human, knew that the short figure must be a dwarf; he had never heard of anything else being so short and wide.

Narz was excited at first; almost too excited. *I have found them!* he thought. His smile quickly faded, though, when he remembered that dwarves were especially fond of traps designed specifically for goblins and orcs, and that he was a few hours travel up their trail.

Moving even slower than before, and double-checking each foot fall, he returned to his group. The fear on his face was evidence enough that he had found them and the orcs descended down the trail as fast as they dared; they were in a full-out sprint by the time they reached the bottom. The only rest they found that night was the minute it took them to find and retrieve their packs left at the base of the mountains.

Narz didn't stop until they reached the raiding party to the south, but even that rest was short lived; nightmares of an army of dwarves falling upon Narz and his group wouldn't let him sleep for long.

Narz was up and headed south before the sun came up. For almost an entire week, Narz kept the same, fast pace. He only allowed them to stop when exhaustion took over and they couldn't run anymore.

Still exhausted, Narz brought the news to King Chorzak.

"What did you find?" King Chorzak demanded, wanting only the important details and nothing more.

"We found the dwarves. We followed a trail leading up into the mountains and found them high up," Narz said. "It's north, almost to the sea."

King Chorzak screamed as his hands flew high into the air and crashed down onto the table in front of him. He hated dwarves; he had fought them before in the underdark. They were about as hard to kill as a giant, but even worse than that were their traps, Chorzak thought.

With a wave of his hand he sent Narz away. Chorzak decided to rest for the night to have a clear mind to plan for the dwarves.

King Chorzak had barely laid his head down to sleep before the mental calling of his master found its way into his thoughts.

The king, not bothering with his armor or weapons, made his way up the narrow trail that led to an empty cave that his master had designated.

"It is time," was the first thing that King Chorzak heard entering the cave. "Pull back your raiding parties and send them south to the woods. I assume all of the supplies are ready?" the voice asked.

"Yes, master. We have everything we need to cut down the trees and make the ships, " Chorzak replied.

"Good, good," the voice said, pleased.

"The scout has returned that I sent out looking for the dwarves. He found a trail leading up into the mountains in the north, close to the sea, and found them high up," Chorzak said.

There was silence for a long moment before Chorzak's master spoke.

"It is too late to change our plans now. I will see to the dwarves," the voice said.

King Chorzak, never knowing if his master who was always in the darkness had left or was still there, waited. After a long silence he left the cave and returned to his quarters in the biggest building in all of Orgath.

Despite the news of the dwarves, an evil smile found its way onto Chorzak's face. Tomorrow he would give the orders he had been waiting so long to give.

By noon the next day Orgath seemed empty and deserted, except for a few dozen goblins left to keep and maintain the place. Thousands of goblins had poured out of the mountain city down south into the plains and towards Long Leaf Forest.

The giant mass of goblins followed the forest west and then south, to the river. There they made camp and began cutting down every tree in the forest. The humans had no outposts or farms so far south, so threat of an attack was minimal. Large buildings were constructed on the bank of the river where the goblins began building their ships.

From deeper inside the forest stood slender figures watching the progress of the goblins. They retreated back with the ever-expanding deforestation and kept in the thick foliage to not be seen. Hundreds had gathered with the passing days, ever staying out of sight in the dense forest. The thousands of goblins had stirred up everything in the forest, causing all its natural inhabitants to seek shelter further in.

"Do we attack?" One of the slender figures asked the figure next to him.

"No," the figure replied. "We will not involve ourselves in the affairs of the humans. We will keep ourselves a secret. Their fate is their own."

With a single wave of his arm, the elves retreated into the forest, leaving no evidence that they had ever passed that way.

One elf, though, stayed behind to watch. He was not left as a spy, or a scout, but stayed out of curiosity. It was not curiosity about the creatures chopping down the forest; he had a natural hatred for the wretched things. It was a curiosity of the events transpiring, the thought-provoking, unknown events that had led to this war between the humans and goblins, and the future outcome. He wanted to witness all of it, unlike the rest of his kin who were content to remain undiscovered in the heart of their beloved forest.

King Bourndrimiur made his way down the long, steep tunnel that led to the sea cave, along with a handful of guards. It had become almost a daily venture; the king had gained a taste for the huge fish that made the large cave-pond their home. The tunnel had been widened and smoothened to allow for easier access, and steps were being carved out from the bottom up.

The opening of the tunnel into the cave created a current of fresh, cool, salty air up into the tunnel and the kingdom beyond.

The king reached the large cave entrance and inhaled deeply.

"Ahh," he said, breathing in heavily.

He wound his way through the long tunnel that led to the large, open chamber, the sound of the waterfall again filling his head.

The large had changed some; more torches had been placed in the room, lighting it up considerably and a path of stone had been laid, leading right up to the pond.

Bornar, the dwarf who found the cave and the king's best mining leader, had been assigned to the cave with a dozen other dwarves.

"Me king," Bornar said, bowing as King Bourndrimiur approached.

"Tell me there's still fish for catchin' in the pond, Bornar," the king said with a chuckle, a slight smile on his face. That was a rare sight; before finding the cave and the pond of fish, the king had had no reason to smile in years. It seemed to most of the dwarves that the taste of fish and the fresh air relieved the king of his stress, which was good news for everyone.

"Aye," Bornar replied with a smile, pointing a finger to a row of large fish on a nearby table.

"Well," the king said, "what're we waiting for?"

Bornar motioned to one of the dwarves next to him to start cooking the fish. It wasn't long before the king and the other dwarves were eating the huge fish.

"Does this pond lead into the sea?" the king asked Bornar.

"I'm not sure," Bornar answered, confused.

"What if we eat all the fish in the pond? Can more come in?" the king asked, a little concerned at the thought of not having any more fish to eat.

"Good point," Bornar said, now staring at the area where the waterfall met the water. "I guess there's only one way to find out," he said and undressed down to his undergarments.

"Can you swim?" the king asked, anxious to see Bornar swim. He smiled at the thought.

"Here," Bornar said, throwing one end of the rope to a nearby dwarf and tying the other end around himself. "Just in case," he said, a slightly worried look crossing his face.

Now all the dwarves around him burst into laughter at the sight; a near-naked dwarf about to jump into water without knowing if he could swim, and a rope tied around him 'just in case'.

By the time Bornar placed his first foot in the water every dwarf in the cave had come to watch.

Step by step he waded out into the pond.

"Ahh!" he screamed. "Somethin' just nibbled at me toes!"

"Well boys," the king said, "looks like we found ourselves some fish bait!"

Bornar, annoyed by both the laughter behind him and at his own over-reaction to the fish, mumbled under his breath and continued out into the pond.

He was soon on his toes, his mouth barely above water. With his heart pounding, he pushed off with one foot and the floor sank away deeper below him. On pure instinct, Bornar kicked his feet and waved his arms up and down; his head stayed above water!

"I guess he can swim," one of the dwarves watching said, a little put out at Bornar's success; it almost seemed anti-climactic with all of their joking and laughing before.

Taking a minute to make sure he could stay afloat, Bornar tilted his body forward and began swimming forward. He stopped just before the waterfall and looked back; it was so loud that close to the waterfall that he couldn't hear what the dwarves were yelling but it was obvious that they wanted him to continue.

Not wanting to get pounded by the heavy water falling down in front of him, Bornar took a deep breath and swam under the waterfall. He didn't have to go far before the light from outside lit up the water around him and he could see that the sea was deep under the waterfall.

He decided to swim out further, to the other side of the waterfall, and get a view from the outside world. He was blinded, temporarily, by the bright sunshine, but he soon saw the waterfall and surrounding landscape around the entrance.

The entire face of the mountain that bordered the sea was a high cliff. Huge rocks jutted out from the water around entrance; they seemed to keep most of the big waves from crashing against the cliff walls around the entrance to the cave.

Bornar swam over to a nearby rock and climbed up onto it. The cliff ran only a short way to the east before cutting south and out of sight. The cliff to the west continued for what Bornar thought was a few miles before sloping down to sea level. Far in the distance to the east there was a narrow valley cutting straight into the mountains heavily forested. The coast to the east, from the mountains north, was green as far as Bornar could see.

Now turning around to see the open sea, Bornar saw exactly that; just open sea. The sun was high and a cool, sea breeze wafted in from the north. With not a cloud in the sky, Bornar stood in awe. He stood there, perched on a rock, staring out of the vast expanse before jumping back in and swimming back into the cave, again going under the waterfall.

Bornar was breathing heavily by the time he pulled himself out of the water at the king's feet.

"Well, what's out there?" The king asked, excitedly.

Still catching his breath, Bornar held up a finger to the king and smiled.

"Me king," he said, still breathing heavily. "The entrance is deep. It's a cliff and leads straight into the sea. It's just open water."

The king stood thinking for a moment. An idea crossed his mind; trade with the humans seemed difficult, with the mountain path being so narrow and steep at parts, he knew wagons wouldn't be able to make it. The king tilted his head slightly to one side as he mentally measured the height and width of the waterfall.

"Is it big enough for a ship?" the king asked.

"Uh," Bornar thought, "I think so. It's deep enough. There are some rocks near the entrance but a ship might be able to make it through."

The king turned to one of the guards that had accompanied him down into the cave, "find Danflorf. Tell him to get a group ready to visit the humans."

With a bow the dwarf was off, back down the cave and up the tunnel to find the king's son.

"Looks like we're going to need to remodel a bit, Bornar," the king said with his hands on his hips. "I'll send down another group to help."

"Aye," Bornar said, standing up with a smile to match the king's.

The king and his guards left the cave to Bornar and his men.

"Well," Bornar said to the men left standing around him. "We have a port to make, what are you all standing around for?!" Bornar's excitement quickly spread to everyone in the cave; a hidden port inside their own cave was exciting news to the dwarves who had never been on a ship before.

Chapter 23

Cade's Trial

Despite feeling like a prisoner on The Mistress, Cade made the most of their time on The Calm Sea; he above on the deck as much as he was able to, gazing out over the seemingly endless sea and breathing in his new found freedom. He figured that even if he had been shackled, it would not have been enough to deter him from enjoying the spray of the sea, the salty, cool breeze or the large fish and huge sharks that often accompanied the boat just under the surface of the water.

For hours he would stare out into the open ocean, forcing himself to untie the mental bonds that were holding him with fear of his past, fear of retribution from his rogue guild. He watched the clouds and how they would turn from snow white to a dark, menacing shade of black in a matter of minutes. Even the small storms The Mistress had to sail through on the way back seemed to call to Cade; being extremely agile, Cade climbed up the front mast to feel the strength of the wind blow across his body. He closed his eyes and he felt as though he was passing from the physical to some superior state of being, the strength and power of the wind taking his mind to a different place entirely.

He had yearned for this freedom for so long that even the to and fro motion of the ship seemed only to add to and heighten his experience, making the reality of his departure from Daley that much more real.

Dryx and Weylor passed the better part of most days recuperating in their cots below deck. They were more familiar with the movement of the ship while sailing and didn't seem to mind so much anymore.

Despite the healing potions that they had taken when Cade freed them, their wounds still took most of their energy to heal. The swelling subsided as the days past on the sea but the discoloration of their welts and bruises were taking more time.

Dryx, especially, could hardly stand being so tired all the time and spending so much of the day swaying in a cot; he felt as though he would lose his edge from the lack of practice and training.

Weylor, unlike Dryx, didn't mind so much the time spent in his cot; it gave him time to look back on his kidnapping and set in his mind how the world was outside of Taris. Every defensive spell that could have helped their situation in the inn went through his mind; but the fact that there had been no sense of danger made Weylor, in the moment, feel no need to use them.

It was a good thing, Weylor thought, that they had lived through their kidnapping in Daley; never again would they let their guard down, even when all seems well and there is no apparent danger.

He spent hours and hours going through his personal spell book and devising new ways of protecting his brother and himself in all kinds of situations. It wouldn't happen again, Weylor was confident.

Cade returned to his cot, next to the twins, one night after spending most of the day above deck.

"How can you spend so much time just staring out over the sea?" Dryx asked, his patience gone. He hated how bored he was and that Cade seemed perfectly entertained at the mere sight of the open sea.

"I have been dreaming of this freedom for a long time," Cade said, feeling a little more comfortable around the twins he had kidnapped only days before. "Almost every night I would climb to the top of a building near the port and stare out of the water, wishing I could just leave and explore what might be on the other side."

Dryx, now understanding Cade's reasons, relaxed. He understood how Cade felt; his entire life growing up Taris, in the Fighter's School, he had dreamt of the day when he would be able to leave in a scouting party to hunt the goblins that threatened his home and that had killed his father. He remembered the day he and Weylor had been assigned to the Silver Dragon's scouting party and how he felt finally leaving Taris behind.

Weylor watched as Dryx relaxed in his cot, caught up in his own thoughts of freedom and remembering when he felt as Cade did now. "Well, Cade, there is a chance that our king will allow you to stay with us," Weylor said. "We have traveled to the dwarven kingdom of Icedome and down through the mountains to witness the goblin city of Orgath. We have ambushed goblins and now, we have been kidnapped," he said with a laugh. Weylor truly believed that he and his brother were now better off than before having gone through that experience.

"How can you forgive and trust me so openly?" Cade asked, feeling even more ashamed than ever at how he had lived in Daley. The twins were showing cade characteristics he had not seen in his rogue guild in Daley; compassion and forgiveness.

"You saved our lives and put your own life at risk doing it," Dryx said, sitting up in his cot. "We have seen men die putting their own lives at risk for others; it takes something more than what an ordinary person has."

Weylor, keeping his smile to himself, was surprised at how open Dryx had become. Weylor had never known another person that Dryx had opened up to besides himself. Cade didn't know that, Weylor knew, but he thought Dryx must be excited to have someone else to accompany them on their adventures, someone he could learn from and better his own skills.

Cade didn't respond to Dryx's compliment; he just lay back in his cot to try and understand if someone could really be so forgiving. Cade's future was beginning to look far brighter than he had ever imagined and he wanted to enjoy the feeling while it lasted.

"Land!" a sailor yelled from the crow's nest at the top of the front mast. He spotted the high light of the tower on the steep hill in Taris.

Cade and the twins made their way to the bow of the boat; the light was a welcome sight in the darkness. It wasn't long before the torches lining the docks were seen off in the distance, marking the base of the cliff that formed Taris' northern border with the sea.

"Cade," came the voice of the captain from behind them.

Cade turned around to see the captain, flanked by two of his sailors, standing just behind them, holding shackles.

Cade took a deep breath and exhaled, walking forward with his wrists out.

"It's only procedure," Captain Terrell said, looking apologetic while he clasped the shackles around Cade's wrists. "You are not under arrest but you will have to spend the night in a jail cell. Tomorrow you will face trial and the king and his court will decide what to do."

Cade, for some reason that he didn't yet understand, was more willing to take responsibility for his own actions than ever before. He did not hesitate or flinch when the shackles closed around his wrists. "Yes, Captain. I understand," was all he responded.

He stared at the ground as he was led off the ship and up the steps to Taris; he was thinking harder than he had ever thought about this new feeling he felt that gave him courage to face the consequences of his actions. Perhaps it was because, despite being in shackles, he still felt the thrill of freedom and of being in Taris, or maybe it was that Dryx's words had sunk deeper than he thought. Either way, Cade was willing to hold his head up when he faced the king and his council. It was now his responsibility to accept, without bitterness towards anyone but himself, whatever judgments they would see fit to pass.

The twins were taken to the temple of Valerum by Captain Terrell himself. He knew the twins had been through enough and wanted to make sure they got the help they needed.

The twins were led into the temple and guards were sent out to bring back two of the more experienced clerics and the twin's mother.

Captain Terrell waited in the entrance chamber with Deli as the clerics worked over the twins; their wounds were not serious, mostly superficial, but the clerics did as much as they could nonetheless.

As soon as Deli heard that her sons had been kidnapped and tortured she ran to their rooms; only when she saw them well and with only bruising left to show from their ordeal, did she follow Captain Terrell back to the benches where he explained what had happened and how they had been saved.

Deli, once the captain retired, spent the rest of the night sitting on a chair in the corner of the room where the twins slept peacefully. The clerics and administered a stronger healing potion and had covered the twin's wounds in a special ointment; by morning the swelling would be gone along with the bruising and discoloration.

The next morning the twins awoke to find their mother asleep in the corner. They both sighed and hung their heads, knowing how much she must have worried during the night.

"Mother," Weylor said in a low, calm voice.

Deli stirred at the sound, her eyes slowly opening; she had found very little sleep that night.

"My boys!" she said, tears instantly coming to her eyes.

The twins walked over to her and she stood up, embracing both of them. She had felt that same fear only once before, when she had watched her sons the night before. A decade before, just before Alruin had faded into the darkness, he had looked back and met Deli's eyes; she knew, in that moment, she would never see him again and it was that same fear that had kept her up the night before worrying over her sons.

"I was so worried," she said, her voice breaking and the twins could feel her slight sobs as she hugged them.

"We are okay, mother," Weylor said in a soft voice, trying to comfort his mother.

"See," Dryx said; his voice just as soft as Weylor's but also trying to lighten the mood. "Even the bruising is already gone. We are good as new," he smiled.

Captain Terrell was just outside the room and waited for the twins to calm their mother down before he entered.

"I have spoken with Captain Strongshield, Cade's trial will be this morning," he said to the twins.

"We wish to accompany him," Dryx said, looking straight at Captain Terrell.

"I thought as much. Come, I will take you to the keep," he said and waited for them. "You can sit with me, Deli, if you wish?" he asked, knowing Deli wouldn't want to return home so quickly after seeing her sons.

"Yes, thank you," Deli said appreciatively, and followed the captain and her sons to the keep.

Cade was in shackles and seated in front of a long table in one of the bigger rooms of the keep. The table had not yet filled with the king and his council.

"You can sit in the seats behind Cade," Captain Terrell said to the twins before leading Deli to one of the rows further back.

The twins made their way to Cade and each placed a hand on his shoulder before sitting down.

He looked back and smiled when he saw the twins behind him. He had hoped that they would join him but he had not allowed himself to expect as much. "Thank you," he said, his head turned back to the twins.

"You saved our life, we are here now to help save yours," Weylor said, happy that he was able to help Cade and repay the debt he felt.

It wasn't long before the king and his council entered the room and filled the seats at the table.

Captain Strongshield was the first to speak. "We have been informed that Cade, seated before us, had a hand in Dryx and Weylor Stormcaller's kidnapping in Daley. He is part of a guild of rogues in Daley that have been working in Daley, we found out, for many years. The twins were tortured and Captain Terrell, himself, saw the damage that was done. Cade," he said, turning from the council to Cade seated in the chair before him. "Do you deny any of these claims?"

Cade, still determined to accept whatever may come, held his head up and answered, "No, Captain. I am guilty of all of those charges." His heart raced with his voiced confession of what happened; it was a very unfamiliar feeling, but it somehow brought a smile to his face.

Captain Strongshield waited for a moment before continuing; he had expected the rogue to answer very differently and now decided to bring to light to the council the rest of the story.

"Now, Captain Terrell also informed me that Cade is the one who, at risk of his own life, freed Dryx and Weylor from the guild's secret hideout and returned them to Captain Terrell. The twins informed the captain that Cade had administered potions of healing to them and led them from the hideout. He had no hand in their torture and agreed peacefully to be shackled and judged. Cade," he said, once again turning to Cade, "do you deny any of this."

Cade stared at the captain for what seemed like, to him, a long time before speaking. "I accept whatever judgment is to be placed upon me. Yes," he continued, "I freed Dryx and Weylor from our secret hideout and traded information to the Daley Guard in exchange to leave with Captain Terrell."

The king's interest was now peaked. He, himself, was as honest as men come and knew there had to be something more to the story. He motioned for the captain to be seated and stood himself. "Why did you save them? And why did you trade the information to be able to leave with Captain Terrell?" the king asked Cade.

Cade hadn't expected to answer those questions in his hearing. "I have longed to leave the guild and Daley for a long time. I have always wanted to travel across The Calm Sea and see what more the world could hold. Trading the information to leave with Captain Terrell was the only way to achieve what I have always dreamed of and," he said, cutting off his sentence. He suddenly wished he hadn't said 'and'; they would want to know what else.

"And?" the king asked in a curious tone.

"I knew that if I stayed in Daley I would be killed," he said straightforward. It should be obvious even to them, Cade thought, that his guild of rogues would want him dead after betraying them.

The king and his council all were silent as they thought about Cade's answers.

"And what about you, Dryx and Weylor, what do you think?" the king asked the twins.

Weylor and Dryx both stood up to support Cade.

"King Ironwill," Weylor began, "we feel indebted to Cade for saving our lives. The other rogues would surely have tortured us to death. He freed us and we have not seen any hesitance from Cade in leaving his old lifestyle." He looked to Dryx, who nodded, then turned back and continued. "We would ask, if Cade is released, for permission that he be assigned to us until we can repay our debt."

The king hid his smile. He understood that the twins would have the best judgment about Cade after spending the voyage back to Taris with him. More than anything Captain Strongshield had said, King Ironwill wanted to know what the twins would have done with Cade. They had exceeded the king's expectations in all of their missions, from leading the dwarves to meet the king to returning with the dwarves to Icedome and solidifying their alliance with them and gaining King Bourndrimiur's confidence and trust.

The king and his council talked amongst themselves for many minutes, yet the twins noticed that Cade, although resigned, was not scared. They saw in his face that he would accept whatever consequence was necessary for his actions. When the twins saw this, they knew they would not be able to leave with a clear conscious if Cade was sentenced to jail.

"Cade," Captain Strongshield said, standing up. "You are hereby sentenced, by order of the king, to serve Taris as a bodyguard to the scouts, Dryx and Weylor Stormcaller, until they see fit that all debt has been repaid."

Cade's eyes widened and his heart raced; he couldn't believe what he heard.

The twins smiled and patted Cade on the shoulders from behind; they were as excited as he was that he was free and could leave with them to a world filled with adventure and surprise.

"Thank you, thank you," Cade said, standing up and bowing to the king and his council. He now felt yet another new feeling that he was unaccustomed to; gratitude. He couldn't believe that the council had been so understanding and forgiving and that they would trust him with the twins.

Then and there Cade vowed to himself that he would never again live as he did before, but would strive to uphold his new responsibility and give meaning to his life.

A guard walked over and took off the shackles from Cade's hands. "Your belongings are waiting in the outer chamber," the guard said.

Cade turned around to face the twins; they were looking at him, smiling. "I cannot thank you enough," he said, "I will always be indebted to you."

"No," Dryx said, "we are indebted to you. Now," he smiled, looking from Weylor back to Cade, "how about we go see where we are off to next?"

Cade, with as big a smile as he had ever had, nodded his agreement and followed the twins from the keep.

Chapter 24

The Bridge to Viltress

The king's council gave the twins a week off of duty to rest and recover. The twins were glad for the brief reprieve, though they had felt almost completely healed when the awoke in the temple the morning of Cade's trial; the cleric's prayers and potions had worked to restore them to full health.

It didn't take more than an hour for the twins and Cade to visit and see every inch of the city inside the walls. Cade had always known that Taris was, by far, a much smaller city, but he was truly amazed at how small the city actually was compared to Daley. *There was nowhere to hide, nowhere to have any sort of secret guild and really,* he thought, *no one to rob.*

Cade enjoyed it, though. The newness and difference of Taris only added to his overall experience of finally traveling to a new land and seeking new and exciting adventures. Being able to stay with the twins, Cade was hopeful that he would soon be able to visit the whole kingdom of Taris; to travel from its western border to its eastern and everywhere in between.

The twins told Cade of the land roundabout that was mostly used for farming and ranching, of their old home of Halsgrove, now New Halsgrove, and of Gander's Forest with The Giant's Steppes behind them. More than anywhere he had heard of, Cade wanted to visit Icedome and see the dwarves and the splendor of their kingdom inside a mountain.

Looking out over the top of the Taris' walls, Cade had replaced his fear with excitement and hope at the promise of adventure and a better life.

Once again, the high tower, the Mage Tower, that marked the eastern border of the city of Taris, came into view. Danflorf, once again accompanied by a dozen bodyguards, sat on the front of a wagon beside a guard from New Halsgrove who drove it.

"Finally," Danflorf said with a sigh, letting out all of the anticipation that had been built up over the slow journey to Taris in the wagon. He rubbed his hands together and smiled, patting the guard on the back. "Exciting news we have for yer king!" he told the guard excitedly.

The guard, who felt as though the dwarf's pats were more like giant hammers hitting him in the back, smiled back as big as he could to calm the dwarf down; he could do without the dwarf knocking the air out of him.

"What's the news?" the guard asked.

"Uh," Danflorf said, a little hesitant, "ah what'll it matter; we found a cave at the base of our home that leads into the sea, it may be big enough for a ship to get in!"

The guard was more than a little confused at why that should seem so exciting to the dwarf; it was a cave big enough for a ship, the guard thought, what's so exciting? He didn't voice his opinion, of course; if the pats from the dwarf could knock the air out of him so easy, he didn't want to find out what a real hit could do to him.

Once again a rider had been sent ahead of the dwarves to give the king word of their coming. The wagon slowed before the walls of Taris and the huge doors were opened, allowing them to enter.

A guard inside the gate notified the wagon drivers to head straight for the keep; the king would see them that same evening.

The dwarves, feeling more comfortable in the presence of so many humans, didn't hesitate to leave their weapons with the guards in the entrance chamber of the keep and follow Danflorf into the large room beyond, where tables and food had been prepared for the dwarven guests.

The king, after the dwarves had left after their first arrival, had sent a messenger over to the inn to find out what the dwarves preferred for food and drink. He thought it a small cost to prepare such a great feast for his new allies when there was so much potential in store with them; both in trade and in defense of the kingdom in their new alliance.

Not a single dwarf could hold back his smile when they entered the long, spacious room to find all of their favorite food and drink that they didn't have in Icedome. Two hours passed and the dwarves never noticed the time; they ate and ate and ate, and drank just as much! The variety and exquisite new flavors and tastes, at least to the dwarves, had them stuffing their stomachs as far as they would stretch, and then some.

Feeling as comfortable as they had ever been, the dwarves passed their time eating with each telling stories of battle and experiences they had each had, both funny and serious. They talked of the minerals in their mountain, new discoveries in their constantly growing network of tunnels, of the rumors that they would be able to fight the goblins alongside the humans; something not a single dwarf in Icedome didn't desire.

"My friends," King Ironwill said with smile, entering the room where the dwarves were. "I hope the food is to your liking," he said, hoping that his cooks had prepared the right meals that the messenger had told them.

"The finest food I have ever eaten, King Ironwill," Danflorf said, scooting out his chair and bending into a bow; he popped straight back up, though. Bending forward had put too much pressure on his already tight stomach and he had to straighten out to keep from puking.

"A good sign," King Ironwill said, laughing at the sight of the near-to-bursting dwarf. "The road from Icedome to Taris is a long one; I imagine you wish to rest before you share whatever message you have for us?" the king asked.

"Thank you, King Ironwill, but if it's all the same to you, I've been waiting almost a week and I think it's news you'll want to hear," Danflorf said, his excited smile returning to his face.

"Very well," he said to Danflorf, nodding his head in respect to the dwarven prince. "Guards," he called.

The two guards at the door ran over in front of the king and bowed, "Yes, King Ironwill?" one of them replied.

"Show our guests to the meeting room when they are ready," the king said.

The king didn't have to wait long before Danflorf was led into the meeting where he and some of his council members sat talking.

The king, along with everyone else, stood up and nodded their heads in respect to the prince as he took a seat by King Ironwill.

Danflorf knew this was a sign of respect but he wished everyone would treat him like an equal and not like a prince; although being a prince had, at times, come in handy to young dwarf.

"There is no way for us," Danflorf started out, not wasting any time, "to make a decent trail through the mountains from the forest to Icedome for trade. Me father also doesn't want to pave the way for any potential enemies."

The king and the other men all looked disappointed but Danflorf knew, from his previous conversations with the king, that he would not try to push the dwarves to try; the king valued their alliance for more than just trade.

"But," Danflorf continued, "We might have found another way!" That big smile on Danflorf's face catching the full attention of everyone around him. "Do you have a map of the sea along the mountains?"

"Tornelius?" the king asked the wizard next to him.

Tornelius was old by Taris' standards; his beard was full and gray and matched the long hair hanging down from his head. He looked frail but moved as if his body was new. His eyes were the color hazel and his skin was smooth.

Reaching into one of the many folds in his robes, Tornelius produced a map and spread it out on the table in front of the dwarf.

Danflorf stood up and found where the waterfall would be from outside the cave. "Here," he said, making a small dot with a quill on the map, marking the location of the entrance.

"And what is there?" Tornelius asked, his curiosity peaked by the random spot the dwarf had chosen to put a dot on his map.

"That is where we will be able to trade. We found a cave at the base of our mountain and it led to the sea. It's hidden by a waterfall but we reckon that a ship can make it past the rocks and through the waterfall," Danflorf said. "We've already started constructing a dock inside."

King Ironwill stared for a long moment at the map. "This does sound good, but," he started saying, but an obvious flaw in the logic of it came to the king's mind, "do you have a ship? Or know how to sail one?" the king asked.

"Eh," Danflorf said. The excitement of the potential trade route had blinded the dwarves to the most obvious obstacle in their way: their ability to sail.

"King Ironwill," Jaspe, one of the council members, said, and idea coming to him. "We could teach them, couldn't we? We could take them the supplies needed and some of our blacksmiths could go work with them," he said.

Jaspe was a short, stalky man whose skin was dark from being on the docks all day. He oversaw all the trade into and from Taris and managed Taris' small fleet of fishing boats and merchant ships.

The king looked from Jaspe to Danflorf, a sign for Danflorf to answer the inquiry.

Smiling once again, Danflorf nodded his agreement. "Aye," he said, "we can return with you by sea, if you have a ship that can take us?"

"That can be arranged," King Ironwill replied, his hopes now higher than ever. Trade would be quicker and more effective by ship and King Bourndrimiur would be able to keep the mountain trail secret. "Tornelius, I want you to accompany the ship. Find the best captain in port and leave when our guests are ready," he said to the wizard, who looked more than happy to get a chance to see the great dwarven kingdom of Icedome.

"Of course, my king," Tornelius said, standing up and excusing himself with a smile and a nod.

A guard entered the meeting room as Tornelius left. He stopped midway across the room to wait for the king to wave him forward.

King Ironwill noticed the guard and waved him towards him. The guard looked scared and anxious.

"King Ironwill," the guard whispered into the king's ear, "the bridge to Viltress has been taken."

The king's eyes shot open at the news. "Quickly, a map of the western kingdom," he said, his voice anxious. "The bridge over the river to Viltress has been taken."

All the council members straightened in their chairs, their eyes wide. One of them opened up a map of the kingdom between Taris and Viltress on the table.

"How did the goblins make it to the bridge without us knowing?" the king asked Captain Strongshield.

"I do not know. We have several outposts and scouting parties to the south; they would not have gotten through them unknown," the captain replied.

"If they have taken the bridge, then," the king's words cut out as he realized the truth to their situation. "War is coming," he said, looking around to the other council members. "Captain

Strongshield, we need to take back that bridge; if they destroy it, Viltress is cut off."

"I will lead the attack myself, King Ironwill," he said and turned to the guard that had brought the news, "how many?"

"At least a hundred, Captain. They came in ships on the river from the south; we were taken by surprise; I barely made it out alive," the guard said, his fear evidenced by his shaky voice.

"Ships?" the kings asked, truly confused.

"Yes, my lord, from the river down south; dozens of ships," the guard replied.

"Captain, take all the men that we can spare from Taris; if that bridge is destroyed, Viltress will be cut off," he said to Captain Strongshield.

"Right away," Captain Strongshield said and left the room.

"Danflorf," the king said, turning to the quiet dwarf, "I will make sure that you and your men return to Icedome on the first available ship."

"And leave when there goblins to kill?" Danflorf asked in return; Danflorf could think of no better way to return to Icedome than having bloodied his axe a few times with filthy goblin blood. "We will go with your men to the bridge, King Ironwill, and help take care of your pest invasion."

If Taris' only bridge to Viltress wasn't at stake, King Ironwill might have tried to convince the dwarven prince against going, but Taris would need Viltress' help when it came time for war.

"We thank you, Danflorf, you and your men. I will have some wagons prepared for you and your men; you will leave at first light," the king said.

Danflorf smiled; although he was still fairly young by dwarven standards, he had been fighting goblins since his ancient home in the underdark and would not miss an opportunity to split a few goblin skulls if he was able to.

"What about the twins?" Danflorf asked. Danflorf had grown fond of the twins and their young spirits, so akin to his own. He knew that Taffer, also, would want to know about the twins; he had spent the most time with the twins out of all the dwarves.

"They recently returned from Daley and are still here in the city. If they are well, I doubt they would miss this opportunity," the king replied.

With a short bow to the king, Danflorf left the room to inform his party.

"Those boys," the king said to the remaining council members still seated around him, "have insured our alliance with the dwarves."

"I will send out my fastest ships to Daley and Viltress. If the bridge is destroyed, it will take Viltress time to organize its men into ships and sail here," Jaspe told the king.

King Ironwill understood the implications of losing the bridge; Viltress would not be able to send enough help in time by sea when the war started. He nodded to Jaspe his agreement.

Word spread quickly throughout the town of the attack on the bridge to Viltress. Guards were sent out to every scouting and war party in the kingdom to find out what had happened. The watch on top of the walls of Taris doubled and the stream of merchants stopped overnight.

Cade and the twins had taken to practicing and dueling in the Fighters School to pass the time. Cade and Dryx could duel for hours a day, each one gaining and losing the advantage to the other through their matches.

Weylor's thoughts were still on the night that he and his brother were kidnapped. While Cade and his brother dueled and practiced their melee combat, Weylor hovered over the many thick volumes of spells and enchantments that were available to him in the Mage's Tower. He studied and practiced the spells until they were as familiar to him as breathing. He copied dozens of spells into his own spell book, which, thanks to a minor magical enchantment, stayed relatively thin and light compared to the ever increasing number of pages in it.

Weylor found one particularly interesting spell that he had never practiced before; a spell that allowed him to change his physical appearance; not just that of his clothes. He thought of the possibilities of what he could do with the spell and realized that any mage could do the same; he was beginning to understand why his master, Tornelius, always said that being a wizard was more about respecting the power of magic than about harnessing it.

Captain Strongshield had visited the Fighter's School and recruited every able bodied man to his command; Cade and the twins were more than ready when the call came.

Dawn found a large war party, led by Captain Strongshield, just outside the gates of the city; a dozen wagons and dozens of horses.

Dryx, Weylor and Cade rode in a wagon with Danflorf and Taffer, and a few other dwarves that they had not met. They were happy to see their dwarven friends again, just as Danflorf and Taffer were happy to see the twins and their new companion. The twins told the dwarves of their trip to Daley and how Cade had joined them, and Danflorf told the twins about the cave they found and their plans to make a dock inside of it.

Cade, more than anyone else in the entire war party, felt the thrill of adventure grow stronger with every moment that passed, bringing them closer to the enemy Cade had never met. He was excited to be part of something that was helping to protect others; an honorable way to use his deadly skills gained as a rogue in Daley.

He felt no particular desire to kill goblins, but he knew that the goblins would not hesitate to kill him and had attacked and murdered many men of Taris without mercy; he would not hesitate either. He was nervous to kill, nonetheless, and feel the guilt that might come with killing but he also knew that it was his responsibility now to protect the twins.

Captain Strongshield stopped the war party on the night of the second day, when the fires burning around the bridge were visible in the distance.

The bridge was wide and made of stone; low walls surrounded the bridge on both sides of the river. The doors were now closed and a dozen goblins stood alert on top of the walls; with many more dozens of goblins inside the gates.

Chapter 25

The Dragon Cave

Captain Strongshield stared out into the night towards the bridge. The goblin force was big enough to easily take the virtually unguarded bridge, but the captain's worries were beyond their taking of the bridge. The goblins, for the past ten years, had appeared to be unorganized and sporadic, not attacking in big groups. It seemed as though they weren't unified as they were last time. But now, Captain Strongshield thought, taking the bridge was a bold move. There would be no point in one lone band of goblins taking the bridge and cutting off any help from Viltress unless Taris was going to be attacked; and the goblins wouldn't attack Taris unless they had a considerable force united under one banner. The captain also realized something else, something that made his heart pound with fear and anxiousness; if the goblins were that organized to sail ships up the river to take the bridge, they would not leave so few to guard it. An army from Viltress would easily take the bridge and the goblins would have taken it for nothing. Unless, he realized, they meant to destroy it.

"You there," Captain Strongshield said to a nearby soldier, "bring me the rogue from Daley, Cade, and the twins."

"Yes, sir," the guard said and ran off.

The guard found Cade and the twins with the easily found group of dwarves near the back of the large camp.

"Cade, the captain wishes to see you. Dryx and Weylor, also," the guard said.

Danflorf motioned with his head for Taffer to accompany them.

They followed the guard to the front of the camp where the captain stood staring out towards the bridge not far ahead of them.

"Captain?" Dryx said as they approached Captain Strongshield.

The captain turned around. "It looks like an opportunity has presented itself, Cade, for which your skills could be of use as a rogue," the captain said.

"What are my orders?" Cade said; he was eager to prove his loyalty and that he could be trusted.

"I fear that the goblins mean to destroy the bridge, not just take it. They will have too many guards out for us to catch them by surprise. I need you to find out if the bridge has been destroyed yet, and if not, if they are planning to destroy it," the captain said to Cade. He felt uneasy about sending Cade and the twins to the bridge and possibly to their death, but the security of the entire kingdom came down to finding out if the bridge was still up and he couldn't march on the bridge and risk losing dozens of men to retake a broken bridge. "Dryx, Weylor," he said, "I know you have been through a lot, but I must ask this of you. This bridge is key to receiving aid from Viltress."

"We will not let you down, Captain," Weylor replied.

"And I'll be going with you," Taffer said, stepping around the twins. "If there's going to be any goblin skull-smashing tonight, ain't no one better at it than me," he said, winking at the twins.

Captain Strongshield thought for a moment about letting the dwarf accompany the group, but nodded his head in agreement when he realized that, if they got into a tight spot, no one would be able to help them more than a dwarf.

"Very well," the captain said. "If you aren't back by sunrise," he said but was cut off by Dryx. Both twins smiled wide that Taffer was accompanying them.

"We'll be back, Captain," Dryx said confidently. He felt as safe as anyone could have felt with his three companions next to him; Cade was as silent as a ghost and his equal in melee combat, he could think of no one more dangerous than Weylor, and anyone he would rather fight less, and he knew that when it came to Taffer and goblins, Taffer would be the only one left standing.

Leaving everything but their weapons, the group headed off for the bridge. It was dark and clouds covered the light of the moon and stars, leaving the torches on the walls of the bridge the only light in the area.

The forest in the area had been cleared away around bridge; had there been more light the group would have easily been spotted. But in the almost perfect darkness of the night, the group moved unseen and unheard almost right up to the wall surrounding the bridge inside.

The light from the torches seemed so bright in the darkness that the group was able to virtually every detail of ever goblin standing watch on top of the wall. They were awake and very alert.

Cade knew, though, that with the torches burning so bright during such a dark night, the goblins would be able to see nothing outside the light provided by the torches. He motioned for the twins and Taffer to stay where they were and left, first to the south side of the wall. He moved like a shadow moving within a darker shadow; even with a full moon out, Cade would have left no more trace of his passing than a gentle breeze over tall grass.

He saw that goblins were doubled up along the entire wall; there would be no going over the wall to get in. He made his way to the northern end; it was the same. Cade did notice, however, that the river was wide, but the current was slow and gentle.

He made his way back to Taffer and the twins. "There is no way in over the walls," he whispered, "but the river flows gently; we may be able to swim and climb up right under the bridge."

With no one opposed to his plan, Cade led them south to the river below the bridge, just out of range of the torches. They slipped into the gently flowing river; Taffer's fear of swimming quickly left as he realized that he was quite buoyant.

The wall came back in along the bank to connect to the bridge, so that even from the river there was no entrance inside the walls; unless you were an expert rogue that was not unfamiliar with climbing stone walls.

Once again, Cade motioned for the others to wait while he climbed the wall to see what he could. There were no goblins along the walls facing the river, only on the outer walls. Once on top of the wall, Cade saw that the goblins were trying to destroy the bridge. They had made a lot of progress; the stone was half-gone where the bridge met the shore.

Cade looked down over the wall and whistled quietly, signaling to the others that the coast was clear.

Cade didn't notice that Taffer had climbed up the wall and jumped when he turned, scanning the area for any potential threats. Cade hadn't heard a single jingle or clink of Taffer's armor and knew Taffer could not be that nimble; he was a dwarf, after all.

Weylor smiled when he saw the expression on Cade's face. He had placed a simple enchantment on Taffer's armor, silencing it for a short while.

"We need to find out how they are destroying the bridge," Dryx whispered to the others after seeing the stone broken up at the bank.

Cade led them down the wall towards the bridge. Dozens of tents and low fires filled the area between the gate and the bridge. There were two rooms on either side of the bridge that they couldn't see into from top of the wall.

Taffer held Cade back a moment; he smelled a familiar smell. He couldn't remember what the repugnant smell belonged to; it had been a long time since he last smelled it. The hair on the back of his head instantly stood on edge but as hard as he tried to remember, the answer eluded him.

The expression on Taffer's face made Cade and the twins feel even more on edge; whatever it was that Taffer smelled, the fact that just its smell put Taffer on edge was unsettling to the rest of them.

"There," Taffer said, pointing his axe to the room on the ground. A huge pick lay on the ground against the entrance to the room, a pick too big for any goblin to use effectively.

A sound from behind the group dropped all of them to the ground. A pair of goblins was walking on top of the wall towards them; they weren't carrying torches.

Taffer pulled out a small throwing axe but Cade grabbed Taffer's hand, stopping him. He might be able to kill one of the goblins but the other would cry out and they would all be dead.

The goblins were still a ways down the wall, and there were no torches. Cade hopped up and ran straight towards the goblins, moving too quiet for the goblins to hear him approaching. Right before he would be noticed, Cade dropped himself off the side of the wall, holding on with his hands to the top of the wall.

Cade waited there, pressed against the wall and hanging only by his fingers, until the goblins passed. Having lived as a rogue since a child, Cade's muscles were honed to perfection for climbing and finding grip where others hadn't the strength. He pulled himself back up as soon as the goblins passed and walked up behind them. He realized how much smaller the goblins were than him, but he wouldn't take any chances on giving either one the chance to scream out. Pulling out both his daggers, Cade, quicker than either goblin could react, thrust his daggers through the necks of the goblins from the outside-in. The blades blocked their throats, letting no sound leave their mouths as they faded into the night that never ends. Cade waited until the goblins reached up to grab the daggers in their throats and pulled them out, only to find the space between their rib cages, piercing both goblins lungs.

Cade caught the goblins and let them down softly onto the ground. He crouched over them for a moment, staring at their dead bodies; it was the first time he had killed anything. The guilt and remorse he thought he might feel was not there when he looked at the dead goblins before him; they were ugly and even looked evil to Cade. *No,* he thought, *there is no reason to feel guilt for killing these vile creatures.*

He crept back to the others and found Taffer staring at the room with the pick in the doorway. The smell had him as alert as he had ever been, both axe and shield drawn out on top of the wall.

"If we don't kill whatever is in that room, the bridge will be destroyed tomorrow," Weylor whispered.

None of them, not even Taffer, wanted to go down to that room but they all knew he was right. Whatever they found in that room, it had to die.

The wall led over the bridge, next to the roof of the room with the pick. Cade hopped over and hung over the side of the building, looking in through the window. He jumped back up, scared. He backed up all the way to the wall, staring in the direction of the window. "Big," he mouthed, motioning with his hands that whatever he saw was massive.

Seeing Cade's hand motion for the size of whatever he saw, Taffer remembered the smell; ogre.

Ogres were huge, powerful creatures that looked like small giants. They grew to over eight feet in height and, although normally not too intelligent, made up for their lack of intelligence with sheer strength.

"It will smell us if it hasn't already," Taffer whispered, his voice serious. "We need to kill it or run, and run fast."

The group heard a snore and a sniffle from inside the room; they had no time to decide. Taffer found a ladder down from the wall and moved over to the entrance, Cade and Dryx right behind him.

Weylor stayed up on the wall; he knew from his studies that bigger creatures, like ogres and giants, had tough hides and that his magic would do little to harm it. He would keep watch over the entrance and facilitate their escape if needed.

Taffer poked his head inside the doorway and saw the ogre, asleep on the ground. He hadn't seen an ogre since before the attack on Brüevelden, but he remembered all too well their power. He turned back to Cade and Dryx and nodded. He entered the room slowly and moved to the back, as close as he could get to the things head. Taffer wished he had a big axe, he wasn't sure if he could sever the thing's head with a hand axe, even if it was asleep and helpless.

Taking a deep breath, Taffer raised his axe over his head with both hands and swung as hard as he could at the ogre's neck.

At the same time, Dryx and Cade tried to find any strategic places to stab that might help take down the massive ogre. The skin was much tougher than they thought, though, and the blades were stopped before reaching the hilts.

The ogre screamed out as the axe tore through its throat. The axe severed the major artery, causing blood to fly out in all directions, but it hadn't had enough force to cut all the way through. One of the ogre's hands flew to its throat, grasping at the damage, while the other instinctively flew around and knocked Taffer back against the wall.

Chills ran up Weylor's spine as he heard the howl of the ogre from inside the room. It wouldn't take long before every goblin in the camp came running to the room to see what happened. Thinking as quickly as he could, Weylor knew that he had no spell that could kill enough of the goblins to help his friends. He reached into the folds of his robe and pulled out a handful of colorful dust, it seemed like normal dirt but was colored and very fine. He tossed it into the air while muttering the arcane enchantment and the dust starting glowing. He sent it down in between the building and the goblins closest to the room below him. The dust got brighter and shone in all colors, weaving patterns in and out of itself like a snake.

Inside the room, Taffer was unconscious against the wall. The wounds caused by Dryx and Weylor seemed to be very minor to the massive creature who was groping at its throat trying to find breathe.

"We need to get out of here, now," Dryx said.

Cade agreed and ran over with Dryx to Taffer. "Taffer, wake up! We need to go, now!" Cade said as loud as he dared. For some reason the goblins hadn't come swarming in yet, but they would soon.

"What the," Taffer said as he came to. "What happened?"

"No time, we need to go, now!" Dryx said, helping Taffer to his feet.

They ran outside and saw Weylor's colorful pattern in the air. "Where do we go?" Cade said, looking around for Weylor.

"To the river, it's our only hope," Weylor said from behind them, stepping off the ladder.

Dozens of goblins stood staring at the hypnotizing pattern in the air. They seemed to have forgotten the scream they heard and their heads turned with the pattern winding its way through the air; until one of the goblins saw the fleeing group and screamed out, pointing at them. The sudden scream freed them from the hypnotism of the spell and dozens of goblins ran up the bridge towards the group.

Cade, Taffer and the twins jumped from the bridge into the water below. They were able to find a log to hold onto as the current slowly quickened on its gradual descent down to the sea. They could see and hear groups of goblins running out to the banks of the river following them.

"Looks like we're going to have to stay in the river," Taffer said, breathing heavily; he still felt a bit light headed from being hit by the ogre.

"What was that thing?" Cade asked.

"That was an ogre," Taffer said still breathing heavily. "They're nearly as strong as giants and just as stupid."

The group floated down the river for an hour and lost the shouts and howls of the goblins along the banks behind them. Dawn was fast approaching and the first light of day lit up the clouds high in the sky.

The coast came into view after another half-hour of floating, and so did the black sails of a goblin ship down the river behind them.

"That's not good," Taffer said, pointing to the sail off in the distance.

"What are we going to do?" Cade said anxiously.

The group looked around for any possible solutions; the only viable option was the sea. They wouldn't be able to outrun the goblins, there were too many and the ship was gaining on them.

As they neared the mouth of the river, where it poured out into the ocean, they were caught up in a mass of logs that had piled up, unable to escape into the sea.

"There's our cover," Weylor said, letting go of the log with the others and grabbing a new one. "We need to free these logs; it will make it harder for them to find us."

The other three swam over and started helping free the logs to flow out with them into the sea. It wasn't long before the group was floating alongside dozens of huge logs, doing their best to keep the logs as close together as they could.

The goblin ship had slowed down as it reached the sea and the dozens of logs now in its path. The ship maneuvered slowly through the logs, making sure that the group didn't slip by them back to shore. An hour passed before the group was crowded into the last dozen logs between them and the goblin ship.

The fog offshore had hidden a huge cliff that extended for a mile in either direction. The shore was no longer in sight and the group had run out of sea; the cliff was now against their backs and the goblin ship was almost on top of them.

Arrows started to fly out from the ship; the goblins were shooting at anything that might be one of the intruders.

Weylor dove down underwater to escape the arrows. The light from the sun was now high enough over the mountains to give them light in the water. Weylor saw a large, dark area in the rock below the water; a cave. He swam back up to the surface, being careful to come up for air in between logs.

"There is a cave underwater!" he yelled out to the others, hoping they could hear him.

"Go!" Dryx yelled back, taking a deep breath and swimming down under the logs. He saw Cade and Taffer both descend from other areas in the logs and they followed Weylor into the dark cave.

The cave was too far underwater for the sun's light to penetrate. Weylor took out one of his exploding pebbles and let it drop to the floor of the cave before he mentally thought the magic word in his mind and the small pebbled exploded into a burst of light. It lasted only a second, but it was long enough for the group to see how big the cave actually was. At least twenty feet across, and the same height, the cave went straight for a couple dozen more feet before turning up.

Weylor turned back to the others behind him them pointed to where the cave turned up. He swam towards the opening and broke through the surface of the cave, the other right behind him.

They pulled themselves up into the cave, all of them gasping for air. The ground was smooth and cold and the air they breathed seemed stale.

"Do you think they'll follow?" Dryx asked Taffer, breathing heavily.

"If goblins can swim this far I'm a bearded elf," he said, also between heavy breaths.

The group rested for a few minutes before deciding to see if the cave let out somewhere else. They followed the cave back into the cliff, running their hands along the side to guide them.

"I think it's safe enough for some light now," Weylor said, remembering and taking out a slightly larger stone than before that had been permanently enchanted to always shine by one of the clerics of the temple; it was one of the many parting gifts from Tornelius.

Weylor was confused as he looked back to his companions; they all looked as though they had seen death itself. Their weapons fell from their hands and their heads slowly looked higher and higher.

Weylor knew there had to be something behind him. As he turned, he realized that they had walked into an enormous cavern.

In the middle of the room was a mound of treasure; gold, silver, gems of every color and size, suits of armor and weapons littered the entire place. The huge pile glittered with the light from Weylor's stone, which also dropped to the ground when he saw what was lying on top of the mound of treasure.

There, stretching across the entire mound was a dragon. Its tail was long and thick, with a fin-like frond of spikes, connected by skin, running up it and continuing up its back. Its hind legs and lower stomach were narrow but very muscular. The front legs, almost twice the length of its back legs, were laid across the mound towards them. Each leg, behind the knee, had another small frond, similar to those on its tail. Massive wings attached to the dragon behind its shoulders, the flap of the wing connecting all the way down to where the tail met the torso. The neck of the dragon was extended vertically, fully thirty feet in the air, with the same frond spike leading up its spine and ending on the top of its head. The dragon had two horns, on either side of its head, which protruded straight back from behind its skull, perpendicular to its neck. The dragon's mouth was also narrow, though it was still big enough for a man to lie down inside of it and still have room.

The dragon bent its neck and dropped its head, extending it out towards the group, and stopped just feet from Weylor.

There, paralyzed with fear, Dryx, Weylor, Cade, and Taffer stared into the eyes of a dragon.